justice
deferred

justice deferred

a novel

Len Williams

WELCOME RAIN PUBLISHERS
New York

Justice Deferred
Copyright © 2002 by Len Williams
All rights reserved.

Library of Congress CIP data is available from the publisher.

Direct any inquiries to
Welcome Rain Publishers LLC

ISBN: 978-1-56649-319-2

Printed in the USA

This Welcome Rain edition 2016

For Michael

acknowledgments

My lovely wife, Christine, who is always supportive. She married a businessman and got a writer instead. Who knew?

contents

prologue

This is a story of three people. Each of them is me.

The first is the youth, Billy Ray Billings. He is grown and gone now. He ceased to exist. He was officially pronounced dead.

For many years any remembrance of him was unwanted and quickly sublimated as something quite repulsive. He was, after all, the root of my devastation.

In truth I was ashamed of him and his ilk: the poor white trash of rural south Alabama.

It is only now, when I have made my way, that I must recall Billy Ray. Without him, my story has no beginning and we have no fulfillment.

Fancy word, fulfillment. Billy Ray would never have heard it in a lifetime, had his lifetime come and gone, as would generally happen in Grand Bay, Alabama.

But now I love Billy Ray. He is like a son, or a younger brother to me, one who was amusing in an uncouth way and caused me pain. But I love him because he is family and he is my family.

Part 1

billy ray

CHAPTER

Billy Ray's memory starts with a beating. That is his first bea-con. He is just six and it is his first day at school. He is eager to go to school; there was never a book in his home or a toy that he did not invent. Rose, his mother, had bought him new sneakers and a white T-shirt for school. She had cut his hair and scrubbed him up with a facecloth until his skin hurt.

Rose was a scrawny woman almost overcome by weak men and unwanted children. Home was four rooms and a porch nailed to-gether by fifty years of poverty. She walked with him the half mile on the two-track dirt road into Grand Bay, handed him his lunch, and gave him over to a big woman in the school yard.

At recess, some bigger boys called him a rube and a hick and told him his haircut looked stupid. At first he was ashamed and frightened, but then a fat kid who'd been hanging back got brave enough to step forward and call him a little sissy chicken. At once Billy Ray saw the fat boy's fear despite the bravado of numbers of-fered by the other boys.

Billy Ray was used to roughhousing and wrestling. That's about all he did with his two friends Ronnie and Dwight. So he hung his head and pretended to turn away to leave. The fat boy came right up to him then, taunting.

The first punch hit the fat boy squarely on the nose as he was leaning into Billy Ray with more sass. The second got him in the temple and put him down. Then Billy Ray was on him, pummeling furiously.

The other kids stood back as kids do to watch a good fight.

The fat boy had to go to the nurse and then home because he was wobbly. Billy Ray got a paddling from the principal, had a little cry, and went back to class.

At home, his stepfather beat him with a stick because his clothes were ripped. They were that poor.

Billy Ray would remember that particular beacon all his life, but not recognize its meaning until much later.

Billy Ray spent as little time as possible in his house. His stepfather was a mean drunk and seemed always looking for excuses to hit him. So Billy Ray ran wild with his pals. There were swamps to the south and small hills to the north, ideal terrain for their youthful energy. With his pals he roamed those woods, loving the freedom and the wild fun. They stole whenever they had the opportunity and eventually took a rusty old twenty-two from a widow's house. Over time they learned to shoot anything that moved. The rifle was their most precious prize and they built a tree house to protect it. Ammo was stolen from fathers, older brothers, uncles—anyone at all.

Pretending to be soldiers, they became minor vandals, breaking windows, letting the air out of tires, or breaking down fences so cattle could escape.

And then came the fire. They hadn't meant for it to spread. All they wanted was the fire department to crank up the sirens and come out so they could hide and laugh. They had become somewhat proficient in that small art.

There was a small shed at the edge of the woods to the north of town, which was part of an old cannery that had ceased operations a few years earlier. What was the danger to anyone? None—no one would get hurt. It would just be a good prank. They wouldn't even burn it down; just get a little smoke rising and call it in. Something to do on a summer afternoon.

So they rolled an old tire into the shed and filled it with rags and newspapers and poured a tin of gasoline on it. The tire was in the middle of the shed, a good many feet from any walls. The floor was concrete. They were experts.

When the tire was well ablaze and the shed filling with smoke, they smashed a window to let the smoke out. But when they opened the door to leave, a sudden draft sent pieces of flaming newspaper wafting up toward the roof. In no time, the roof was smoldering and then it burst into flames. The boys could only watch and swear with fear and excitement.

When the fire truck arrived, the shed was already consumed in red shooting flames. The heat was amazing. The boys had not called the fire department, a passing truck driver had called it in on his CB, and he told of the three boys running down the road. He knew one of them. He knew Ronnie's father. He knew Ronnie.

In the early evening the sheriff's deputy came up to his house looking for Billy Ray. Ronnie and Dwight were already in the sheriff's car. What was the use of denying it?

The judge gave them each sixty days in reform school for vandalism, and took his time telling them that they wouldn't have to go there this time. Instead, they would be on strict probation for a year, and he hoped fervently that their parents would take them in hand.

That's all Earl needed to beat Billy Ray with his belt until he bled.

That fall, shortly after the fire, in grade six, Billy Ray met Lenny Fox, who had been held back and was almost two years older. Lenny taught Billy Ray and his pals to steal from stores. There were several techniques, but the main ingredient was always nerve.

Since Billy Ray was by then somewhat of a tough guy, nerve was not a problem for him.

Stealing came easily because there was nothing in its way!

Retrospect is another word alien to Billy Ray. It is only for us now to judge him. He could never imagine the life I have now. In retrospect, Billy Ray was already well down the wrong path.

I remember it like a movie seen many times; it's sometimes the whole thing, other times only a scene. It is the beacon of that time.

We have been taught to boost. That's the word we use now to elevate our new craft. Ronnie is small and wiry, so he is usually the runner if we need one. Dwight is big and clumsy. His role is distraction. Lenny tells us what to do. I usually do the stealing.

Lenny is older and tougher and meaner. We are in his gang. Nobody messes with us.

We enter the old department store on Saturday mid-morning when it is busiest. Lenny has determined that we are ready for bigger things. He wants a transistor radio, which, he tells us, we can all listen to. We are excited.

It's one of those old three-story stores with the main stairs in the middle and an old elevator and more stairs at the back. The radios are in the basement. Each of us has gone in by himself during the week and know where the radios are displayed and which one to take.

Our plan is the usual one, the only difference being the stairs up. So far we have only boosted from drugstores and five-and-dimes or grocery stores for a chocolate bar or cigarettes.

We stand out among the women and men who shop on a Saturday morning in November, but we are unaware of that.

Lenny will loiter near the main doors and watch for managers or a deputy, should one walk by. Ronnie will stay close to me in case we have to run. In that emergency, one of us runs and the other gets in the way of any pursuers. This has only happened once and it worked well. At the supermarket, Ronnie ran with the candy and I let myself be knocked down by the clerk in pursuit. Since there was nothing in my pockets, I was let go. We had the confidence of experience. Being on probation attested to my toughness. I'd been threatened by punishment and I loved it.

Dwight is going to create a distracting disturbance.

We enter by different doors over a ten minute period.

I pass Dwight on the aisle near the towels and tell him that I am ready.

Then I close in on the radio. It is inside a glass case with a sliding door on the back. The lock is open for the day so that the clerk can bring things out for customers to look at.

Dwight's diversion was excellent. He stumbled into a pot and pan counter. It sounded like a minor traffic accident. I looked at Ronnie and he smiled and then nodded that the coast was clear. The only clerk ran to Dwight's noise. I reached in and grabbed the radio and then another. Walking quickly, I gave one to Ronnie and he stuffed it under his loose shirt like I did. I went up the main stairs in the center and Ronnie went up the smaller stairs at the back.

When I approached the main doors, Lenny was not there. That was okay; sometimes he hid or went outside to wait.

As I stepped on to the street, I felt good and turned toward the town square. The big hand that grabbed my shoulder stopped me and hurt me. A thick thumb dug into my neck. The shock did not stop me from reacting and I turned and swung my fist at the same time. I hit a large man on the hip and he swore at me and slapped my face so hard I went down on all fours. He grabbed my hair at the back and picked me up. I screamed and cried all the way back through the store to the office.

Ronnie was already there. Soon they brought in Dwight, who had tried to help Ronnie and been caught by a clerk.

We waited for the sheriff to come, too stunned to understand what was happening.

When you're young and bad, you think all the adults are conspiring to ruin your fun. They are the natural enemy. Those in authority, like teachers and ministers, are a pain in the ass, but the ones in uniform are the worst. Whatever they said was bullshit. I wish to God I'd believed this one. But I obviously did not.

The sheriff came in with a deputy. That was not good news at all.

"These the ones?" the sheriff asked.

"Yup and that Fox boy, Lenny, but he ain't around this time."

"Humph. Okay. Woolworth guy be able to make these three, you figure?"

"Yup, and the Piggly Wiggly too."

That sheriff was a heavyset older man with a big belly, but he was clean shaven and his brown uniform was neat on him. He looked at us and sighed. Then he asked the deputy and the manager to give him a minute with us alone.

As they left, I thought he was going to beat us. But he sat on a chair in front of us and looked us over thoroughly. We could not move because we were too stunned.

"Boys," he said. "You ain't the first or the last to pull this kinda foolishness. The police is always gonna be a whole lot smarter than a bunch a dumb crackers like y'all. You remember that and this little bit a trouble here will be good for you. But if you don't stop this kinda thing right here and now, it's gonna be real hard, I can promise you that. I seen a lot of smart alec boys like y'all end up in jail or worse, so I always take time to make this little speech. Sometimes it works, sometimes it don't, but it makes me feel better myself. Now I'm gonna do y'all a favor."

He did not smile and I thought we would receive a stern warning and be on our way. Lenny had told us that the cops never bothered to arrest kids for shoplifting. So I waited for some more bullshit and threats. We were pretty used to that.

"Boys, the radios are both over fifty dollars and that's theft. Premeditated, that means y'all planned it. I'm gonna have to make an example here, so I'm takin' you into the courthouse and I'm gonna book the three of you for theft. You'll have to stay in the juvenile lockup until I can get the judge. You the boys still on probation for that fire over at Sweeny's, ain't you? Not a real smart thing to do, stealin' on probation."

He got up and called the deputy, who took down our names and addresses and then marched us through the whole store to the patrol car out front. He locked us in the back while a whole crowd of grown-ups looked down their noses at us. I tried to look tough.

We sat in a locked room with wire over the windows all afternoon. Finally, a woman brought us a sandwich and a Coke and a deputy had took each of us to the bathroom.

Jesus, Mary, and Joseph, I had never been so shocked in all my life as when they took us upstairs to the courtroom. There was my mother in her waitress uniform, Dwight's father looking madder than hell, and Ronnie's grandmother who he lived with. They were not sitting together. Then there was the supermarket guy we made fun of because he was so stupid, the two men from the department store, and Mr. Hartstone the druggist. Shock would not hope to convey my emotions.

The sheriff was there with his deputy, talking to an older man and a young woman with glasses. The woman came over to us at the table where they made us sit. God, we must have been a wild-looking trio of desperados. Dwight started crying when he saw his father. Ronnie just looked at his shoes, and of course I looked tough.

The young woman sat with us. "My name is Madelaine Wilson," she said, saying each word clearly like a teacher. "I am your lawyer. The judge appointed me because your folks didn't have a lawyer. Boys, it's my job to make sure that your rights are looked after here and to advise your folks what to do. Now we need to talk for a few minutes. We can go to a room over there or we can do it right here. Are you okay here?"

We nodded our ignorance, as she had anticipated.

She checked our names and addresses, what school we went to and how old we were. We were all twelve, born in 1964. It was November 1976. Seen from this distance, it could as easily have been 1876.

"Alright, boys. I'm going to ask you some questions and you tell me the truth. That's the only way I can help you. If you lie, it only gets worse, you understand me?"

We all nod again.

We admitted to her that we had stolen the radios. What else could we say? The guys were sitting right there.

What about the drugstore and Piggly Wiggly?

Ah, just some candy and stuff.

Did we plan those?

Nah, just took some little stuff, you know.

She made a few notes, then went to talk to the sheriff, while the older man read a book behind a desk.

When she came back, she was not at all happy. "Boys, the sheriff wants to make an example of you. You are all still on probation. That's just like a prior conviction. He wants to bring three charges against you: shoplifting, theft over fifty dollars, and resisting arrest. The problem we have is that you did all that and he can probably prove it. I'm going to talk to your parents or guardians now and tell them what I recommend. It's their decision, not yours."

The old guy turned out to be the judge and we had our hearing right there and then.

Miss Wilson argued with the sheriff and the sheriff stayed pretty calm. The judge asked some questions.

In the end the sheriff dropped the shoplifting and the resisting arrest and the judge gave us all sixty days in the juvenile reform school and read the riot act to our parents. He hoped this would straighten us up because probation obviously had not. I wish it had.

No one ever asked about Lenny. We at least had enough dignity not to mention his name. But we didn't forget him.

They gave us a few minutes with our folks. I got my face slapped and my mother told me I was a smart-ass little prick to cause her all this trouble. At least Earl wasn't there.

CHAPTER

e'd heard about the reform school, but only in the mytholog-
ical sense of someplace we could imagine but never see. It
was a place in the black-and-white movies with tough guys and
kindly priests. If a kid had been to reform school, he was idolized
as blooded and feared.

They sent an old gray school van for us that night. The deputy
put us on the bus and signed papers for the driver. He locked the
cage door and told us there were box suppers and milk at the back.
If we made a fuss, he said, it would only make it worse for us. He
needn't have worried.

The Alabama Juvenile Reform School is just outside of Mobile. We
got there at about nine o'clock on the same day as we committed
the crime, Alabama justice being swift.

We went into the under-fourteen side, which looked like a
church to me, but the guard showed us the over-fourteen side because it looked like a real jail with a big wire fence around it.

I may be the only boy who ever liked reform school. It wasn't at all like the movies. The guards were mostly women and mostly nice. There wasn't any point in being a tough guy in there. They explained right off that fighting just added time.

We went to school most of the day and did jobs before and after. Every day you had to read what you were doing when they woke us up at seven o'clock. There was helping the cooks or taking out trash or helping in the laundry or yard work. We had to make our beds and keep our area neat.

The food was better than I got at home and I went to church there for the first time in my life.

There were only about fifty kids in there and we were split into four groups according to age, so Dwight and Ronnie and I stayed together.

Mostly we were treated okay, but they definitely stood for no nonsense. The odd smart-ass would spend hours with a toothbrush cleaning the johns or scrubbing the mess-hall floor.

We were there until the middle of January. Dwight and Ronnie took the furlough to go home for two days at Christmas. I stayed put. What would be the point? I'd already decided what to do about my stepfather when I got out and I didn't care any about my mother. Besides, we were having a real turkey dinner and I could watch the bowl games on TV in peace and quiet.

We each got a present of a little bible book and had two days off school. I guess the women felt sorry for us, so those of us who remained were treated very well.

Dwight came back with a black eye, but said his mother had bought him a bike which he could keep if he stayed away from me. He said he would do that after we had taken care of Lenny. I felt bad but let it go. Dwight had a regular family with older sisters and a nice mother. He really had no choice.

Ronnie was happy. His grandmother was sending him to his aunt and uncle in North Carolina because she couldn't handle him anymore. He was excited and told us it was only for a tryout but that he wanted to stay with them because his uncle was a hunter.

In reform school, we all wore cheap blue pants and shirts. When we left they gave us our own clothes back, all folded and clean. They even cleaned my old jacket.

The superintendent warned us to get on the right side of the law and I certainly intended to do just that.

Nobody came to the courthouse to pick me up, but Ronnie's uncle and Dwight's mother were there for them. It was around noon, so I walked over to the diner to see if my mother was working. She was, but she just told me to go home and wait for Earl.

Earl came in a little while after I got home. He had that mean look on him that I had expected. Not much made Earl happy, but beating on me and my little brother, Mitch, did seem to satisfy him.

Earl was not big and was older than my mother by a good ten years. Some of his teeth were missing and most of his hair.

"Stand you up, boy!"

"Earl," I said. "If you ever hit me or Mitch again, I'm going to wait until you're asleep sometime and I'm going to stab you with a butcher knife. Now fuck off and leave me alone before I do it right here and now."

Just in case the threat would not be enough, I had a small baseball bat behind me on the chair. You know, like for Little League.

Sure enough, old Earl couldn't quite get it or resist his urge to beat on me.

"Stand up, boy, when I'm talkin' to you."

"Earl, you're making a big mistake." I'd learned that kind of talk in reform school. But Earl came to pick me up out of my chair. In the three or four steps it took him, I could see that he'd been drinking. When he reached out to grab me, I swung the little bat and whacked his hand pretty hard. Then I stood and whacked the other hand before he could retract it. He screamed bloody murder and tried one more time. I banged his hands until he ran outside yelling and I went after him.

I guess all those beatings he gave me kind of built up, because I jumped on his back and put him down and whacked away for a while until I was finished. I never hit his head or face or balls.

Then, real calm, I told Earl that if he touched Mitch or me again, I'd sure as Christ kill his sorry ass.

He lay there for a little while and then sat up and looked at his hands and at me.

"We got a deal here, Earl?"

All the poor fool did was curse and go inside for his booze. Then he went out.

My mother, Rose, was surprised to see me with Mitch all happy and playing snap when she got home.

"You seen Earl?

"I beat the hell out of him and he ran off to get drunk I expect."

She went a bit nuts when I showed her the bat. "Maybe he's in the emergency room. I whacked his hands pretty bad."

She left too.

On Monday, Ronnie, Dwight and I were back in school. More warnings and threats from the principal and our teacher and the adulation of our few friends. The others kept their distance. We were different animals now, hardened cons. We told a few lies to enhance our image.

We wanted to hear Lenny's story. Either he'd just lucked out and got away or he'd seen trouble coming and deserted us. We suspected the latter but wanted confirmation.

He pulled his usual cool act, welcoming us back with pats on the back and not a word of explanation. All day he hung with his other pals and barely acknowledged us. After school we walked him home like we were still his gang. He still didn't bring it up.

"Lenny, what the fuck happened?" Ronnie finally asked.

"Where the fuck were you?"

"When?" He was not good at this and his face said he knew when.

Dwight was now as big as Lenny and his recent experience had honed his courage. He put his hand on Lenny's shoulder and stopped him up short. "When the fucking managers spotted us. That's your fucking job. That's fucking when."

Dwight was usually a calm kid who went along for the ride. Even I was surprised to see his anger.

Lenny lost his usual bravado with that and tried to convince us that he hadn't run out on us before we even accused him of it.

So we just beat him up pretty good right there and told him there'd be two more coming because there were three of us. And if he told on us, we'd kill him. I kneeled down by his ear and said, "I've got a gun, Lenny. Just take your beatin' like a man. You're gettin' off easy."

We never touched him again. Dwight dropped me like the plague and Ronnie went to live in North Carolina, never to be heard from again.

CHAPTER

3

I try to remember the emotions of the time. Perhaps I can. Perhaps Billy Ray can.

We have to work together to remember. He's been shunned for so long that he is reticent to reappear, especially emotionally.

But it's clear enough. Even he has to admit it. He was a tough kid who'd been to reform school. That part he showed them. Never overt about himself now, he didn't need to fight anymore. They'd seen Lenny and the word had gotten around about his stepfather. Those two wrongs which Billy Ray righted in his own dumb physical way had set him apart as someone without fear. It's strange that after all the years of ridding myself of that dumb kid, I must admit a grudging admiration for his courage. Especially with Earl.

What no one was allowed to see was the kid who needed a little affection. After he beat Earl, his mother refused him everything. She would not even buy him clothes. Meals as a family had never existed for him, even before his real father ran off. Now he ate what he could find and got all his affection from his younger brother,

Mitch. And the cat. God, I'd forgotten the cat. Mitch had brought home a kitten just a year or so before Billy Ray went to reform school. His name had changed several times as he grew and Mitch saw him differently. Rose told him to get rid of it, but Mitch kept the cat. He fed it outside and let it sleep with him when it was cold.

The final name was Smoke, because he was gray I guess.

I remember him because first thing I'd do every morning was find him for a big hug. He'd purr his ass off because that meant food was next. And I'd hug Mitch too whenever he'd let me.

So I can see now in my excellent hindsight that Earl and Rose were only out for themselves and that Smoke and Mitch were my family.

CHAPTER

For the next four years, Billy Ray grew through adolescence, stole seldom, always had a part-time job and spent all the time he could in the woods with his friends.

School was just the way time was passed. It neither interested him nor annoyed him. He progressed from year to year in the middle of his class and rarely studied for tests.

In high school he played some football. Being only average size, but quick and tough, he was a decent defensive back. He liked the way girls treated him and he enjoyed the hitting. Practice was a pain, but there was the fun and companionship with the guys.

As the school work became more difficult, Billy Ray didn't change his study habits, so the work passed him by. His assignments and homework were done poorly or were late.

He'd always felt inferior because of his family, and the disgrace of failing grade ten finished him off. He could not recover. There would be no football and he must repeat the year. He quit.

The letter had come in late June. He'd failed. The shame was intense. To this day, I feel the heat of it on my neck.

Billy Ray told no one. He could not. Nor could he stay in Grand Bay where everybody would know it.

All summer he worked two jobs. During the day, he stocked shelves and delivered on a bike for a grocery store, and in the evenings he bussed tables at the diner where his mother worked. She was gone when he started at six.

No one remarked at his industriousness. Who would? Rose and Earl drank every night and Mitch was too young.

I can remember thinking that if I had a suitcase and some clothes that I would be a man and I could get on the bus and go someplace bigger and start my life.

As happens sometimes when we daydream, or imagine things, they come true.

On a hot September day, as school was about to start, Billy Ray Billings, sixteen years old, packed his new suitcase, told his mother he was leaving, and got on the bus to Mobile. He had some clothes and three hundred and fifty dollars.

I stayed with my Aunt Wilma for a week or so. She was my real father's sister. But she had no room for me except a couch on the back porch, so as soon as I could I moved on.

Wilma was good to me. I could go there for supper or to use her washing machine whenever I liked. She had two little kids and a husband who was a baker and worked weird hours. It was always a good place for me to go and I never took it for granted or went there empty-handed. It was the only place I was known at all.

CHAPTER

5

The line, for Billy Ray, was crossed after he'd been in Mobile for about two years. It was his discovery of Orville's Pool Room. Up until then he'd led a somewhat reasonable life. He worked in a big deli-bakery doing odd jobs. He cleaned up, cut meat, and served at the counter. It was an okay job with a few tips. He lived in a room of his own in an old house full of similar castaways. He smoked some dope and drank beer at night, but he always got to work on time and worked hard. It was a life of sorts.

Orville's was a tough-guy pool hall. Billy Ray was a pretty good pool shooter, but had stayed close to the house he lived in and played at a big public kind of place nearby. It was called the Metropolitan and had over twenty tables and served fast food.

Orville's had an older crowd who drank a lot of beer and the code was different there. It was full of men, not boys. That was its reputation.

I suppose this is like the movie I play of Billy Ray's famous arrest at the department store, equally vivid because it was the evening I met my future.

I played pool sometimes at the Metropolitan with a guy in my house named Benny. We went over there a couple of nights a week.

Benny was about nineteen or twenty and was tall and skinny. One night he just said we should go someplace else for a change, so we went to Orville's. Just like that. That's how your life can change.

So we go to Orville's and sign up for a table and sit watching some motorcycle guys play. I'm sitting on a stool, sipping on a beer bottle, and we're beside a black guy and a white guy. Nobody's talking. We're just watching the chain-and-leather guys shoot pool. They were terrible, and if I'd had the nerve, I'd have asked for a little action.

One shooter was fat and loud and hairy. He had tattoos as well. He was shooting from our end of the table and he told us to move so he'd have more room. We moved.

Then he noticed the black guy alone with three white guys and told him to get the fuck back or he'd whack him one. The black guy just smiled at him and moved farther away.

"What you smilin' at boy?" The fat biker barked out at him.

"Nothin', boss, just happy I guess."

The hog grunted, took his shot, and miscued. His pals laughed and we all smiled too. He only noticed the black guy.

"You laughin' at me boy?"

The black guy stood up from his stool. He was bigger than I'd supposed. He just looked at that hog and never stopped smiling. "Yeah, I suppose I am. You want to shoot some pool for some money, big shot?"

The biker stiffened and then laughed as he turned to his buddies. "You hear that boys? Nigger here thinks he can shoot pool with white folks." He turned back to the black man. "That right, boy?" he yelled.

The place was still. The black man said, "White trash, cracker. White folks are nice enough. You know what I mean, cracker?"

Well, shit, I couldn't believe my ears. We were all glued then. A second passed and then the hog lunged at the black guy with his cue stick. Big mistake. With no effort, the black guy let the cue stick thrust right past him and as the hog stumbled to catch his balance, he was hit as hard as I'd ever seen anyone hit, right in the middle of the face with a large black elbow.

We all heard the crunch and saw the blood spurt as the hog went down like a shot bull.

The black guy held up his hand as the other bikers came toward him and he yelled, "Stop right there!"

They hesitated and he said, "This guy asked for what he got. You'd best be leaving it at that."

One more biker came at him, fists flailing. Two terrible punches to the face stood that biker up with shock, then he was hit in the stomach and went down as well.

A third biker came at the black man and the fourth was about to jump him from behind, when, on instinct alone, I reached out and grabbed his shoulder so that he spun toward me.

He started to yell something and started to take a swing at me. I guess I was in pretty good shape from slugging boxes around the deli, and he was probably a little drunk. In any case, I went nuts on him and really let him have it. He was bigger than me and very close, so I hit his ribs as hard as I could and kept my head down. I must have hit him seven or eight times before he ran out of breath and stepped back. Then I pounded him any place I could until he went down too.

When I looked up, the whole pool room was just standing there staring at me. There were four groaning bikers on the floor and the black guy and me looking wild at each other.

Then the black guy smiled and said to me, "I think this table is free now. You want to shoot a few games?" He stuck out his hand.

"Name's Maynard." He had to stop again to catch a breath. "Appreciate the help."

I shook his hand. "Billy Ray. No problem." I was panting, too, and shaking.

Orville was a large man who had some Indian or something in him and he had seen everything. Apparently it wasn't the first time the bikers had caused trouble, but it was the first time they had gotten their asses kicked. They were helped out to their bikes where Orville informed them that they could not come back. Ever.

Maynard's friend was a very good shooter. His name was Eddie, short for Eduardo, but he didn't look Mexican or anything. He was all shaggy hair and bright colors.

Eddie looked up from a shot as if a strange thought had just that instant made itself known.

"Billy Ray? You a fighter?"

Not understanding fully, I replied, "You mean like a boxer? Shit no."

"No. Like do you fight a lot?"

"No. Last fight I had, I was twelve years old."

"So why'd you help old Maynard out here, you don't fight?"

"I don't know. Wasn't fair I guess. The last guy was gonna jump him from behind."

"Didn't you think I might grab him myself?"

"Never thought."

"Man, you was bangin' him good. He was tougher'n he looked. You worried maybe they'll come back?"

I thought, then said, "Nope."

"'N why's that?" Maynard put his cue down and smiled at me.

"Because they'd have to kill us and the odds on that are not too good."

That seemed to get Maynard's attention. "You that tough, Billy

Ray? You're so tough how come you ain't fought nobody since you was twelve?"

"I didn't need to. No point in fighting unless somebody makes you."

"So who'd you fight when you was twelve?"

"A guy who left me to get busted and my stepfather."

"Jesus. Your stepfather? And you was twelve? What'd he do?"

"He beat us. He was a booze hound."

"Okay, tough guy, how'd you beat up on a grown man when you was twelve?"

"With a kid's baseball bat."

Maynard laughed out loud. He was almost tall and very solid, with a face ready to smile. He had a friendly laugh. "Yeah. That'd do it pretty good. You white folks . . ." He shook his head, wondering about us white folks I suppose.

"He was black," I said.

Maynard smiled again with less mirth. "You anti-black, Billy Ray?"

"No, Maynard, I'm not," I answered. "But I am anti-asshole."

Maynard laughed and Eddie and Benny smiled with relief.

As he resumed his shot, Eddie said, "Well I'm glad we got all that cleared up. Now we're gonna whip y'all's ass at some eight-ball here."

"You can try. Dollar a point?"

We shot pool and fooled around until midnight. Benny and I made a couple of dollars. It was that close.

Nobody drank much until the pool was over. Then we had a nightcap at the counter where Maynard explained my anti-asshole stance to Orville who seemed to like it a lot.

"So what do you boys do?" Eddie asked over a beer.

Benny answered, "Billy Ray works for a deli and I work for the parks department. What do you do?"

Just conversation.

Eddie answered, "We steal stuff. Mostly cars."

"You're kidding, right?" I smiled.

Maynard said, "Nope. That's what we do. Been doin' it pretty good too, last little while."

There was nowhere to go from there, so we let it drop.

After that night, I became a regular at Orville's, dropping in a couple of nights a week. Benny came with me some of the time. When we'd see Maynard and Eddie there, we'd play pool and drink beer and shoot the shit. I loved it and it felt good to be somewhere where the owner knew my name and I had some history. Somehow Orville made you cool or not. We always tipped the waitress real good and were very well behaved. But you could tell the biker story had made the rounds. We'd paid our dues, it seemed. We were tough.

Eddie and I had some great games, just the two of us. We got pretty good, but never hustled anybody and kept mostly to ourselves.

One night when I was there without Benny, Eddie pulled a roll of bills from his pocket to pay the waitress for the beers. The roll was about a half inch thick. I made some comment like business must be good.

Eddie tossed me the wad. It was all hundreds. Maynard had one too. They'd just been paid for a delivery, they said.

"We broke our cherry yesterday, Billy Ray," Maynard said. "We're in the luxury-car business now. Ain't that right, Eddie? Got ourselves a big Mercedes. Like new too."

They were proud. It was like a promotion for them or something.

I didn't know what to say, so I asked, "Shit, how can you sell it? What about all the numbers and stuff?

"Not our problem," Maynard answered. "We're in the C.O.D. business now."

I guess they trusted me by then, so Eddie asked me if I wanted to know how it all worked. Later, they told me they'd talked it over before and agreed to try to take me on with them.

We went out for a sandwich that night and sat in the back patio of a takeout place by ourselves. They explained how it worked, stealing cars.

What a story. They were both twenty-one and they'd been at it together for over three years. Full-time. There was a pecking order among car thieves. They'd moved through stealing cheap imports so the chop shops could cut them up for parts, through older cars for the same purpose, to their current elevated business of receiving orders from a man who paid them cash for the cars he wanted. He then looked after the numbers and everything else and sold them as used cars into the wholesale market.

Whatever the blue book wholesale was, they got a third, cash.

With the new work came more risk because of alarms, cops, security guys, and all that, so they had to invest like in any business.

They'd had to buy a truck and some tools, and Eddie had to read all the handbooks for mechanics about alarms.

Would I like to see how it worked? Why not? Shit, they'd been doing it for three years and only needed to steal a car every month or so. And the bankrolls were more than I made in six months.

As we left the patio, Maynard put his arm around my shoulder and said "We just keep this to ourselves, okay? This not a good thing to be talkin' to nobody about, y'all know what I'm sayin'?"

CHAPTER

6

We met a couple of weeks later on a Friday night to talk about things.

They offered to cut me in. All I had to do was help them spot a car they wanted and then watch for problems from someplace nearby. I wanted the money but I was really scared of getting caught. We were having a few beers and shooting some pool on the corner table at Orville's where it was all right to talk. They talked me into taking a twenty-percent cut as a lookout.

"Man, we been doin' this for three years. We're pros, boy." Eddie was full of confidence, and I guess it rubbed off, so I told them about Lenny and said I'd do it and be real serious about it too. We shook on it.

There had never been any talk about how they actually did it, nor did I know where they lived. The only thing I knew about them was that they drove an old Pontiac GTO and had bought a truck.

I was off work on Sunday and Monday, so on Saturday we met

around five at Orville's and drove out toward Pensacola in the Pontiac.

You could tell right away in the car that Maynard was the man. Eddie was jumpy and excited, but Maynard just drove along with his arm out the window listening to his music.

"Here we be, gentlemen," Maynard said, as he pulled into a big mall parking lot just off the interstate.

"This here's an outlet mall, Billy Ray. People come from all over. Them rich folks love a bargain. Tomorrow's the big day. Be busy as hell tomorrow after church, about one or two. Now we just gonna drive around here for a spell and get a good idea about the exits, where the rich folks shop and like that."

On Sunday morning, they took me to their home. It was in the suburbs, west of Mobile. I was really surprised. It was quite a nice little ranch-style house with big trees, a big backyard, and a two-car garage. The furniture was new-looking and the house was clean. Eddie explained that Maynard was a neat freak and even had a lady friend of his clean up once a week and cook some things and leave them in the fridge.

I guess I'd just assumed they'd live in some dump like I did, but here were two happy-go-lucky car thieves living quietly in the suburbs.

Maynard never ceased to surprise me with his reasoning. When I asked him about what the neighbors might think of a black guy living with a white guy in the suburbs, he smiled and explained.

"Well, Billy Ray, it's like this here. There's some other black folks out here. You know, teachers and lawyers and such. We tell folks we're partners in the sellin' business and we sell stuff for people over the phone. You know, like distressed stuff that needs to be sold quick. So we come and go and keep to ourselves out here. Ain't no landlord 'cuz I bought this place myself. Got it in my mama's name."

Then they took me into the garage to see their truck. That was an education. Maynard looked on with pride as Eddie showed me his masterpiece.

"If it's gonna rain, we're in trouble," he said. "All the letterin' washes off. Not bad, eh?"

Not bad was right. The spotless white service van had both sides lettered perfectly in medium blue ACME SERVICE INC, with an 800 phone number under it. "Maynard does the letterin'. Takes him two whole days, he's so particular. Looks good, eh?"

"Jesus, I'll say, it's great," I said. "But what if you're already on the road, going some place, and it starts to rain?"

"First," Maynard answered. "We watch the weather forecast, and second, if we do get caught up short with some rain, then we got two sheets of white plastic we can slap on till we get back here."

The van had sliding doors on both sides. That was a custom job because they usually came on only one side.

Inside were tools on a rack at the back, all in their place, clamped on. Eddie said he'd built the rack himself and custom designed some of the tools as well.

"I been doin' this for a long time now Billy Ray," he said. "Started before I run into Maynard here. They get this old van, man, and we're cooked. We got about everything you need in the car stealin' business."

He showed me his alarm-system manuals and all the special tools for each make of car. All were either factory equipment or gadgets he'd made himself at a machine shop he used.

Maynard explained how it all worked and why they could use me.

We got to the mall about one and parked at the edge, waiting. The lot was filling up slowly.

"There's our boy." Maynard said quietly. "See, over there by the light post. The silver Mercedes. Must be new. He's parkin' it way out so it won't get scratched."

The van's windows had a dark tint and Maynard was using small binoculars. No one could look in and see us.

"Okay. That's real good. Got Florida plates. Okay now here's the folks. Two old folks that's walkin' real slow. This gonna be good, boys. Here Billy Ray, take a look."

I did.

"Okay, now Billy Ray, you go on in with them a-ways and come on out when they shoppin' or whatever. Got to make sure they're busy, you see?"

The couple were in their seventies and I walked behind them into the mall, until they sat down for a cup of coffee in the food court. Then I went outside and nodded my head. The van drove right over to the Mercedes and parked close to the driver's side.

Maynard stayed at the wheel with the motor running in case of security or police or somebody else driving up. I watched out for the same thing plus the old folks.

The Mercedes alarm went for two honks and stopped before anyone could tell it from anybody honking his horn. Two minutes later the van drove off and the Mercedes backed up and drove off in the other direction.

I spent a half hour at the mall buying a few clothes and then took the shuttle bus back to Mobile. There was little fear in me. They were pros, and I was getting a bankroll just for watching.

The Mercedes was almost new and the blue book was forty-five thousand. I got three thousand dollars in hundred dollar bills that night.

I helped them twice more over the next month and a half and got five thousand more. Then they wanted me to go on a trip with them to Puerto Rico and I couldn't resist. My boss wouldn't give me the two weeks off, so I quit, because I'd never been on a vacation before.

Man, did we have ourselves a time in Puerto Rico. We found three nurses from Detroit down there for some fun, and we partied with them for a whole week. I'd never seen anything like it: boats, good food, girls in string bikinis. We spent money like there was no end to it. It's still the best two weeks of my life. Unfortunately, I had too good a time. I was hooked. Not so much for the money. It was the freedom and the fun and being with Maynard and Eddie.

CHAPTER

My room at Maynard's was at the back, with a good breeze and trees to shade the windows. Maynard's friend, Brenda, changed our sheets every week and washed our clothes. It was, by far, the best I'd ever lived.

Once I settled in, I started to read magazines and the newspaper for the first time in my life and I watched a lot of television. So I wouldn't get flabby, I did all the yard work and took to running early in the morning.

Eddie showed me all about stealing cars. We practiced in a big compound where they put old cars before they squashed them for scrap. Eddie knew the guy there so there wasn't any problem. Maynard said Eddie was the best and could teach car stealing at college.

I was never as good as Eddie, but he said I had a good touch. Maynard agreed.

They started me off on some old cars downtown at night just to practice. We just left them someplace after I stole them.

We always wore gloves. None of us had ever been printed anyway, but Maynard wanted to be safe.

My first personal theft was a new BMW. Maynard called it breaking my cherry. We took it from a restaurant lot by the beach on the way to Pensacola. Eddie sat at the bar watching the owner while Maynard and I did it. I got a third: four thousand.

We were busy then for a while at our stealing. There was never a hitch. We'd get a car every two or three weeks, and my bankroll was really growing.

Eddie and I wanted to take a trip to Mexico or even France, but Maynard wouldn't let us because he didn't want us printed for passports. So we went to Hawaii that next time. God, we hiked and rode horses and went snorkeling. Two weeks in a big hotel. We took a suite to be together. The three musketeers. Big tippers. Cocktail hour at the pool. We were "phone salesmen on a vacation." Surf and turf. Nothing cheap for us.

CHAPTER

We had over two years of good times before we got caught. I was almost twenty.

It turned out that some old guy had caught a glimpse of Eddie working on a car door from the van's side door. It was really a fluke because the guy was two rows away. In court he said the sun glinted on a tool or something and caught his eye. So he drove over to the mall door and told the security guard.

There was only one cop car at first. Maynard saw it and I guess he thought he could scare the cops off. He ran up to us shouting to get going, then went for the cop as he tried to get out of his car. The cop was small and white and he stuck a big pistol right in Maynard's face and that was it. Two other cop cars came up right then, and they cut us off and cuffed us quick.

Talk about shock. I could hardly breathe. All I could think about was prison. There was no way I wasn't going to prison. There wasn't any delayed reaction either. No hope at all. When the cuffs went on, I knew. In those few minutes, my life as a big spender on vacations vanished as if it had never been real at all.

CHAPTER

The police took the van apart and they found some notes that Eddie had kept on some of our bigger scores. He had been careful and kept them under the rocker panel. But the cops found them and they had us for at least four counts of car theft, they said.

We had enough money for our own lawyer. Since we were caught in the act and the police could prove four other thefts, he said we should all do the same thing, which was to let him try to get the number of counts reduced to one or two and then plead us guilty and let him try to get us as light a sentence as possible.

He told us about the three-strike rule and how we could live with two counts but no more. He explained that the State of Alabama had a habitual-offenders act that some people called the three-strike law. We'd heard about that. But it was really a four-strike law. After three convictions for any felonies, the fourth one put you away for good. Life without parole. We were nervous as hell and he had to explain the three-strike stuff several times. I got it after a while and it made my knees weak. If they charged us with three, and if we were ever caught again, we'd get life. I couldn't believe my ears. Could we get four now? The lawyer said it never happened like that.

He did a good job for us and talked them down to two counts of grand theft auto. He argued hard that we had no prior record, but the van and the tools and Eddie's notes were all against us.

Maynard had his mom put the house up so we could make bail. Nobody thought about skipping because they had our prints now and we'd get caught eventually. The lawyer said we could get anything from probation to ten years on each count. He guessed, with the van and all, that we'd get five or six.

We all got five years on each count, but the sentences would be concurrent, which meant we could be out in two or three if we behaved. The lawyer thanked the judge. We had two convictions each. Two strikes.

The judge said not to thank him yet because he was sending us to the Alabama State Penitentiary at Bessemer which was the toughest, so we would not be too eager to go back to stealing cars again.

I called my mother at the diner in Grand Bay to tell her and she hung up on me. She never said a word after I told her I was going to the penitentiary for stealing cars. For once, I couldn't blame her. It hurt, though. I'd have been happy with anything she said, no matter how bad.

CHAPTER

10

Reform school is no preparation for prison. In reform school they're trying to help you out, especially the ladies. In prison, no one likes you or themselves. It is an evil place.

We went up to the prison with a dozen other guys in a drab prison bus with bars on the windows. It was rainy and cold. I almost cried, I felt so stupid and ashamed. And I was scared. God was I scared. I was twenty years old and going to a real prison. What was the matter with me? Was I just that dumb? I knew I was.

Well, I caught a break. The guards took us into the prison where we were signed for and then they made us sit on benches and wait for the warden. None of us felt like talking or even looking up from our shoes.

The warden came in. He was a lot younger than I'd have imagined, and well dressed in a brown suit, white shirt, and shined shoes.

There was a blackboard there and he just started to write on it with yellow chalk after looking us over.

1. Three strikes
2. Good behavior
3. Roads or inside

Then he turned and talked to us very calmly. The first part was about the three-strike law. We all had one or two now. I remember telling myself that I'd never be back here. That was for fucking sure. I'd learned my lesson twice already now and just wanted to be alive in three years to get the hell out of there.

The warden took a long time on the three strikes just like our lawyer, but I soon tuned out because it would never apply to me. I'd haul garbage first. Happily.

Then he went on about not causing any trouble here because they'd make us serve the full sentence and add to it if necessary. No problem here, I'd be a model prisoner.

Last, he told us we had only this one chance to decide if we wanted to work on the road gangs for the State, or stay inside and be assigned to one of the shops. They had to know now because the clothes and shoes would be different and the road gang had cells someplace different from the rest.

When I was the only one who raised his hand for the road gang, I thought I'd made some really stupid mistake, but I wanted to be outside and I wanted to be tired at night so I kept my hand up.

It was one of the few decisions I'd made that worked out well.

The road crew were all in Block D and we never mixed with the others so I never saw Eddie or Maynard again until we got out.

They put me in a cell with a guy named Cecil from Birmingham. He was doing eight for robbing a 7-Eleven and assaulting a cop. He'd done two already and knew the ropes.

For twenty-two months I shoveled, raked, pick-axed, and hauled. And I did not mind it at all because I was outside getting tired. We never sassed the guards and they treated us okay, all in all.

Every day at noon time we got a box lunch and milk and we could sit together and talk or sleep. I always liked those lunches because I felt free there, sitting outside on some dirt or grass.

I just concentrated on the freedom of being outside and the exertion.

On bad weather days we could watch the TV for a few hours in the mess hall.

At night, I listened to Cecil's radio and went to sleep as quickly as I could.

We were worked hard but got lots to eat, so I bulked up pretty good and got a good tan. Later, I learned it was the bad history of road gangs that kept others from signing up. I suppose it was those old movies of chained black men with the bosses on horses with rifles.

There was one day off a week, on Sunday. Then we mostly just laid around the cell waiting for Monday, or watching some TV in the mess hall.

No one bothered with me. I was just as quiet as I could be to avoid any notice by anyone. Our routine was such that there was little opportunity for trouble anyway.

I never once went to the exercise yard on Sunday when I could have because I was hiding from anything that would remind me of where I was.

So for twenty-two months I wore bright orange coveralls and hat and made two dollars a day breaking my back on Alabama roads. You'd think I would have learned.

I thought I had. Maybe I should have stayed inside and seen real prison life instead of the road gangs.

CHAPTER

The prison was overcrowded. Some cells had three inmates. We were released after less than two years. All three of us came out on the same bus back to Mobile. It was the prison bus but we were freed by then and weren't locked in. The driver said he was picking up a new batch, including a couple of four-time losers. I felt for them, the poor stupid bastards.

We all went back to Maynard's house. His sister lived there while we were away, so it was nice and clean for us to come home to.

But it was never the same after that first time in prison. We tried to go back to our old selves but we had seen the result of our old selves and were not impressed enough to rejoin them.

But it was okay, certainly a big relief from incarceration. We had each hidden money at the house, so there was no immediate need for work. I had a little over three thousand and I think Maynard and Eddie had more.

We hung around the house just watching TV and laying

around, not even talking that much for about a week. In the evenings we'd go to Orville's to shoot some pool and go to a bar that had good burgers. The life, however, had been taken from us.

We all wanted a real vacation but could not risk our bankrolls, so we went to the beach near Pensacola for a week and stayed in a motel. We did pretty well in the female department there with some waitresses. More than anything else, that finally lifted my spirits. I hung out with this big old fat girl named Helen. She was always kidding around and making me laugh. I went back to see her for a year or so after that. She lived in a little apartment of her own over the garage of a big house on the beach and looked after it and cleaned for the owners who came on weekends from Montgomery. I spent some nice times there with her.

Anyway, by the time we got back home, after that first week on the ocean our outlook had brightened.

Getting a job when you're an ex-con is not easy. We all had the same probation officer and he helped us some, but all that was available to us at first were day-labor jobs.

Eddie and Maynard wouldn't go, but I did. Every morning I went and stood with other men outside a small strip center and waited for contractors or gardeners or anybody else who needed some hands for the day. The pay was always the same, five dollars an hour, cash.

I learned fast how to be selected and got work almost every day. If you were clean and stood alone, you went first.

It wasn't easy work and never much fun, but I could pay Maynard my rent and live on what I made. The other money I'd saved went into the bank.

After about three months of day work, I got a steady job as a laborer on a big construction site downtown. They were putting up an office tower and I'd have work for a year or more. The pay was better because I was in the union, but I had to pay taxes. It was okay, but it was still a little like prison work. I had to exhaust myself every day in order to sleep without thinking about what a lowlife I was.

Mind you, this is all upon reflection from the grand heights of my current literacy. At the time, there were no such thoughts, just work every day and make a living and get tired. A twenty-two-year-old laborer with a prison record, trying not to think.

We started going over to Grand Bay every month or so to hunt and so I could see my brother, Mitch. By this time, Earl was long gone and my mother, Rose, was an alcoholic. She could still work during the day but never came home until she was drunk. Mitch said she let old drunks stay with her sometimes.

It was a little embarrassing, but Maynard and Eddie were always nice to her, which I appreciated. I'd sleep with Mitch, and Maynard and Eddie would sleep in my old bed. Mitch was seventeen and already bigger than me.

We had some good old times up there on a Saturday and Sunday. We all bought cheap rifles and got hunting licenses like we should from the county courthouse. Man, I wouldn't even park illegally.

Mitch was real good in the woods by then and I let him show us what to do. We got some deer and wild hogs and saw a lot of alligators and snakes.

We'd give what we shot to the butcher in town and he'd give us meat to freeze and to barbecue.

By that time, Mike had joined us and he started coming up there too for our weekends. He slept on the old couch in the parlor, which he said he preferred to sleeping with any of us.

Mike was sitting out back at Maynard's house with Eddie when I came home from work one afternoon.

Eddie said Mike was from Texas and that they'd met him in

prison. He was tanned and happy-looking and I asked how come he looked so good if he just got out.

He smiled that relaxed smile of his and told me he'd gone to his uncle's farm for a couple of months so that he could work and sleep and eat. I understood right away and told him about the road gang and what I did on my construction job.

Mike slept on the living room couch at Maynard's for a week or so and we all got along great. It seemed a happier place with him there because he was always kidding around and he could cook too.

We talked it over, and we made kind of a room for Mike in the basement which was concrete and dry and had casement windows. We put a rug and a bed and a couple of cheap room dividers down there and Mike fixed it up nice. It worked great for me because of his cooking and my rent went down a little.

I was the only one who worked. The others got busy stealing again when their stash was depleted.

It didn't matter to me. They were my friends and as tight as Eddie and Maynard were, that's how tight Mike and I became too. Mike was like me in some ways. He'd had two fathers and his mother had finally left him with his uncle. He was happier than me though, and tall and good-looking. He seemed to be what I could have been if I was smarter. It made me feel good that we were pals. It helped me a lot to have a real close friend.

What they all did was their business. We never even talked about it much. Mike worked alone. He said he always had and felt safer that way. Maynard and Eddie were stealing from cheap condos and apartments that were easy to break into. They still used a van and Maynard was always changing the sign on it. We used to sit around drinking beer and watching television thinking up funny names to put on the van.

Usually they'd be a repair service and wear coveralls. I never asked what they got or how they sold it but they told me anyway.

They'd get all excited when they'd score big. It was nothing like luxury cars though—just TVs and stereos and sometimes money or jewelry. They kept the stuff in a U-Rent and every couple of months or so, they'd fill the van and drive up to Montgomery to sell it to a fence they knew.

Mike never talked about his thing. All we knew from him was that he kept a car in a garage he rented someplace near downtown and he only used it when he was working. Otherwise he took the bus or a cab.

Mostly though, they hung around the house and I worked at my construction job. All I ever asked of them was not to bring any stolen stuff home in case we were raided or something. No problem, no one wanted hot stuff around anyway.

Mike needed to exercise a lot to burn up energy like me, and he liked to look good. He was as tall as Maynard, about six feet, but he was rangy where Maynard was chunky. Every night almost, Mike would have a good run and pump some weights before he cooked us supper. He played racquetball sometimes at a place nearby. We never went with him because he never asked us to. Crooks can be very considerate.

We were our own thing there. We were our own family. In a way we were like four old farts living together. Mike shopped and cooked. Eddie did the dishes and put out the garbage. I did the yard work and Maynard cleaned and fixed things. We could have been four old ladies sitting there almost every night eating our supper in the kitchen. We played a lot of penny ante poker and shot some pool or just kicked back and watched TV at night.

Each of us had a girlfriend or at least a woman to sleep with, but we seldom brought them home. I went to Helen and the other guys used motels or the woman's house. We joked about them some, but they were not something we shared.

Nobody knocked me for having a straight job. In fact, sometimes Mike would pack me a lunch from leftovers.

Usually nobody worked on the weekends and we took to hunting more with Mitch and fishing sometimes up on the Alabama River by Millers Ferry. Mitch would drive up and meet us there sometimes too. We'd get day permits from the guy who rented rowboats, and fish out there and drink cold beer and chew on beef jerky. Those were some great days of freedom.

Whatever we did, Mike got good at it right away. He'd buy a magazine about fly fishing and buy the stuff and make us lures, or he'd read about butchering hogs and start cutting them up himself on a table behind the house with a hose and ice all ready to go and plastic to wrap the meat in.

We swam a lot up on the river too. Mitch and Mike were the best. Eddie couldn't swim at all and wouldn't even try.

Except for the fact that the three of them were stealing for a living, we had an ideal setup. I'd never been as content as I was during that time we had together. I set this down for you, because without it you could not possibly appreciate what I eventually lost.

So passed a year and a half. My construction job ended then and I was not unhappy to take a few weeks off before finding another. My three thousand was still in the bank along with two more I'd saved. I had no car, no debts and lived cheaply. I'd coast for a while.

Where Maynard was a little thuggy-looking now with that little black ski hat he wore and a goatee, and Eddie was always wild-looking with long curly hair and a big droopy mustache, Mike looked like a college student or something. I looked like what I was, a muscled-up, dumb-looking laborer.

Mike always shaved and showered in the morning, and if he was going to work, he'd be dressed very quiet but nice in slacks and a sports jacket. Sometimes he wore a tie.

Finally, I asked him what the hell he had to get all dressed up for.

"Well," he answered, with that big smile. "Two reasons I guess. One is that I like to feel good in nice clothes and the other is that if someone is looking for a crook, I want to look more like a guy who sells real estate. It might give me a break when I need it."

Eddie and Maynard were there when I asked Mike that question and they nodded sagely.

All at once we were into a full-scale business talk. For over a year everybody had kept to himself about their work. Now, in half an hour, it all came out. Actually, it turned quickly to bragging. It seemed that although Maynard and Eddie worked together quite a lot, they also did singles. They all did pretty much the same thing, although where Eddie picked locks or forced windows, Mike went in the front door with some snow job and left a window or door open for later. We had a few laughs at some close calls and then the conversation ran out of gas.

They were all doing pretty well, but Mike seemed to score the best goods and he was getting a good price for them. That definitely interested Maynard.

CHAPTER

Mike asked, "Why do you guys drive all the way up to Montgomery to fence your stuff? You got something going I should know about up there?"

Maynard was always serious about business. "What we got is somebody we know real good and the stuff is outta Mobile so nobody is gonna see it again."

"Sounds good. What's he give you, you figure, on retail?"

Eddie answered. "'Bout twenty-five percent."

Maynard said, "More like twenty."

Mike said, "I'm getting thirty and the stuff is leaving town too. I've been working with this guy a couple of months now. Pretty big operator. Guy's from Birmingham, so he sells their stuff here and Mobile stuff up there. He's a big fence in Birmingham.

What the hell, thirty percent was huge, Maynard said, they'd take a looksee at this guy with Mike.

Mike set up the meeting for a couple of days later and I didn't have anything better to do so I went along. This was all new to me.

I wasn't stealing anything and we were only going to talk. It was fun for me to go with the guys.

We all had good clothes on like we were going to a business meeting in Maynard's car.

I had to admit that the fence was very well set up. It was in a thin two-story building on a downtown side street. The sign said Roberts Electrical Repairs, and there was a counter and a man there who took in items and actually fixed them. We went through to the back, which was a little warehouse with shelves full of used appliances with repair tags on them.

Mike led us up a wooden stair to the second floor. Up there we met two men in their thirties in a kind of combination living room and office. We all shook hands and then sat down to talk.

The head guy's name was Frank and the other guy was Ernie. Frank said he had a big operation in Birmingham and another one in Memphis. This was his third. He backed a truck up to the back door once a week and took everything to his warehouse upstate. He said he paid a bit better than his competitors but he only took in first-class goods.

Ernie said that Mike was doing real good for them and that if we produced goods like his, they could handle us too. They were looking for good earners. Everybody was feeling good up there with the big operator.

During the meeting Maynard said okay, it sounded good to him. No more driving up to Montgomery for a while. He'd give Frank and Ernie a try. So we got instructions on how to contact them and what the procedure would be and we all had a beer and left.

You are going to think I'm really dumb and you'd be right. I slipped again. Not only that, but the same way. Maybe it's like being a drug addict or an alcoholic. You think one hit or one sip is just going to be that, and you can handle it just fine. In my case, it was probably true that I could have cut it off easily. In fact I'm sure it is.

I got kind of caught up in the spirit of things though, and went a couple of times with Mike to drive and be a lookout.

Those next few weeks, he worked really hard because he said he didn't want to show up with Maynard and Eddie and look like a piker in front of Frank.

His car was a station wagon. It was a few years old but a good model and clean with good paint. Mike kept a couple of dark blue sheets in the back to cover stuff up.

He got in houses and apartments by just ringing the bell, he said, and giving whoever answered it some bullshit about a charity he was collecting for. Usually it was for toys for underprivileged kids. He took small donations and gave a receipt when they offered money. He said he only asked for a couple of dollars so most people gave him that just to get rid of him. Then he'd have to go to the bathroom. Then he'd admire the place, and all the time he was casing it. Were the windows locked? Was there an alarm system? He'd ask if the person worked. Mike said it was amazing how much ladies would tell you. He'd been fed, laid, and complimented on his good work.

About half the time he'd get enough information so that he could come back in a few days and knock them off. He said he never touched anything in the houses that he didn't wipe off, and when he went back he wore gloves and took only one or two things.

For three weeks I drove him around and when he hit a place, I'd pull up so he could put the stuff in the station wagon.

He usually took small things. Never TVs or microwaves or stereos. Mostly small appliances and jewelry and money. During that time he hit about a dozen places and had no problem whatever.

When the time came to cash in, we put all of Mike's stuff in the van with Maynard and Eddie's haul. It was pretty full and everybody was excited to sell it. We were just like farmers, going off to market our produce.

Frank told Mike to have us drive up to the back door of the repair place at one o'clock in the afternoon. It was a Tuesday, I remember, because we sat up and watched Monday night football the
night before.

There was no question of me not going along. Although I had
done no stealing myself, Mike had promised me a quarter of his
take for the times I went with him. It was fun too, going to deal with
a fence, especially a big one from upstate.

Frank was impressed with our haul, especially with two brand-
new stereo units the other guys had gotten, still in their original
boxes.

Mike had some good jewelry that Ernie appraised with an eye
glass. There was some good-natured haggling, but in the end we
sold it all to Frank and left with our money.

Frank said he was a little light on inventory and could use more
goods as soon as we could get some. We were on to a good thing
here.

In a little more than a month we were back with another load. This
time, I'd gone into a couple of places with Mike to help him carry
out rugs. I was just along for a lark though, and was thinking of getting a construction job again.

We made the second drop at the repair shop and again were
paid well and congratulated on our merchandise. Eddie had
scored a whole box of transistor radios off a store's receiving
dock, which Frank said were gold to him because they sold like
hot cakes. One rug I'd helped Mike with was real Persian. We got
five hundred dollars for it alone. It was fun bullshitting with the
fence guys. Eddie and I acted tough. We were so full of shit, I can
hardly bear to remember it.

That second drop at the repair shop was on a Thursday night
and we decided to go up to Grand Bay in the morning and do
some hunting. We were high as kites. Things were going great for

us and we could really kick back up there now because my mother had moved in with some old farmer and quit her job. Mitch was working in the sawmill and living by himself in our old place. He was nineteen then, and after the ladies.

CHAPTER

13

I t was a typical hungover Sunday morning in Grand Bay. Mike was already up when the police bull horn started. He had no idea what was going on. By the time he woke me up, I could see Mike running around and yelling for us to run for it. The thought of a fire passed through my brain but was quickly supplanted by the loud electric words *police* and *hands above your heads.*

Mike ran out the back door in his underwear. Then there was some shouting and someone fired off a couple of rounds. The bull horn was clear after that because we were listening for anything. I thought they'd shot Mike. We just did what they said after those shots, and came out the front door with our hands on our heads.

Will I ever forget that scene? If I was an artist I could paint every detail.

There were three police cars and an old van. One was the sheriff, one was Mobile police, and the third was state troopers. There were at least ten cops with their guns out and some had all that black swat-team stuff on. The local sheriff was the only one who didn't have his gun out. He just looked at me and shook his head and walked off a piece by himself.

We were cuffed and had to sit against the porch while they searched the house. A big state trooper stood looking at us with his pistol hanging in his hand. He swore at us a lot.

I started to protest that Mitch wasn't in with us, but Maynard told me to keep my mouth shut until we got a lawyer.

One of the Mobile cops started telling us we'd better tell them everything there and then. While he was talking, Maynard just talked louder right over him. "Don't say nothin' but your name and address. He's gotta read us our rights. Don't say nothin' 'til we get a lawyer."

The cop was pissed, but the state trooper sergeant took him aside and then he came back and read us our rights. I had long feared those words, and couldn't look at the guy.

When I finally looked up, I saw Frank and Ernie, the guys we fenced through, walking over to us with another Mobile cop. Then I knew we were in deep shit because it looked to me like they'd busted our fences and they'd ratted us out.

The cop asked Frank and Ernie if we were the ones and they said yes, three of us were. The didn't know who Mitch was.

The sheriff told them it was Mitch's house and that he was my brother.

"You want to do this?" the Mobile cop asked Ernie.

Ernie said, "I sure do," and he pulled out his wallet and flipped it open. While I stared at the gold badge, I heard him start his little speech. "I am Detective Ernest Collins of the Mobile Police Department—"

I looked at Frank who showed us his badge too with a big grin. I never heard the rest. Not the words anyway, only sounds. We'd been selling our stuff to undercover cops. All I can remember is shame and fear, and they overwhelmed my brain.

We were hung over that morning from too many beers, so the shock of being arrested by ten cops with guns and then seeing Frank and Ernie flash their badges was just too great. We couldn't even look at each other. We were going away for a long time. I can actually remember thinking that I hadn't stolen anything, but I knew at the same time that it wouldn't matter.

After Ernie said whatever it was he had to say to charge us, it went real quiet until I suddenly remembered Mike.

I just blurted out the question without thinking. "Jesus! Mike! Did you fucking kill him?"

I guess I tried to get up because Frank pushed me back down.

"No we didn't shoot anybody, now just stay calm there so we won't have to shoot you."

Then I heard Maynard again. "Don't have to tell 'em nothin' Billy Ray."

I shut up for good then.

At the county jail beside the courthouse they separated us and kept asking all kinds of questions. Trying to find out the names of other fences and other thieves. They told me it would help me if I told. If I'd known any I'd have probably told, I was so scared, but I didn't know any and all I kept telling them was that I wanted a lawyer.

Back in Mobile, Maynard got us all the same lawyer we'd had the last time. He talked to us and then went to see the prosecutor.

When he came back that evening he was very business-like and calm. We might as well have been puppets.

At least he didn't mince his words.

"Boys," he said, sitting across the old beat-up green table from us. "It's not looking good for you."

Maynard said something to the effect that we'd figured that much out and he wanted to know how bad it was going to be.

"Well, here's the thing," the lawyer said, "they have got you

on videotape, they have still pictures and they have your fingerprints. They have you admitting stealing the stuff and they have
positive identification on some of the goods. The prosecutor said
he'd recommend a middle sentence if you just confess to a count
each of grand theft."

Maynard tried to tell him that Mike was the main guy on my
end of it and I'd only gone along for a lark. We talked about that
for a while, but with Mike gone and me on tape with them, acting like a big shot, I knew that wouldn't fly and I told the lawyer
not to bother.

I felt so frustrated I could have exploded. All I could think of
was how I'd stayed away from anything crooked and had just
helped out Mike for a lark.

It was just like the first time. I was so stupid that I couldn't believe it. I couldn't believe this was happening to me again. Again!
But it was. The whole thing was out of control.

The lawyer said there were no weapons involved but we'd have
to be charged with a felony A because it was our third offense. That
meant we were looking at ten years to ninety-nine, depending on
the prosecutor's recommendation and the judge. He could not pre-
dict anything except that it would only get worse if we didn't cooperate and plead guilty to the charge. Ninety-nine! I was limp.

After we badgered him, he guessed we'd probably get fifteen or
twenty. Maybe we'd be out in six or eight. But it could be more. He
couldn't promise anything, except that a trial would only make it
worse.

We listened then to the charge. It was for stealing two stereo
sets from a truck and a bracelet from an apartment. I was surprised that there wasn't more stuff mentioned, but the lawyer
said that was how they did it, just used the goods that were ID'ed
so they'd be sure of the conviction. That made sense and he said
if that's all the prosecutor mentioned that he'd have a good argument for a lighter sentence.

Our lawyer wanted to see all the evidence before he committed to our confessions. When he got us together after seeing the tapes and the IDs on the goods he just told us the quicker the better, in case the police decided to up the ante. He said the videotape was a half hour of us bragging and drinking beer. He'd never seen anything like it.

Since there wasn't going to be any trial, they set the preliminary hearing for the next week. Our lawyer said he'd pulled some strings to get it on the docket at once. We thought he was real smart. Under normal circumstances he would have been.

There were eight or ten little groups in the courtroom that morning. Our little group was us three, the lawyer, and Maynard's sister who'd brought us better clothes to wear so the judge would think we were nice clean-cut guys.

When the courtroom was empty except for us, the prosecutor read the charge and introduced Frank and Ernie who described the evidence. Frank did most of the talking and he used a lot of cop lingo like "perpetrators" and "surveillance equipment." He identified us in a proud voice. I couldn't even hate him, I felt so stupid. Everybody I saw there was smart. The cops, the lawyers, the judge, and even the clerks and sheriffs. They had jobs and education. I just had to be the stupidest person there.

How did we plead? The judge asked our lawyer if we were prepared to plead. He said yes and the clerk read the same charge three times and each of us stood up straight and said "Guilty, Your Honor."

Would we agree to the sentencing right now? Sure, our lawyer told us it would go better now. The judge would see us as very cooperative.

The sentencing hearing lasted thirty minutes. The prosecutor said nothing much, just telling the judge to be fair to the people we had robbed.

Our guy had his notes ready because he'd asked for this to happen. He sounded good and I felt like he meant what he said about our contrition and learning a hard lesson and we'd benefit more from a lenient sentence.

The judge took notes and went into his office or someplace to think it over for a while.

When he came back we had to stand and he read the sentence to each of us very formally. We got twelve years each and a stern lecture about citizenship.

Our lawyer was elated. He had gotten us almost the minimum for a felony A. It was the third felony conviction for each of us. The limit.

On our last visit with him that evening, we paid him with checks that Maynard's sister had gotten from our house. He got a thousand from each of us and we were all happy to pay him. He'd guided us well.

Twelve years meant we'd be out in five or six. I was relieved, knowing the end of it. Prison was not a mystery to me. I'd just dig more ditches and get the hell out of there. I could do five more years on the roads. I knew how to do that.

When you are thinking ninety-nine, five or six sounds like a reprieve.

CHAPTER

We had to wait in the county jail for a few weeks before our transfer to the penitentiary could be arranged.

Mitch came to see me there in jail and it made me feel awful to see how he pitied me. I tried to act cool and he tried to make me feel like I had somebody who gave a shit. My mother had heard about it before he saw her. It was all over Grand Bay and in the paper. They even had my grade ten picture. I wouldn't let Mitch show it to me. Mitch said the article had called me a three-time loser.

All I wanted then was to get up to the penitentiary and get on the road gang. I told myself that I could do the time that way and that I still had a bank account with five thousand in it for when I got out. Considering everything, I was getting off easy. That's what I told Mitch and he said I could live with him when I came out.

We were separated in the Mobile jail and I didn't see Eddie or Maynard much until three weeks passed and they put us together in a room with a green metal table and old wooden chairs.

Before they brought me there they put on the leg chains and wrist chains, so I figured we were going up to the penitentiary. Maynard and Eddie were already in the room when I got there. There were three guards in the room with us. I asked one if the bus was here for us. He said he didn't know anything about a bus. All he knew was what he'd been told—just to bring us here.

Our lawyer came in with the same prosecutor we'd had for the hearing. They did not look happy. Behind them was Frank Babcock in a suit.

Before we could think anything at all except that we were mildly surprised at the sendoff, Frank pulled out a paper and began to read very quickly. They didn't even sit down.

It just sounded to me like the stuff we were going to prison for, so I assumed it was some formality they did to felony A guys and I kind of tuned out.

Frank finished and the prosecutor said that he'd saved us the trouble of calling our lawyer and talked to him himself.

I looked at Maynard and he shrugged.

When I looked back, Frank and the prosecutor were leaving and the guards went with them. Our lawyer stayed with us.

Eddie asked, "What was that all about?" He was his usual cocky self.

"They're charging you with another set of thefts," he said. Then he looked up and held up his hands. "I'm sorry."

Not one of us got it.

Maynard said "We already been convicted. This is bullshit. What's the prick want? We been sentenced. It's over, right? They can't charge you for the same thing twice, right?"

Eddie and I joined in. What more could they do to us? Nothing, right?

The lawyer just sat there with his head down and waited for us to stop.

When we did, he let out a big sigh and said, "I guess they called me first, so I'd be the one to explain it."

He was a nice enough guy, our lawyer. His name was Fred Gray and he was about forty, a little pudgy, and a little bald. I must admit he always told us what he knew and what he didn't. What did I know? He was from some college and I was a convicted thief.

So he told us to listen to him until he got finished.

"Boys, I think they set you up."

Eddie could never keep quiet. He jumped right in. "That's not a newsflash, Fred. We were on TV, remember?"

Usually Fred would come right back at him to keep him in his place. This time he didn't even seem to notice and kept on talking, looking at his yellow pad.

"Please pay careful attention. This is very serious. I'm sorry to have to tell you this but you have been charged with another offense. This isn't just more on the old one. This is completely separate."

We started to yell and swear and he just sat there with his hand up for us to stop. We did because we had to hear the rest, although nothing was really registering at that point. All we knew was that it was not good.

He continued without his notes. "I think they set you up for this on purpose, but the police swear they just figured out these latest charges this week. I called them every name in the book, but they had the department's lawyer with them and they stuck to their story.

"They don't have to bring these charges, and ordinarily they might not, but with the three-strike thing now . . . I don't know . . . well anyway they charged you for stealing a box of portable radios and a Persian rug. They have all the evidence they had for the other stuff. The problem here is the three-strike thing."

We could not talk. My heart was set pounding by the third-strike stuff.

"Technically," he said, "you have three previous felony convictions. Do you understand the three-strike law?"

Maynard jumped up and his chair went over backwards. He yelled and cursed until the guards had to come in and settle him down. An interlude seemed to calm him while the guards acted tough and he acted docile. Then they left us alone with our lawyer again.

Maynard said, "They fucked us, didn't they Fred? Why the fuck would they go and do that? We're just some two-bit thieves. All we do is steal, for Christ's sake."

"I don't know for sure, Maynard, but you can be sure that it's not you boys in particular. I think it's something they dreamed up to make themselves look good."

"Well, can we fight it at least, for Christ's sake?" I asked.

"Yeah, we can, but I don't hold out much hope. These are separate crimes and you do have three convictions. Let me talk to some people and then I'll advise you, okay?"

"You need money for this, Fred?" Eddie asked. "We got money."

"Not now Eddie. Let's see what I can find out from some other lawyers and a judge I know. Give me a couple of days. This part is on the house. I feel like those fucking assholes have set me up too. They have a weapon on this one too. They have Eddie bragging about his knife and how good he is with it."

Then I knew it was bad. Fred never had talked like that to us. He always talked lawyer talk to us before that. Eddie yelled that he was only bullshitting about the knife. Fred said he'd seen the tape and it didn't look like that.

The following two days were dreadful for me. We three were separated. I was in a four-man cell. The other men were there for a month or two and that made it even worse. All I could do was sit on my bunk and think. All I could think was three strikes. I still thought Fred Gray would beat it for us. It was too unfair. Surely the judge would see that. Wasn't it just a little more of the stuff we were already convicted for? My moods were alternately hopeful and dejected. The only peace I got was sleep, and that never lasted long enough.

Two days later Fred was back to see us in the interview room. He got right to it.

"Look boys, I have to tell you right off that it does not look good. The police are sticking to their story that the cases are separate and that they didn't solve the second until after you were convicted of the first. Technically that makes this one your fourth. I even checked their notebooks. They kept everything separate. The knife makes it armed robbery. But that's really beside the point. Any conviction will be the fourth for all of you.

Maynard said "Jesus Fred, they had to know. Why the fuck would they set us up like this? We go down on this one, we're gone for good. Why the fuck would they do that? What'd we ever do to them? The knife is bullshit and they know it."

Fred shook his head. "They are policemen. They judge themselves on convictions. You're a big deal for them. It's not personal. Just the opposite."

We just sat there shaking our dumb heads. There was no way we could understand that stealing from people's houses could get us life with no parole.

Fred continued, "Look, I've spent all of the last two days on this. I talked to some other defense lawyers, a couple of prosecutors I know and a judge. The bottom line is that there is only one shot and that's a jury. If we go before a judge, he'd have no choice. You did it and he'd convict you. A jury might cut us a little slack but it would take an unusual judge and a very sympathetic jury. They'd have to find you not guilty of something they'd know you did. I'm not even sure any judge would let me introduce the things I'd need to persuade the jury. Frankly I don't think we would win but I think we have to try. There is no other chance. The police are not going to change their story and no judge wants to look weak on habitual criminals. You're in a very bad spot. I can't say it any plainer."

I learned a lot from Fred Gray. He was practical, direct, and terse. That realization would come to me many years hence when I had reason to reflect. At that moment in that interview room I was stunned to the point of immobility.

Words are often imprecise. I was stunned in the same sense as when a bull is hit with a sledgehammer before its throat is cut or a boxer is still standing but can no longer raise his arms. I knew in that moment that we would fight but that we would lose.

Can anyone comprehend a life sentence with no possibility of parole? The road gang was gone from my thoughts. I'd been in prison. Long termers never get on the road gang. They had all been together in a cell block. We used to joke about them. All I could picture was me sitting on a gray bunk in my blue clothes, looking at a concrete wall. It was not possible for me to be going there. All I wanted to do was work construction and shoot pool. I hadn't really stolen anything. All I'd done was help Mike. So I was stunned.

"Mike," I said. "Where's Mike?"

Fred was puzzled so Eddie said, "You know, the other guy with us. The one that ran."

"Oh him. He got away I guess, or else he's dead. They said he went into the swamp. They had dogs after him but they lost him at the swamp. The paper said he just had his underwear on. It'd be pretty bad in there with the mud and the alligators and bugs and snakes and all. What was he like? Could he get through that?"

"Shoes and shorts and wallet," I said. The picture of Mike flashed out the back door of my mind.

They all looked at me, questioning.

"He had his shoes and shorts in one hand and his wallet in the other. I just remembered now. He yelled at me to come and then he took off," I said.

"Well I'd take those odds any day," Maynard said. And he was right. We nodded our agreement.

"How much this gonna cost?" Eddie asked very quietly. "We got some money."

Fred flipped through his yellow pad until he found what he wanted.

"My estimate is about eight to ten thousand. It depends on how long it goes. I figured on three or four days and I need help on this. I need a junior and somebody to help with the jury selection."

CHAPTER

15

Jury selection took most of one day. Fred had hired a woman who was a jury expert to help him. She was quite stout, about forty, and looked out of place to me with all this dyed red hair piled up on her head and big glasses with those pink plastic frames. She and Fred would talk and then Fred would ask the juror questions. Fred said she was a shrink of some kind and not a lawyer, so he had to ask the questions.

He told us that the ideal jury for us was black and young. Our jury ended up mostly white and middle-aged.

The woman never once talked to us although we were there at the table. She left the moment the jury was selected. Fred told us she thought the two black men and a couple of women might be sympathetic. He tried to sound positive.

When the judge talked to the jury before the trial started, you could tell it was going to be tough for us. He told them their job was to look at the facts of this case only and to render a verdict. Their job was to apply the law, not interpret it. Fred stared at him, but he never looked at Fred.

The prosecutor this time was different. He was lanky and in his fifties with gray hair and good clothes. He sat with his legs stretched out, smiling at the jury. The prosecutor from our first case sat beside him with a lot of paper in front of him. Fred said the new guy was the chief prosecutor and only came to court when he could get good publicity. I wished he hadn't told me that.

The prosecutor's opening statement was terse. He never talked about our record, only the portable radio and the rug and Eddie's knife. We were on videotape, he said, bragging about our thefts, so he hoped we wouldn't have to waste too much of the jury's valuable time.

The moment Fred started talking about our last conviction, the prosecutor jumped up and objected. The judge stopped Fred from answering and took them into his office for about ten minutes. When they came back, he called a recess and Fred told us that the judge would not allow any talk of our records in opening arguments.

The trial took only that afternoon and the next morning.

Right after the lunch break the prosecutor put Frank Babcock on the stand and about ten minutes later the jury had the whole story. How Detective Collins had found one of our gang in a bar bragging about his thefts. How we came to their fence house all thrilled to be such good crooks. It was all true but I hated to hear it said like that, like we were such stupid scum.

All these people looking at us. I could see us too: Maynard stone-still looking at nothing; Eddie, trying to be cool but fidgeting with his hair and mustache. I felt like a man in another man's skin, in a bad dream that I knew was real.

They played the videotape then. We had not seen the first one, only Fred had. I'd never seen myself on TV before. The thing went on for half an hour. Every minute of it was true and awful, except I shouldn't have been in it. I should have been working at construction. I only went because it might be fun. But there I was, talking my ass off, sounding like a big shot. We swore, drank their beer, bragged about what good earners we'd be, and then we took the cash. I shouldn't have been in a police video. I suppose I was in shock, or depressed. There was not a thing I could do. A hopeless fool in a courtroom with men intent on locking me up.

Then they showed the photos to the jury and had the goods identified by their owner. There were even serial numbers on the radios and a certificate on the back of the rug. Frank and Ernie were in nice suits, Ernie's beard was gone, and they both had new haircuts. They usually looked at the jury and only looked at us to say we were the ones.

There was a fingerprint expert and then a clerk who gave our previous convictions.

Fred got a turn at Frank and Ernie after all the damage was done. He tried to make them admit that they could have put this case with our other one, but the cops just kept saying it only came to light after, and besides they were completely separate crimes.

I remember Fred getting all indignant and asking Frank Babcock why they hadn't just arrested us when they got the first goods to fence. That sounded like a good question to me, but Frank's answer just took the wind out of Fred's sails. Mine too.

"Well, you see, that would have blown our cover, wouldn't it? That was a real good operation we had there and these were not our only customers." Frank smiled for the jury and Fred went back to his notes.

The sad thing was that what Frank had said made sense to me.

If any doubts were in the jury's minds, the prosecutor got rid of them in his re-cross by making the cops look like nice guys doing a tough job.

In his summation to the jury, the prosecutor dwelt on the same thing. It was not the police or the jury who made the laws. It was us who had broken them. He said our defense was just an attempt to make the jury feel sorry for obvious criminals. Fred always told us to look at the jury to see if we could find somebody looking back and then to smile a little at them. When the prosecutor was calling us lowlifes, I made eye contact with one of the women on the jury and she stuck out her chin and looked away.

Fred was good, but he had no facts. All he had was a suggestion and his outrage. I actually thought he might get to a couple of them to at least hang the jury.

The judge laid it out for the jury before they deliberated. Only the facts introduced in this trial could be considered. Their job was this case and this case only. He even told them what a good jury they were, paying attention to everything.

We adjourned at two-thirty in the afternoon and we had a verdict two hours later.

As the charges were read out, the foreman said "Guilty, Your Honor" to each of them.

The judge thanked them and dismissed them. Before they had left, he told everyone else to stay where they were.

He said he might as well get the sentencing over with, as there were no arguments possible with the three-strike law.

He had no choice but to give us life with no possibility of parole. That's what number four called for. Even without an actual weapon. And we had a weapon.

Mitch was there and he cried when I looked at him so I started crying too. I had lost myself.

Part 2

TB18078

CHAPTER

The twenty-two months I'd served for the car thefts had been in a different place. There we labored outdoors and we were getting out. Then I had actually looked forward to being an ex-con. I'd be a tough guy. Girls would be impressed. It's hard for me to imagine how abjectly stupid I was.

Being back in jail was bad enough, but the way I got there was the absolute crusher. How stupid could I be? Imagine if it was you or a relative or a friend. They had snared me like a rabbit. When I had seen the fence guys at our house, I almost had a heart attack. I couldn't breathe. When they spoke I knew what had happened. I'd been trapped. But I'd had no idea how trapped.

I'd stolen cars, and a rug. I'd received a few thousand dollars and I was in prison for life. For all of the rest of my only life.

They had a statistic and I had life by myself with no hope, inside.

Since I'd been in prison before, it took only a month or so to settle in, if you can call it that.

Maynard and Eddie were in different blocks. I'd only see them on Sunday for a couple of hours. Mike, of course, was not with us. Of him we knew nothing.

They'd worked us over pretty hard about Mike, but how can you give up a buddy? Besides who knew where he'd gone? All I knew was how he ran out and I'd be damned if I'd tell them anything else.

After the final trial, and before we went up to prison, the cops had tried again to find out what we knew about Mike. We were four-time losers so I guess they thought we wouldn't care anymore.

Well, I'd thought, fair enough. I might as well have some fun. So I told the bald guy, the one playing good cop, that I'd think about it. The next day he had his tongue hanging out, ready for me to hand him Mike so the record would be perfect—four for four.

When we talked to those guys, it was in a little interview room. One side had a big mirror, so we figured the others were in there watching. We had leg chains and hand chains on. The furniture was bolted down.

So I got dumber every time these guys talked to me. The dumber I got, the more they relaxed. They had me.

I told the bald guy I'd only whisper it because they might have recorders and such and I didn't want it getting back to Mike that I'd ratted him out. They wanted to know where he would hide out.

So I'm sitting there all dull and dejected and I tell him finally that I'll tell him where Mike might be. He leans in a little closer and I whisper so he can't hear. He comes even closer and I whisper again. Finally, the fool gets up and I see him wink at the mirror and he comes around so he can hear me.

Again I mutter and he gets pissed and gets right in my face. I can smell his cigar breath. But he stays real nice because I'm going to give him Mike.

He came right to me, his ear to my face where I wanted him.

When you hunt you learn to move smoothly, not quickly or slow. Normal does not spook. I casually stretched a little and then just kept on going. I put the chains that joined my wrists over his fat neck and smashed his face down on the table. I got four good ones in before his pals pulled me off.

They wanted to kill me on the spot but I got lucky. The little guy in charge screamed at them and they backed off. He told me they'd get me in prison. I told him I'd be waiting.

I broke the bald guy's nose and some teeth.

So that was how stupid I was. That was Billy Ray at his finest. Four-time loser, bashing a cop.

At the penitentiary, they gave me an older black guy named Leonard for a cell mate. Leonard was in for murder. He'd been in for ten already and figured to get out in another twelve or fifteen. He'd killed his girlfriend when he was twenty-six. He'd been drunk and caught her with another man. He said he was sorry as hell that he'd done it.

I'd only been there a couple of months when Leonard taught me to play checkers and gin rummy. I got pretty good and could beat him sometimes.

He was always reading, and he stayed calm. Nobody bothered us because Leonard was huge and looked mean and was a killer and they knew I'd bashed a cop up pretty bad with my chains on. So we were cool. There were a few remarks about me being his bitch. All he'd say was, "You be careful boy or you gonna be my dead bitch." We were generally left alone.

One evening Leonard was reading on his bunk before lights out. I was agitated, playing solitaire and feeling desperate.

"Hey, Leonard, want a game of rummy? I'm goin' nuts here, man."

Leonard got up and stood looking into my bed. Now this was a six-foot-two, two-hundred-fifty-pound, iron-pumping murderer. His head was shaved and he always had a little wild look about him. His eyes were too big and his lips were huge. Even his teeth were big. I thought he was going to tell me to shut the fuck up, and I would have.

"I know you are, Billy Ray," Leonard said with a sadness and feeling that absolutely contradicted his appearance. "You been handlin' it real good, though," he said, "but you gotta get a new focus. If you just lie there, they got you, man. You have to fight."

I was confused. I didn't get it at all.

"Fight? Fuck, fight what? I'm gone."

"Only your body is gone. Not your head, boy. You have to use your brain. You want to know what I'm readin'?"

I was still confused but just having this conversation was perking me up. I'd been very depressed and alone just moments earlier.

"Sure. Yeah. What?"

Leonard showed me the book. It was *A Tale of Two Cities* by Charles Dickens. The print was small, there were a lot of pages, and the cover was plain green. It looked like a Bible to me.

Then he showed me his notebook, which was filled with neat writing. "These," he said "are the notes I make as I go along so that I'll remember the story and the characters."

"Characters?"

"The people in the book."

"Oh—why?"

"Why the characters?"

"Why everything. What's it about? Why take notes? Christ, it's like school work."

Again Leonard was calm. "It is school work. It's part of my English Literature course."

"That's what them other books are too?"

"Yup."

"That's your work?"

He smiled. "That's my work."

"You go to school?" I was incredulous. "But I thought you cleaned the offices and such? How can you go to school?"

"I do that too, but I'm fast, man."

That night Leonard explained his scam to me and just how it had occurred. He spoke softly and we talked well after lights out.

At first, he said, he'd only wanted to brown-nose and be regarded as a model prisoner so that his parole would be granted as early as possible. He knew from his community at home that the minister was the main guy so he cozied up to the chaplain to see if he could score any brownie points. This chaplain, it seemed, was on to Leonard, having seen many of his ilk previously, so the chaplain told him he could prove his goodness by preparing himself for life on the outside by bettering his education. At the time Leonard was twenty-seven years old and had a grade-eight education in rural Alabama.

Leonard continued his ruse with the chaplain and enrolled in a grade-nine correspondence course. The chaplain corrected his homework. Then the unthinkable happened. Leonard started to enjoy it and did well. After eighteen months, Leonard had finished grade nine and moved on to grade ten. The chaplain interceded on his behalf and got him the cleaning job in the prison office. Soon he could do his work in two hours and the chaplain let him study by himself in a holding cell they have for new arrivals. In a year he was in grade eleven and was studying at night and in the morning too. At the end of his story that night Leonard really shocked me.

"Billy Ray, I killed a good woman and I'll be here till I'm forty-six or forty-eight or even fifty. When I get out I'm gonna get me a smart woman, live in a nice little house with some kids, I hope, and

I'm gonna teach school. I know I'm gonna do it and that book I showed you tonight is second-year college. I'm gonna have a masters degree in education and be the best educated elementary school teacher in Alabama. And I'm gonna straighten up a few little punks like you and me so I can keep 'em outta here. I'm gonna have a little satisfaction before I'm through."

"How come nobody knows? I been in here three months and nobody told me a thing?" I suppose I sounded skeptical.

Leonard laughed that big low rumble of his. "It's better that our fellow inmates think I'm a stone killer. I have a lot of privileges on the other side. There are only three of us and we keep it to ourselves. The chaplain has his job on the line with us."

"So why are you telling me? Who are the others?"

"How far did you go in school?"

"Me? Grade ten but I quit before it was finished."

"How were your marks?"

"Okay, but I didn't go all the time."

Then he said it. He said it only once but I will always remember.

"Billy Ray, you're a smart guy but you don't know it. I can show you how to live in your head so this place won't bother you so much. I want to practice teaching on you. But whether you do or don't, you have to keep my work to yourself. I'm going to sleep now. Good night, Billy Ray."

The next morning our daily deadly prison life continued. Contrary to what you read in the newspaper or see on TV, prison inmates do not live in fear. They live in stultifyingly boring, numbing monotony. First, they count us. Then we line up for chow, which is always awful. Then they count us again. Then we go to work for a dollar fifty a day. My job was in the laundry, running a presser. Then they count us, then we line up for more awful food. Then they lock us up for a couple of hours, then we can go in the yard for an hour if we like. Then they count us and we get locked up again. Then we line up for chow. Then they lock us down for the night. We have to shit right there in the cell. There is a shower twice a week. That's it, except that on Sunday it's even more boring.

Leonard was not bored. He read in the morning before breakfast. When he marched off with the cleaning detail, he was happy because he went to another world, where he knew people who were not prisoners, and he studied there.

When we went to the yard, we stayed together for protection and for company. In the evenings we played a few games of checkers or gin rummy and then he read some more.

Leonard had the only life I could see in that whole awful prison.

A week after Leonard had told me his story I made a decision. I had to make it or go mad. I was twenty-three years old, facing all the rest of my life behind bars. My head had to escape.

So I enrolled in the Leonard Mossgrove School. He had all his correspondence school books and notes neatly stacked on the floor between our bunks and the wall so they could not be seen by passersby. Almost none of the guards knew about Leonard's work. He was very good at keeping his own counsel.

And so I learned from Leonard. Algebra is more fun in prison than in high school. I suppose it's the lack of competition. In high school there are girls, sports, pals, and pool. In prison there is nothing.

Leonard was an excellent teacher. He made me teach myself. He cajoled, kicked my butt, sympathized, and laughed, but he would never ever tell me the answer. I had to find it myself. Step by step. He'd tell me where to look or how to figure, but the looking and the figuring were up to me.

It was not easy at first. Leonard said my study habits sucked. He started me back in grade nine. I felt really dumb.

Every afternoon and night we studied. Others noticed. Occasionally we'd be the subject of a remark from some tough guy, something like, "What're you two asshole buddies readin' in there anyway? How to butt-fuck better?" Others would laugh. Leonard would smile and ask the inmate's name. I remember one new guy, his name was Howie. He was a big dumb white boy with an obvious dislike of blacks. He asked us what the fuck we did together.

"Well Howie, we are currently reading about the intra-familial marriage among the white trash in Alabama and how it has spawned ignorant assholes such as yourself and we have decided to kill you at the earliest opportunity. Ask around, Howie, I am bigger than you, much, much smarter than you, and except for my good friend Billy Ray here, I hate crackers ardently. I am a stone cold killer, Howie, and I am not at all amused by your rhetoric regarding our choice of literature. Howie, you have fucked with the wrong brother. Now be a good fellow and get the fuck out of my sight." Howie was just smart enough to see the downcast eyes around him. Leonard had an aura of brains and physical power. Howie would have hurt me.

The transition was painful for me because I fought the fact of my incarceration every hour I was there. Over the next year, however, I started to see it. I had something to live for. I looked forward to the work. I could think about it while I ironed clothes.

I missed Leonard at chow. He ate with the blacks and I ate with the whites. We agreed it looked more normal. He was very clever about looking normal.

He never asked me if I wanted to see the chaplain or try to work his gig. Nor did I ask to be considered. This was to be our way.

In fact, he didn't tell the chaplain about his project until five years later when I was ready to graduate. By then I was ready to really graduate.

CHAPTER

What I loved the most was reading. It took me away. When Leonard told me I had passed grade nine, he gave me a book. It wasn't a school book, it was a mystery. It was about spies in Berlin: *The Spy Who Came In From The Cold* by John LeCarré. It was way above my head. The writer was British and used words and phrases I was completely unfamiliar with. Leonard smiled his big know-it-all teacher smile and said, "Billy Ray you need a little pushin', boy. Wade on through this one. It'll do you good. Just take your time, you'll figure it all out."

Whenever he talked to me like that I took it as a challenge.

Pretty soon I had a mystery of some kind or another going all the time, as well as my regular work.

I can't tell you exactly when I decided to escape. It wasn't that I woke up one morning and thought about it or that a series of events led to it.

Probably it was the mysteries. They put my mind on the track of convolution, on the track of the unusual.

Deduction would be my only chance and there would be but one.

And I had all the time in the world, a lifetime to think about it.

Leonard had a goal, teaching. I got a goal too; to join Leonard, but in a different way. I would be like the heroes in my mysteries. I would deduce a plan and right a wrong.

I know it sounds corny. You must remember who I was then. I was a lifer living in his head. It was my home and my only salvation. The mysteries took me away. Nothing was impossible there.

The only person who ever visited me was my brother, Mitch. My mother moved to Meridian the year I was sent away and she never came back. Mitch got a few cards and then nothing. She gave up, I guess.

I suppose Mitch learned his lesson by watching my stupidity. He had a decent job at the sawmill and was soon to be married. I was happy for him.

He came up to see me once a month without fail. Words can never express what it meant to me. I got the local news from Mitch. It kept my brain connected to my head. He could stay an hour and he always did. I could hug him when he came and when he left, and in between we could sit and talk with the guards watching us.

CHAPTER

3

Five years passed in the crushing monotony of incarceration, forever. I escaped at every possible instant into my twin cerebral worlds: fiction and my education.

Leonard had earned all the credits he needed and was a graduate of the University of Alabama. He showed me his diploma only once and then he gave it to the chaplain for safekeeping. His studying intensified after that. I loved him like a father. He is a great man.

In April he told me that he'd told the chaplain that I was ready to try the high school graduation exams and the SAT for college entrance.

The chaplain called for me one day and, for the first time, I was admitted to Leonard's other world. There were offices and women and normal. I'd been in the can so long, I'd forgotten normal. But I did not feel normal. They had me leg-chained and handcuffed and a guard kept me marching with a billy club in my back.

The chaplain was an older man, maybe sixty or so. He was short and stout with wispy white hair.

We were alone in his little bare prison office.

"Leonard's been teaching you I hear."

"Yes sir, he has."

"What's your I.Q., Billy Ray?"

"Don't know, sir. Never took a test."

"So—" he chuckled. "That Leonard's a piece of work isn't he? He never told you, did he?"

"Told me what?"

The chaplain sighed. "Billy Ray, Leonard has given you three I.Q. tests. Do you remember taking some tests? Several pages of general questions?"

"Oh sure, sure. He gives me one at the end of each grade. I thought they were part of the program. You know, something else to pass."

"Billy Ray, do you know anything about I.Q.s?"

At least, Leonard had explained that to me. "Yes sir, it means intelligence quotient. Average of the population is one hundred. Eighty is borderline moron. One twenty is good. Over one forty is top one percent. Over one fifty is genius."

"Guess yours."

My mind deduced that I'd probably graduate from high school and that would be a little above average. "One ten."

"Billy Ray, it's over one thirty-five. On three different tests. Mine is one twenty and Leonard's is a little more How in the name of heaven did you ever land in here?"

I told him, plain and simple. I was a thief but they trapped me. I never had a chance.

"Do you believe in God, Billy Ray?"

"I suppose so. Everybody does, but I've only been to church a few times. My mother never went."

I saw the opening as if God Himself had presented it to me. The chaplain lived in Leonard's other world. Normal, if only once a week, was still normal and it would stop the abnormal for that time. Abnormal, minus a little normal equals a little less abnormal.

I knew what was coming next. It was in his face. What he got from me was encouragement in the form of a hopeful look.

"Billy Ray, would you like to receive some religious instruction? I think it might help you to cope in here."

"Yes sir, I surely would."

"Have your been baptized?"

"No sir, not that I know of."

"Have you ever come to the chapel service on Sundays?"

"No sir, I haven't."

"You know how to do it?"

"Yes sir. They call it out on Sunday mornings and we have to flash our lights to be let out. Why doesn't Leonard go?"

"He's too damned proud. Thinks he'd be found out besides, he says."

"Does he believe in God too?"

"Ask him. He won't tell me."

"But— But you help him anyway? Even if he doesn't believe?"

"Billy Ray, Leonard is finding God the hard way. Maybe when he's that great teacher ten years from now, he'll know God helped him out. You don't push Leonard. He has to do it his way."

"You sure got that right, but I'll tell you one thing, Reverend, he's saving my life in here."

"Mine too, son. He's the only reason I keep it up here. I'm retired now. I don't have a church anymore. Now don't you be telling him that, you hear?"

"No sir, I surely won't."

"Good. Start coming to chapel and we'll start there, all right?"

"Yes sir."

Another little world to see. The Reverend Lester Smith needed work. I'd be it.

"Billy Ray," Reverend Smith said. "Leonard asked me to get

high school examinations for you. I have them and I'm prepared to administer them. There are eight and they take two hours each. We'll do one a day starting today in the afternoon. That fit your schedule okay?"

I laughed with him. "I think I can work it in."

I got first-class honors, and the Reverend Smith and Leonard and some of the office people had donuts and coffee to celebrate. I cried like a baby to be that normal and to have real people shake my hand. They just let me cry it out.

"Well, son," said Reverend Smith, "you going on to college now?"

Everyone chuckled, even me.

"Yes sir, I am. Professor Leonard here has started me already. I'm enrolled, just waiting for the courses."

"Well good for you. What's it to be? I hear you are fond of literature?"

"That I am, but I'm going to be a lawyer."

That stopped the chuckles.

"Maybe I'll be the first con lawyer on the Internet. My fees would be attractive—a dollar ninety-five a day."

The chuckles reappeared.

The reverend would be my man. He was the one to work on.

CHAPTER

Well into my first year as a college undergraduate, Mitch brought me the news that would change my life again. Mike was back.

"God, Billy Ray, I'd never have known him in a hundred years. He's in the goddamned Marines and he's stationed down in Pensacola. He just called information and called me up. I went to see him over in Mobile. He's a fuckin' corporal. Head's shaved, looks like one a them guys on TV. But still neat as a pin. You remember how he was?" Mitch laughed. "Always cleaning my refrigerator."

So I did. Mike was also fearless and he could talk his way out of anything.

The reason he didn't get caught with the rest of us dummies was that when he saw them walking around our place that morning and told us we had to run, we hesitated. He didn't. We'd all been in bed just getting up, hung over as usual. Mike grabbed his pants, took his shoes and wallet, and took off out the back.

The sheriff's guys were fat and slow and I guess they couldn't decide whether to chase him or get us. They chose us.

"Man, he's lookin' good, Billy Ray. We talked for a long time and he told me how he got away. He went to our old tree house and grabbed a few cans of beans and stuff we kept up there and then he went straight into the swamp. Said it took him four days to get out and he was all bit up by bugs and such. But he slept up in the trees and nothin' big got at him. He came out way over where the railway tracks go over the river and hopped a freight goin' north. He got all the way to Birmingham before he could get off. So he went homeless, pretendin' he was nuts for a while, then he went out west. Billy Ray, he got his name changed back to his real father's and he's clear as a bloody bell. But he won't come to Grand Bay and he says he can't come up here. But the bugger came back. You got to give him credit. He came back and he told me to tell you he thinks about you guys all the time. He said he'd do anything, but there's nothin' anybody can do."

Maybe, maybe not. I did have one little idea.

"How long will he be at Pensacola?"

"Just got there. Said probably a year anyway. He's learning how to be a gunner on a big new helicopter. Do you believe that bugger? He must be smart as hell to do that."

"Yes, I suppose he is. Smarter than me anyway. He's in the Marines and I'm in stir. Tell him I'm real happy for him and I'm impressed he looked you up. That means a lot to me. Mitch, keep in touch with him. Tell him to stand by, okay?"

Mitch looked straight at me. "You can't break out of this place, Billy Ray. It's not possible. They'd kill you."

"I know that, Mitch. Tell him anyway, okay?"

Mitch shrugged. "You goin' to tell me what you're thinking, Billy Ray?"

"No, I'm not."

"Well, fuck you very much."

"Mitch," I said. "You are my whole entire family. You're all I've got. Just tell Mike to stand by. What you don't know is best for both of us, okay?"

Mitch shrugged. "Sure," he said, but he thought I was hallucinating, that much was evident.

A month later, Mitch was back. He'd seen Mike again and he'd re-stated his promise to help. I told Mitch to tell Mike to stock the old tree house; fix it up if it needed it and put a pair of big bolt cutters up there. "Make sure the ladder is easy to climb. Don't you go near it or even think about it or ever tell anybody, not even your girlfriend, about this or you'll end up in here. We're never going to talk about this again, Mitch. Can you do that?"

"Billy Ray, if you think—"

I cut him off. "Do it, Mitch. I've got just this one chance. Do it for me then never think about it again. This never happened."

Again I got that "you deluded bugger" look from him. But he agreed to tell Mike.

CHAPTER

5

I got the idea in an old-fashioned mystery from England. A prisoner had one of his own family killed so that he could get out to attend the funeral. He escaped in the hearse. It was a stupid, kind of obvious plot, but it stayed with me.

One day at lunch, about two or three years after I'd read the book, I saw a possibility.

In front of me was a quart of two-percent milk. I read it like I read everything I see. Just a habit. I'd seen a lot like it, but nothing registered before. On the milk carton was the drawing of a young man's face and a little personal information. It was about the kid having disappeared. There was a reward for finding him.

One of the toughest things about prison is getting information. Inmates can make just a few calls a month on the pay phone by reversing the charges and the calls are listened to. Computers are normally out because they can be used like phones, but Leonard and I used a computer sometimes for research. The chaplain got us a used one. It was slow but it serviced our needs.

The problem would be using it for my purpose without being detected.

But a convict has one thing. Time. He can wait.

It must have taken me ten tries before I found the right Web sites. After that, it was easy. Whenever the reverend left the office he had to lock me in and tell the guard. So I always heard him unlocking the door and I could change the screen before he reentered.

The boy on the milk carton was James Erwin Randolf. Born April 12, 1974. He'd been missing for nine years and he was from Montgomery, Alabama. There was a picture, a brief biography. He had run away from home.

Then I worked on it. Lies should be big and bad or they are not important enough to be believed. So I worked on a big one.

James Erwin Randolf had been missing for a long time. The Montgomery newspapers both had Web sites so it was technically easy but tedious work to find the few articles on him. I must admit to luck here. James came from a prominent family and they had made quite a cause of finding their son. His father was a self-made owner of a big building supplies business. He'd taken out ads on his own, offering a reward for his son's return. It was the ads, not the fact that the boy had gone AWOL, that spurred the journalists. In the ads and in the body copy of the articles were some of the details of young James's life. I memorized them in rhyme form because they never could be committed to paper or put on the computer. Every time I learned something, a line or two was added to my poem.

It became my mantra and it was the skeleton upon which I built my story. And I built the story as my reality, telling myself over and over and over of its happening. In bed I lived and relived every detail of it, night after night after night.

It would have to be a true story by the time I was obliged to tell it, capable of showing its truth, even to a lie detector. When you have but one chance, nothing will do but perfection.

They would have to coax it out of me and they would wind up believing it.

Jimmy Randolf in between
Sisters Gwyneth and Noreen
Daddy Wally has ten stores
Full of stuff for all your chores
Mom is Helen, has red hair
Poor old Wally lost his hair
Live in Sherwood on the lake
1205 Archer Drive
Three-car garage and patio
Horses for the rodeo
Johnny went to Sherwood High
Played the trumpet, just got by
Friend was Willie LaJollet
Not in heavy-hitter set.

And on it went. I can only remember that much, but there was enough minutiae to let me spin my yarn.

In three months, I was pretty well set. I had the entire story committed to fact. There would be no tripping me up. Self-interrogation continued incessantly as I probed the universe for questions.

Jimmy was my pal. My secret.

His pictures were the key. There had been two of them, both taken a few months before his departure. He'd posed for both. One was in his band uniform and one was a school head shot. I had to trust my intuition on Jimmy and his father.

Before I'd read all those mysteries, none of this would ever have occurred to me.

Mitch came each month as usual. He told me that Mike had repaired and stocked the tree house.

The week before I started the campaign, I had to tell Mitch one more thing.

"Mitch, if you ever hear something about me or if anybody asks you any questions, you have to tell the truth. You know nothing. And it will be the truth because I'm not telling you anything. That's the best way for both of us. But if you hear anything about me, tell Mike. Just tell him what you hear. You'll only be repeating gossip. Nobody can blame you for that. Tell other people too. Don't ever mention Mike to anybody, okay?"

Mitch surprised me there. "I told him to put a blow-up little dinghy in the treehouse too. It's in a backpack. Some food's there too. I had to do it, Billy Ray, there's snakes and gators out there. There's a net too. You can sleep in the dinghy. It's only a big toy one but it's green. I know you told me to stay out of it and I figured you were full of shit anyway so I thought, 'What the fuck, Mitch, if the silly bastard wants to live in fantasyland, he might as well have a good one.' Billy Ray, they could cut my heart out, I'd never tell a soul. Fuck, I sound as crazy as you now. But you know what Mike said? He said, even if you had no chance we had to be ready. He said to tell you, you were pretty smart and you'd figure it out. Now ain't we three dumb bastards?"

I just sat back and started to laugh. He started too. It was fun to fantasize.

We said no more about it then or the next month when he visited me again.

CHAPTER

6

I was baptized on a Sunday morning. Twelve inmates, including Leonard, watched. Leonard had not found the Lord as I had, but he went to chapel with me now and he seemed to enjoy the ritual. You could never tell with Leonard which base he was on. It did me good with the reverend though, to have Leonard in tow.

I took the classes with the reverend by myself. Leonard wasn't ready for anything personal just yet. It was better that way. I needed the reverend to myself. Over the next few weeks following my baptism, I worked Reverend Smith around to the subject of confession. He was Episcopalian and at least had some thoughts on the subject.

He told me that confessions as practiced in the Catholic Church were possibly helpful as cheap psychotherapy, but that he couldn't hold with celibate men hearing personal things from women. I wove the conversation around to just getting things off your chest and then dropped the subject immediately. He told me I could come to him with anything and he wouldn't repeat it unless I said it was okay.

I let that sit for weeks, moving on to other topics.

I was reading the Bible and his old sermons and we'd pray a little together after every session we had together.

My schoolwork was going well and I was being prepared by Reverend Smith to join the church.

He didn't know it but I was watching my diet as carefully as I could to lose the ten pounds of fat I'd put on, and I had taken to jogging, and lightened up on the iron pushing. If Leonard noticed, he said nothing. Maybe he thought I was purifying myself for God. That's how I wanted him to think about it, but I'd never say anything. Leonard was far too clever to be led anywhere. We studied, we played cards, and we were our little family in block C, tier three, cell seventeen. I was almost happy, but I couldn't be because the risk of failure made my heart stop. This was once only and the odds were dreadful.

Fearing the gravity of doubt, I refused to entertain it. Once I started, it had to be true.

I prayed and even tried to believe that God had provided the reverend for this very purpose.

For a while, weeks in fact, I fed the good reverend a menu of far away looks, downcast eyes, little head wags, and long slow exhales.

He finally bit one afternoon in his office after a session on the Good Samaritan.

"Billy Ray, is something bothering you, boy?"

"No sir—well—no, nothing really."

"You know you can talk to me if you have something on your mind. I know it's hard in here. Is somebody bothering you?"

"Oh no." I chuckled. "Nothing like that. I've got Leonard. Nobody messes with Leonard."

"Well that's good. Nothing else, then?"

"No—not—no I'd better—you know it's just old stuff. No way out of it now anyway."

I let him coax me some more, then I said, "Reverend Smith, if I tell you something you can't tell anybody, right? The secrecy of the confessional and all that?"

"Billy Ray, are you in some kind of trouble?"

"Hell, Reverend, can't be in any more trouble than this, can I?" I pointed to my coveralls and leg chains.

The reverend said the magic words. "Son, it's your soul you need to be worried about, not where your body is."

Looking at my feet, I said, so he could barely hear me, "Reverend, I killed a boy. I did a terrible sin."

CHAPTER

It took Reverend Smith two weeks to get any more information out of me. He did it by appealing to my new Christianity. How must the victim's family feel? I must help them.

Once he'd managed to get the gate ajar, I let it all out in one overwhelming confession.

I'd met a boy, a teenager really, on the street one night in Mobile. It was outside a bar and I was drunk on beer. The boy was queer and he wanted to give me a blow job for five dollars. I said okay and let him do it in an alley thinking I'd whack him in the face when he finished and maybe more. It turned out that I liked the blow job and ended up liking the boy. His name was Jimmy. Anyway, I took him to this room I had in Mobile and he stayed there with me for a month or so. He was real quiet and neat. He had some money, so we just hung out. I took him up to Grand Bay on a Sunday to show him how to shoot a bow and arrow. We had some hidden in a tree house in the woods. I didn't want anybody to see me with him in case they thought I was queer. He looked kind of queer. So we drove in by the old sawmill and parked there and went in the woods. He couldn't shoot the arrow worth a damn and he was all nervous and jumpy. We had a bottle of bourbon and we got pretty drunk. Then all of a sudden, out of nowhere he starts to kiss me and talks all kind of trash how he wants me to fuck him in the ass and be his—well—I guess I flipped out or something like that, because I couldn't get him off me. So I grabbed his hair and pulled his head way back and then smacked his face hard into my forehead. I figured out later that I must have driven his nose cartilage up into his brain because he went out like a light. There was blood all over the place. I never touched him after that. He was dead right away.

I left off the story there and looked as dumbfounded as I could, not daring to look up at the reverend.

The reverend didn't let me down. "Billy Ray," he said, almost out of breath. "How did you know he was dead? What did you do to him?"

I had him. "The blood stopped coming out fast. That's how we'd know deer and such were dead."

"Oh my Lord," said the reverend. "Did you feel for his pulse?"

"No need. You could see his eyes were dead."

"Oh my merciful heaven, Billy Ray. What did you do with him? Tell me you didn't just leave him there. There's alligators and possums and all manner of creatures in that place, isn't there?"

"Sure is. No, I wouldn't just leave him out like that. I looked after him as good as I could."

He looked a little relieved at that. "Oh, my soul, Billy Ray, you called nine-one-one or something? That's right isn't it? You wouldn't just leave him out there, would you?"

"No sir. I buried him."

I'd said it. It was alive and out there between me and Reverend Smith.

"You buried him." A flat ending.

"Yes sir, I did. It was an accident and I was a little drunk. I couldn't think what else to do."

"I see." He became stern with me now. I was a prisoner and he was on the other side. He went to his desk right away then and pulled out a pad and pencil. "What was his full name, Billy Ray?"

"You going to take notes? This is just between you and me, right?"

"Billy Ray," he looked at me stone-eyed now, "we have to tell the authorities. We have to tell his family."

I protested and even had a cry before I broke down and told him the boy's first name and when it happened. I'd trust him to help me make it right. He convinced me to talk to the state police, but I did not make it easy for him.

The guard came to get me after supper that night and took me to the warden's office. I'd never been there before and, quite frankly, the whole thing hit me all at once when I saw the warden, the state police, and other men in suits. The reverend was there too. He looked dog tired.

I was away from the safety of Leonard and my cell. I was in chains and all I had with me was my lie, which had come along to be tested by all these smart men under bright lights. In retrospect I think the shock that I felt, with my stupid lie about to be undone, probably worked in my favor. I went into a sweat and could hardly talk.

They sat me down and let the reverend start on me. Since I'd planned on caution and nothing overt whatsoever, my near-catatonic state gave me time to regroup my shattered emotions, and get on with the job of letting them feel clever as hell putting the pieces together.

One absolute cornerstone of my strategy was not to know

Jimmy's last name or where he came from. If he was a good AWOL he wouldn't have told me anyway.

Reverend Smith didn't last long. He was being far too nice to me. I suppose they let him start off because he'd gotten it out of me in the first place and was due his brownie points. The warden looked pretty pleased too. Here his fine institution was helping law enforcement from the inside.

I knew I could have a lawyer, but that might work against me. If they told me I could have one, I'd decided to take them up on it so as to look scared. They never mentioned it that night.

CHAPTER

Over three sessions, one that night and two the next day, I let them have all the clues they'd need to figure out who I'd killed.

They sent in their psychologist and then an FBI guy. I trotted out my tidbits about Jimmy while seeming unaware that they meant anything at all.

I said Jimmy used to brag about wearing his sister's clothes. Once he picked up some guy's old trumpet and blew taps for us. He liked redheads because his mother had red hair. He laughed at bald guys because his father was bald. I did my very best to look like a somewhat rehabilitated fool.

And I always carried with me the remorse that had caused me to seek dispensation from the good reverend.

Strangely, they all seemed to believe me.

The third session was the last because they showed me his picture late in the afternoon. It had been faxed in by the Montgomery police. I identified it without hesitation, showing the appropriate relief that the sessions would be over.

"What'll they do now?" I asked the warden. "Tell his folks?"

I was actually bewildered why they had not asked where the grave was. I needed to find out what they were thinking.

"The Randolf boy's father will be here in the morning. Then we'll see. He's a pretty important man. We'll see what his lawyers say before we do anything. This one'll be by the book," the warden said.

"Who is he?" I asked.

"Big money guy. Friend of the governor."

When you act for your life, it's probably no different from any improv group. I had to act on instinct, and mine told me to play hard to get. If this guy was some powerhouse, a contest would be stupid. I'd have to cower.

"No way I'm talking to his father, or any lawyer either. I need a lawyer too. I have rights too. Prisoners have rights to be represented in new matters. I read that." I sat back and folded my arms. "I want a lawyer before I say one more word and I'm not talking to his father. Period." Then I shut up and looked at the two state detectives and the three other men I didn't know.

One of the suits gave it away. His face dropped and he looked at his partner and said, "Nice goin', genius."

So then I knew they had taken the risk that I could be railroaded right along without a lawyer. I made it a little tougher. "In fact," I said, "I have never been read my rights or offered a lawyer, so I believe everything I've said before is not legally available to you in any proceedings in this matter." Spoken in a lawyerly fashion, I was completely flying blind here, way off my carefully crafted script.

Their mouths dropped and one of the state guys started to call me names and threaten me. Very calmly I stared him down and when he shut up at the insistence of the others, I put in a line I'd had prepared for any suitable opening.

"I'm a lifer, sergeant. There's not a hell of a lot you can do to me. I volunteered my confession to the chaplain in order to help save my soul from eternal damnation. All this lawyer talk is making me very nervous. I'm done. You're on your own now. Don't even bother with the lawyer. Just tell the guard to take me back in. I'm done."

And I was. I refused to talk. Once committed to being a hard ass, I had to follow through. Not one more word came out of me that afternoon. They did everything but hit me. I would not talk to them.

Leonard knew nothing of all this nor did he inquire. Leonard had taught me to stay in my own lane and he let me be.

That night I came back thoroughly shaken and confused. Had I just really been a hothead like in the old days? Had I, in fact, fucked it all up?

He saw my demeanor and laughed. "Billy Ray, you're the whitest white boy I ever did see. What you're needin' is a good old-fashioned ass whippin'. Get them cards, boy. Tonight's my night." He did whip my ass and he crowed about it. I had to smile. Well if I lost everything else, I still had Leonard.

They came for me at my pressing machine at about mid-morning. I had not slept well and I was jumpy. The guards showed a little deference, which made me even more apprehensive.

In the chaplain's office sat a bulky bald man with a country-club tan. He got up and Reverend Smith introduced us.

"Billy Ray, this is Wally Randolf, James's father. Mr. Randolf, this is Billy Ray Billings." The man put out his hand and I shook it. My knees almost gave out. In that instant I felt his troubles, not my own. He didn't even seem to hate me. His voice was kind.

"Sit down, Billy Ray," Mr. Randolf said. "Reverend Smith told me you came forward about Jimmy and that was a good thing to do—for all of us. I'd like you to help us bring this thing to an end. I need your help."

There was Mr. Randolf, Reverend Smith, and a fat guard named Toohey in the little office, but there was also Jimmy. His Jimmy had been gone for years and now he was dead. My Jimmy was pounding in my chest and head, telling me to come to him. His Jimmy had already been mourned for, and he wanted an ending to it. His time was well on the downstroke. Mine was at hand. I felt like two people, three really. I had real sympathy for Mr. Randolf. He was just a sad father trying to be brave. I had terrible fear that I would fail and lose my moment absolutely. And I was Jimmy's lover and his killer.

The choice was there and I took it. I was a killer looking for salvation.

"What about the lawyer?" I asked, looking at the reverend. Now I didn't want one but continuity demanded the question.

Mr. Randolf replied, "I thought we could handle it simpler, Billy Ray. Would you agree to no lawyers, either side?"

I did not answer, so he continued.

"Look Billy Ray, here's the long and the short of it. The most you'd get is murder two and you're already in here for good. I don't want you prosecuted and I'm pretty sure I can guarantee that if you confess to involuntary manslaughter, the whole thing can be over in one court appearance. Of course, you'd have a lawyer for that. All I want is to give my son a Christian burial and let his mother finally grieve for him properly."

He looked at me and I just started to cry. What the fuck was I doing? These were nice people and I was such a stone cold bastard. Let his mother grieve for him properly.

He mistook my tears for remorse about his son, I suppose, because he teared up too.

"You did a good thing telling the reverend, Billy Ray, I want you to finish this for us. I want you to take us to where you buried him."

The actor in me kicked in instantly and instinctively. It was like a visitation. There was nothing planned about it.

"No way man!" I said. "You're gonna get me out there and they're gonna shoot me tryin' to escape. No way. I'm staying here. I don't have to go. I want a damn lawyer."

For a half hour I let Wally Randolf and the reverend talk me into the only thing I wanted in the world. I was not easy to convince. Reverend Smith would have to go with me as a witness, or I would not go. He agreed.

Oh, how I wanted to limit the number of guards and weapons, but I could not tip my hand. The only hope I had was my own reluctance.

Finally, I said, "Look Mr. Randolf. I'm gonna do it, but I don't want any freak show. No reporters or anybody else, okay? Just take me out there real quiet and get me back here."

Then I let one of my other selves pop out for a second. "And I gotta tell you how bad I feel, sir. I didn't mean to kill him. I only was tryin' to get him off me. I sure never meant to hurt him bad."

"They told me what you said, Billy Ray, how it happened. You did right to tell the chaplain."

I stood up abruptly, the actor once again. "Okay, let's get it over with. It's right near Grand Bay. We can be there in a couple of hours."

"Oh no, we can't go that quickly, Billy Ray," Mr. Randolf said. "We've got to notify the local sheriff, and there's some paperwork apparently to get you released for this."

There I had it. There was now a chance that Mitch would find out. Grand Bay is a small place and while the sheriff can keep his own counsel, his deputies never could.

I looked to the reverend for help.

"It'll be a couple of days, Billy Ray. You're doing the right thing here. Just a couple of more days and it'll be over."

Amen! One way or the other. Probably the other.

Two guards and the chaplain took me to Grand Bay in a dark blue prison van with steel mesh on the windows. I'd told them where our start-off point was by the old sawmill ruins, because that's where I said Jimmy and I went in, and because it gave me a good three hours walk to the tree house through some pretty dense woods and some bog. It was all part of my mystery.

We ate box lunches on the way and got there about eleven o'clock on a Tuesday morning, four days after my meeting with Mr. Randolf.

He was there waiting with Sheriff Bobby Cutler, one of his men and two state troopers in fatigues. There were no rifles but they were all wearing pistols on their belts. The sheriff was cordial and he shook my hand and said good morning. His deputy was new and he nodded. Nobody else said anything to me.

The deputy had a shovel. He handed it to me, but I showed him my wrist chains. He shrugged and kept it.

One of the State police was a sergeant and he took charge.

"Okay, the prisoner will lead, one guard on one side and Ferguson here on the other, about fifteen feet out. The rest of us will follow.

Everyone understood. We set out.

I shuffled along as best I could with my ankle chains. There was ample time, so I never complained or tried to fall. All I could do was my best, all hobbled up in the thick woods.

It was August and hot as hell and steamy in there. We started off where the ground was hard and dry, but after a half hour we got near the bog. There were a couple of alligator slides down black muck banks into stagnant water. The bugs were awful.

I got cut up some falling over branches, but I never complained, just got up and kept going. A man on a grim mission. I was half there and half in my own head. It did not seem completely real. But it was.

After an hour we stopped and had water from canteens.

"How much further, boy?" the sergeant asked.

"Another couple of hours," I said. "Maybe less."

He looked at his watch. "Shit, that'll take us to two o'clock. C'mon Henry—you guys too." He motioned for the deputy and the guards to follow him out of my hearing.

I could see them bickering for a minute or two and then the sergeant raised his voice and that stopped the conversation.

They came back to me. The older guard from the prison was not happy.

The sergeant spoke to me. "Okay, pal, we're gonna take off those leg irons, so you can walk faster. This whole thing's takin' too long. We gotta be outta here by six. I'm not havin' a whole lot a fun here in this miserable shit hole and I got Little League tonight." He waved the guard in toward me. "Take 'em off."

The actor, to my surprise, had not deserted me. He was totally unwanted but had to persist. These guys would take all the convincing he could offer.

"No way!" I shouted and turned to the chaplain, who was pretty tired by now and none too happy to be where he was either.

"See," I said. "I told you they'd do it. They're gonna shoot me, sayin' I'd run for it."

Then I looked at the sergeant. "You can't make me. I'm not that dumb."

The sergeant just looked at me like I was a piece of dirt and shrugged. "Hey boy, they're comin' off and you better pick up the pace or I will shoot your sorry ass. Take 'em off, boss."

They took off my leg chains while I acted nervous and cowed.

I picked up the pace all right. These guys were all paunchy except for the new deputy but he was loaded down with a backpack and the shovel.

It surprised me that no one tried to slow me down. The sergeant was too ornery to give in and the other officers were all civil servants, keeping out of the boss's sights. In a less arduous situation it would have been amusing or at least psychologically instructive, I suppose.

We headed due west. The sergeant was nobody's fool and I could see him check his compass to make sure I wasn't just out for a walk.

Keeping the sun on my left and edging right as it went away from us, I kept us in a good line.

My plan was simple enough. I'd take them up close to the swamp and when I got the chance, I'd dive into the black water and get as far as I could underwater. I had a straw I'd saved for two months in my pocket, that I'd gotten out of the trash at the prison office. I'd keep going away from them using the straw for air. I knew it was a dumb plan but in my mind I saw it working. Mitch and I had done it when we were kids. At least I was experienced. If I could get them to rest by some water and take my boots off to rub my feet, then I could swim better.

But I'd never figured on having no leg chains. That had never occurred to me. All my planning, or dreaming, had me shuffling along a foot or so at a time. All the running and conditioning I'd done was for my run after the tree house. I'd expected to go to the tree house at night when the guards had gone for help. I'd figured they'd look for me for a couple of hours and then go back. They could call out for help but they'd have to go and meet them and helicopters couldn't land out in the woods. I'd get out further and further in the water then and come out at night. Finding the tree house in the dark was iffy, but it was my one chance.

That whole plan went out the window the moment I had started to walk free of chains.

The sergeant was a serious asshole and a macho macho man. I could see he was enjoying harping at the others to keep up. He never once told me to slow down. This was his little show and he was the big guy. His gut bounced and his jowls quivered but he kept up. After a half hour or so they were straggled out behind me. He'd pulled in the two wing men because they were not keeping up anyway.

My pace was not obviously quick, but I was in very good condition and got over logs and water and rocks easier than them.

The tree house was northwest of us now, about two miles. There was no trail to take me there, but the land was drier and the timber bigger. The going would be easier. In daylight I could get there in well under an hour.

The new plan replaced the old with great relief. I edged a little north to avoid the swamp and kept the pace as brisk as I could. The sergeant had a hard look on him. I never turned overtly to see it, but when going over a log or around a tree, there he'd be, getting hotter and wetter and more pissed off.

Even I was getting thirsty and tired. Then I heard one of the guards puffing and calling out, coming up to the sergeant.

All I could catch were isolated words but they were my signal.

"Old guy's beat—fuck man, he's a hundred years old."

The sergeant slowed to talk to him and called to me. "Hey, boy, slow down a minute, we're talkin' here."

I slowed. They slowed. I came to a little crest where a high boulder stood on my left and the ground fell to the east.

"I'm gonna take a piss, okay?" I yelled back.

"Yeah, okay," the sergeant stopped and leaned over, his hands on his knees. I went behind the rock for some privacy and took off as quietly as I could down the hill. It was only about thirty yards or so and not steep. I was at the bottom in twenty long fluid strides and turned hard left into the heavy timber. Still no sounds from them.

The sun was over my left shoulder and I kept it there.

Shouts erupted after a minute but I was running free in my woods. There wasn't anybody in that group who could catch me. They'd have to look for my boot prints but I'd turned off where there were dead leaves and rock. They'd have to guess which way I'd gone.

The orange jump suit felt like fire on my body, but I couldn't stop to strip because of the wrist chains. I suppose the jumpsuit gave me speed. Man, I was flying. Part free, part fear. Good fuel.

I never heard any more shouting after those first few minutes and I couldn't think of what was happening back there.

There were no trails but the woods were not too dense. It got hillier as I went north and the crests were easier to get through than the damp lower ground.

It would take them a little while to figure out they couldn't find me and call in that they had fucked up. Then who knew what? Helicopters, dogs, the works I guessed.

All of this added speed.

You see the movies where the escapee is falling down and cutting himself and knocking his head on rocks. Not me. I never even stumbled. I was on air and I flew. It was like I was twelve again with my buddies playing war. I could see three moves ahead. My muscles ran perfectly on adrenaline. My chained hands were out in front of me for balance.

Alone in the woods, I was fairly quiet, even with boots on. They were my old ones, all broke in and recently resoled. Every day I had put oil on them from the pressing machines.

A small clearing with seven spruce trees told me I was home. The seven sisters. They had grown and had a few babies but they were my welcome. I laughed out loud and hung a left. I'd only been a few degrees off course, and only half a mile from the tree house.

CHAPTER

The bolt cutters were hard to hold and I grew desperate after several tries. Then I calmed and told myself only a couple more tries and then I'd split and take them with me to try later. But I lay down up there and put the bolt cutters on the floor to stabilize one handle. The other I sat on and in a couple of tries I cut a link and my arms were free.

There was a backpack. I did not open it. I ripped off my coveralls and tied them around my waist and climbed down in my underwear. The tree house had been empty except for the backpack and the cutters. I took them with me. On the ground I put the cutters through the strap and took off. This time south toward the swamp.

Again I ran. The bolt cutters fell out a couple of times, so I carried them in my hand. There would be no trace other than footprints and I couldn't help that. It was mid afternoon and hotter than hell. I needed water badly so I stopped and went into the backpack. There was a plastic bottle of Gatorade on top. Thank God for Mike. I drank half of it and took off again, full of energy and fear.

The helicopters were north of me but audible. When one got loud I took to ground under a tree. It went south to join the others.

What I really feared was dogs and there were none yet. Nothing was in my mind but fear of them, and it drove me to the green-black fetid swamp.

When I came close to the edge of the swamp I turned west again away from the helicopters' noise. There was not enough cover to risk the swamp in daylight so I decided to put more miles behind me.

I ran west until the sun started to send horizontal light through the trees. In re-creating that day later, I figured I'd run for four hours and covered six or seven miles after leaving the tree house until I finally stopped.

There was no noise now except the birds and insects.

Near the north side of the swamp, I stopped to look in the backpack before it got dark. It was not a big pack but had side pockets and a big extra pocket on its back.

Mike was a genius. The Marines had trained him well. Everything was in big baggies with writing on them. The side flaps had one package each, one was labeled INSECTS/WATER TABS/PILLS, SUN, SALT. The other was FAST FOOD FIRST. In it were chocolates, rice, raisins, and dried fruit. I ate a little supper right there with the rest of the Gatorade and I kept the plastic bottle because it had KEEP printed on it.

In the big flap was the kid's blow-up raft. It was dark green. There was also a piece of green netting and some binder twine.

The main part of the pack had four waterproof packages in double zip-locking bags. The labels read COVERALLS, HAT; MORE GRUB; C-RATIONS. And finally NEW CLOTHES, RAZOR, SOAP, MAP.

Under it all was a tin box which held a kid's compass, two lures, a hand fishing line, a small penknife, a small file, three books of matches, and a little airplane whiskey bottle of Jim Beam.

By last light, my wrist cuffs were off and I had buried the prison coveralls with the file cutters and cuffs in the muck by the swamp. Then I pushed a log on top and scooped water all over the place to hide my marks.

Using a small tree limb I'd broken off and trimmed, I pushed the silly little child's raft out into the swamp with the last light of day. In it with me were my brother and Mike and my love for them.

Mike had been smart. There was no note and the printing was awful. I figured he did it with his left hand. Even the C-rations were Army. He was Marines.

But none of this occurred to me then, other than my profound gratitude.

I could remember this part of the swamp some from my youth. It was the part closest to town. It was quite open after you got through the tangle by the edge. The skin of the raft was pretty thick plastic but I could take no chances with sticks piercing it. So I poled slowly from the front or paddled with my hands when it got too deep, until I got clear.

There was just enough afterglow to see the open water and I knew how far it went. I'd have to be through it by daybreak.

Bump! The raft hit something big. It was a huge log. Perfect. I cut a piece of heavy bark about two feet long and a foot wide off it with the knife. I had a paddle. It broke in two and then I had two paddles, but they were strong enough to use then without further splitting.

Fueling up on some more rice and raisins and putting a tablet in the Gatorade bottle, I filled it with swamp water. Fuck it, there was no choice. When the pill dissolved I drank the crap and started my crossing.

There are startling moments in your life that never fade. All of my life until that moment had led me to this wonderful place. The stars appeared, then the quarter moon, giving off just enough light to see the flat water and the occasional stump or tree. I was euphoric, not because I had escaped, for I had not as yet. It was the euphoria of one mind drinking in the planet, which had been removed. I would have kissed a gator, but fortunately none appeared. I was safe and on the water in the new coolness of the swamp night with the heavens to look up to.

The little compass was luminous so that part was easy, but I didn't really need it. If I went right I'd go aground and left would be mangroves. I dug in and paddled in good long strokes, changing sides with every one.

Many hours later, when I reached the heavier vegetation on the other side, I was really tired, but sunrise was still a way off so I went for a while longer into the heart of the thing until I really couldn't go any further without risking a puncture.

I tied the twine through a metal eyelet on the boat and around a small tree. I'd stay in the water even though there were little islands. No point risking snakes or gators. All at once I was utterly exhausted but I knew I had to be careful, so I rubbed insect stuff on my face and hands and took another good pull on the swamp bottle before putting the net over me.

The sun did not wake me until it was well up. Maybe ten o'clock or so.

There was none of that groggy stuff or thinking this was a dream. The first thing I thought of was the elapsed time. Five or six hours of sleep, no bug bites, but I did have diarrhea. There were pills for that but I knew with the swamp water even the chlorine pills wouldn't kill it all.

Dehydration could be a problem. Fuck it, I'd just keep drinking and eating and shitting. What was the alternative?

So I stepped onto a little island and let it go, popped a pill, and continued paddling into the swamp, staying very close to overhanging vegetation.

The decision I took then went against all my planning, which was to follow Mike's example and head out with all possible speed and try to hop a freight or hide in a truck. Anything.

The helicopters made up my mind for me. No sooner had I untied my raft and pushed off, than the *whir whir whir* of a helicopter came up behind me. If they'd been looking down they would have seen me. I was lucky, and they did not change course. I did. Right back to my little island where I stayed put under a runty cottonwood tree for that whole day.

After two more helicopters came near in the next hour or so, a new noise approached. It didn't come near and I just caught a glimpse of its big-blade motor and stern as it passed in the open water I had crossed the night before.

The only place I knew of where boats could be launched was where I wanted to come out—by the railroad tracks. A second boat came by in the early afternoon. The helicopters were low and slow. I counted three different ones through the leaves.

After the second boat went by, I made my decision. There was a larger island about two hundred yards further into the dense thicket of branches and scum. I could see the bigger trees. No boat could come near it and I figured they'd never imagine I could swim that far anyway, so I charted my course and at dusk I moved camp. It was tricky and the danger of puncturing my little raft was always present, but I made it there by the end of dusk and pulled everything ashore.

The thought of alligators and snakes was there, but thoughts of capture and a life of twenty-three hours a day of confinement made short work of any fear. I'd rather die than be shut up again. There was no doubt that I'd be sent to one of those single-cell places without TV, radio, or books. I'd kill myself first.

I'd stay there until long after the helicopters had gone. Dead or alive, I was not coming out. The clarity of my decision made me calmer. I could breathe.

I slept in the raft with the net over me because it still afforded some protection against things that crawl. Strangely, I slept well. Fatigue, I suppose. Or perhaps it was the knowledge that I was going to camp here for a while. My running was in limbo and the adrenaline-laden fear that accompanied it would be sublimated as well, for a while. Not a real vacation to be sure, but nevertheless a time to rest and think.

The helicopters started an hour or so after dawn. By then I was at the center of my island, well out of any possible view from the air or the water.

During that morning, I laid out all of my possessions and repacked everything by day. There were twenty two-water pills, twelve diarrhea pills, four days of C-rations, a plastic container of rice, some raisins, and fourteen pieces of dried fruit. Twenty-two pills; twenty-two days.

If I'd been from anyplace else, I might have just died there or given myself up, or run for it. It was hot and humid and smelled of all the rot imaginable. Perversely, I loved it because I was home and I knew how to survive. Maybe I couldn't cook what I caught, but I could sure as hell eat them anyway. So I put up twenty-two days of my meager sustenance, in five baggies. I never opened the last package with the final change of clothes because I wanted it fresh and free of the overwhelming humidity.

Then I set about my exploration.

CHAPTER

On my new island I thought of Leonard and what my escape had meant. I tried to imagine what was going on back there in my nightmare life. Leonard was there, and as it turned out, a good observer.

—as to the reaction to your departure, let me recount it as faithfully as I can. You must bear in mind that the outcome was still in much doubt and I had substantial fear for your white hide. I teach a journalism class now and I shall try to follow the principles which I coax my students to use.

You left me without a word, for which I am grateful. When I asked to be taken to the office of Reverend Smith that fateful afternoon, I was told that he was away, but that he'd left instructions that I could work at his computer with a guard present, which I did.

Toward the end of the afternoon, there was much shouting and bustle and I was taken by the guard to the warden's office.

It seems the warden and his chief guard (you remember Captain Marvel?) wished to psychologically jolt me into an instant confession. The warden sat behind the desk and nodded to the captain who confronted me with his stick in my gut. He got very close to me and said something like, "You don't wanna spend the next ten years in the hole, you're gonna tell me where he's goin' right here and now."

I said, "Who?"

He said, "Don't fuck with me boy, you know who."

I said, "Who what?"

He said, "Don't fuck with me boy."

And so it went for several more "Don't fuck with me boys," until the warden pulled him off me and started treating me as he usually did. He was always a pretty good guy but he was not at all happy that a prisoner had escaped. I guess he'd feel somewhat of a failure. I know I would.

In any event, he concluded that I was either unaware of your situation or not about to tell him. Fortunately, I was credible to him. It is hard for me to imagine any guilty man being as flabbergasted as I was at your story.

The warden, Captain Marvel, the guard, and I waited in the warden's office for a couple of hours getting bits and pieces of your exploits, until the good reverend and guards Rafter and Shultz got back. Why they ever allowed a convict to witness this is certainly beyond me. I suspect that had you had any other cellmate, it would never have been countenanced. The warden and the chaplain were used to me, I suppose, and so I stayed.

Perhaps they thought a group interrogation would loosen my tongue. Probably they just forgot I was there. If I had a video of it, I'd be rich.

Picture this. We're eating sandwiches and watching some of the first TV coverage from Mobile and in come the guards and Reverend Smith in a state of severe agitation, to say the least. They are dirty, sweaty, and very apprehensive.

They had good reason. The captain started at the guards with a fury but the warden bade him be quiet. This was the warden's show.

The guards were obviously in very deep shit for having permitted your departure. This much was made clear quite quickly. They were so exhausted, scared, and defensive that the reverend inserted himself in their defense, or at least to attempt a lucid explanation. It was probably a good thing because they had just said that your leg chains had been removed so that you could walk faster and the Captain had to spit out his Coca-Cola.

The reverend stood and raised his hand like a traffic cop to hold back the sputtering Captain. He raised his voice and implored the warden to let him tell the whole story, beginning to end.

I, at the time, was attempting to become invisible so they would not remove me.

The chaplain was brief but clear. He had been duped, he supposed, and they all had been duped as well. It seems you had resisted going for fear of your life and that they had to talk you into it to help save your soul.

He described the meeting at the old mill and the order of march with the state police sergeant in command. The guards corroborated that you strenuously resisted the removal of your leg chains. The warden paid you grudging respect for that. He commented that you must be one stone cold son of a bitch to pull that off.

The reverend then described the arduous trek through the woods and how they had to beg the sergeant to stop for a rest.

Apparently, the scene after your flight was tragicomic. The sergeant took his fellow trooper and—guns drawn—they took out after you, telling the others to stay still. The guards wished to help but the local sheriff explained that Billy Ray had a good head start and could certainly outrun two fat tired cops. Besides, he explained, the sergeant was very excited and would most probably shoot anything that moved. The sheriff pulled out his two-way radio and called the state police headquarters to tell them what had happened and to meet him at the sawmill with choppers and dogs. Then he set off with his deputy back the way they had come.

When the sergeant and trooper reappeared a little later, they were apparently very agitated and did not take well to the news of the sheriff's call and subsequent departure. They set off after said sheriff with the others in tow.

It seems the sheriff made good time because he was not seen again until they reached the sawmill, where he stood beside a helicopter and some chap with dogs.

The sergeant attempted to upbraid the sheriff for not getting his approval before calling for help. I hope I can do his rejoinder justice. Something to the effect of: "Listen asshole, you just fucked up the guarding of a hand- and leg-shackled prisoner with six armed guards. I'm going to try to find him for you. Now get the fuck out of my sight or I'll arrest your sorry ass for incompetence." The sergeant took a swing at him only to learn that the sheriff was quicker. The sergeant was cuffed, read his rights, and informed that he was under arrest for assaulting a sheriff. The sheriff then informed the sergeant that Billy Ray had gotten a dirty deal in the first place and that if he got shot in this fuck-up he would personally come to see the sergeant for rounds two through twelve.

Billy Ray, even the warden smiled. The reverend did not mince his words and got the guards off the hook as much as he could. When the captain was finally allowed to speak again to his guards, I was taken to another room, but I could hear some of it. It was not pretty.

My interrogation continued well into the night, first with the locals and then the state police. I was patient and pleasant and finally asked for a lie detector test because I feared reprisals by the prison.

The state police called my bluff and around midnight, produced a machine, a technician, and a lawyer so that I could sign away my rights.

Before I was allowed to return to my cell, they tossed it looking for anything that might tip them off. Everything was on the floor when I got back.

After the lie detector test, while I waited with the chaplain, I heard some of the preparations for your recapture. It was impressive: choppers, dogs, swamp boats, a five-state alert, TV and radio warnings of a desperate lifer on the loose presumed to be armed. They might have said "just shoot the bugger," but that's against the law.

I was proud of you, Billy Ray, you shouldn't have been in for life. But I was mortally afraid for you.

Since I knew nothing and it wasn't an escape from the prison itself, the warden didn't do a lockdown. He was right too. No point making a bad situation worse. He came on the P.A. at seven in the morning and just told everybody to keep quiet and not be stupid and they could avoid a lockdown. The warden got a lot of marks for that from the long timers. Anybody who got a little frisky was brought up real quick.

Hell, we all wanted to watch it on TV. I spent eighteen years in that place and it was absolutely the highlight of my stay.

You were a hero. Even the guards said it was a work of art, although they expected you back real soon. Most of the rest of us expected you to be shot resisting arrest. But we cheered for you, Billy Ray, not very loud because we wanted those TVs and radios to stay on. Many prisoners thought I'd helped you and congratulated me. I must admit my stoicism in the face of those compliments was interpreted as tacit concurrence. I did not disabuse my fellows of their notion, as it made me feel superior for a few days. Ah, vanity!

But I digress. A day passed, two days passed, and no news of you. Then one unexpected fruit of your scheme came on the evening news of the third day.

Mr. Randolf had been interviewed by the TV reporters and had given the world your scam, including the bit about his boy being a faggot. You were widely congratulated for that twist by your fellow prisoners but it apparently upset his parents greatly because of the stigma attached.

Jimmy Randolf apparently saw his mother crying on TV and just telephoned her because he felt so bad. Seems he had a new name and a wife and two kids over in Mississippi and was making his way in the world despite his pa.

The joyful reconciliation was right there on TV for us and you were accorded some credit, if not by the immediate family.

Yours truly, Leonard

There was an article in the Grand Bay newspaper a few days after my escape. Mitch saved it for me. The sheriff, who asked about the charge pending against the state trooper sergeant, is quoted as follows: "I should have stepped in when the stupid bugger was taking off Billy Ray's chains, but I figured a good walk in the woods would do him good. It did do him real good I guess, unless them gators ate his butt."

CHAPTER

It must be obvious by now that the gators did not eat my butt. The truth is that I ate theirs.

Once I was camouflaged with mud and had a big helmet of branches, I could reconnoiter the island. There were no alligator slides so at least none of the big guys lived here. If I'd found one, I'd have left that night.

I was tuned into rotors and motors and stopped every few seconds to listen. Think of a squirrel who scuttles along and then stops and sits up, twitching his ears and nose. That was me.

There was a safe place to fish under an overhang and that first day I ate a small catfish and a few crayfish, skinned but raw.

The second day brought some luck. I found an old rusted tin can; one of the big fat ones they use for juice. The top was gone but it still held water with no leaks. I scrubbed it up with dirt and leaves and that night I made my first small fire and boiled water in it. The next night I boiled some crayfish and pieces of a brim I'd caught. The fishy water tasted pretty bad but I drank that too. Rust and all. There was lots of vegetation under the water and I boiled some of that and ate it with my fish.

I was constantly sweating in the long hot late August sun, which made me drink more swamp water, boiled or with chlorine. Either way, it went right through me. I was always hungry, thirsty, and always looking for food.

The helicopters and boats stopped after the fifth day but I knew the police would still be waiting for me any place I could come out, on the off chance that I was still in the swamp and not dead.

After a week of little experiments with underwater plants, I was confident of one tuberous ugly red plant that tasted like dandelion stalks but did not make me sick.

One afternoon when I was fishing, an eighteen-inch alligator came close enough so I could whack him on the head. I stuck pieces of him on a stick and cooked them over my fire under the biggest tree. I even had little walls of branches to hide the fire.

Every day I allowed myself a portion of the C-rations and a piece of dried fruit. I ate them with my night meal of seafood and seaweed. The diarrhea calmed down to twice a day.

In the early dawns I swam back and forth near my fishing spot for exercise.

The longer I could stay, the better my chances of escape.

That interlude on my small island remains with me as a wonderful time. Survival became security. They'd never find me there.

The transitions were gradual. Week one was solely a question of survival. Week two was the euphoria of survival and week three was working up the courage to give up this safe nest of mine in the swamp.

At night I'd lie in the raft, which I'd put about two feet off the ground on old logs and mud, and watch the stars. The place was always noisy with various creatures fulfilling their destiny, so I never felt too lonely.

In the interlude between the hovering searchers and my leaving, there were many days of peace. Each day was like the others. When food ceased to be the critical issue, I swam and stretched and lifted logs to keep fit, and I rested.

The rhythm of my life there was mesmerizing and I lived for a time the life before ours.

CHAPTER

13

With two days' provisions remaining, I made my move. Reaction had so often supplanted planning in my escape that it took over quite naturally. My original plan would be there if needed, but I'd learned to trust my instincts more.

Without having thought about it the night before, I got up and left my camp immediately. It was a dark cloudy morning, with rain threatening—not a good day for helicopters. There'd been none for two weeks, but a man escaping with his life can risk nothing.

I paddled over the last piece of open water in light rain with thunder above the low black clouds to shield me. When I neared the thicker swamp, close to land, it was past noon and I needed rest.

Knowing that I could easily come out of the swamp that night, my thoughts turned to the last waterproof package in my pack. Careful to keep it dry with my body, I opened it with almost religious interest. It was my chance, probably my only chance, because anybody who spotted the wild man I'd become, would certainly have been shocked.

I could only imagine how I looked. The prison buzz cut would be grown in. My beard was three weeks old and since I'm not very hairy, it probably was uneven and wild looking. I'd applied mud camouflage daily, though I rinsed off in the swamp every day while swimming. And I'd been living in my underwear and prison T-shirt most of that time. My boots had been washed and dried and were each in a big baggie along with their gray cotton socks.

For escape purposes, my size was excellent. I figured I'd lost ten or fifteen pounds so I was a skinny man standing five feet, ten inches. Not someone to notice unless he's covered with mud, has three-week-old underwear on, and looks like the missing link.

The last package was bigger than the others. Mike had packed it with no real hope that I could ever get to it. The contents, which told me he must be a good Marine, deserve listing in military style.

> Comb – small – one
> Shampoo – hotel – one
> Razor – plastic – one
> Soap – hotel – one
> Washcloth – blue – one
> Nail clippers – small – one
> Cap – old – Bama – one
> Shorts – tan – one
> T-shirt – Budweiser – one
> T-shirt – Green – one
> Sandals – black – two

In the shorts were five twenty-dollar bills, two fives, and two ones. There was no note.

On a little hillock of an island in the pouring rain, I bathed, shampooed, and shaved. Then I cut my nails and cleaned them as well as I could. Using soap on the washcloth I did the best I could with my teeth. The rain washed me clean of soap and I put my new toilet things in a baggie.

I scrubbed the backpack and rinsed it as clean as possible in the rain water. The rain grew heavier then and I loved it even as I shivered.

Naked, I continued my voyage through the swamp thicket, and with little incident other than hard going, came within sight of real woods in the late afternoon.

I buried everything except the backpack and its contents in the swamp mud before I went ashore, and put on the sandals to walk through the woods. My prison boots and socks were left behind.

Picture me, if you will, a clean recently coifed naked man with a backpack, walking gingerly through the woods. It seemed quite natural to me. I was clean, my feet would not be hurt and my only change of clothes was clean and dry.

Well before dark, the rain stopped and the sun came through occasionally. I was on higher ground now in a pine wood where the going was easier.

Without warning I came to the edge and a wire fence. Beyond it was a rising field of something green, planted in long rows across.

The cautious animal I had become waited. The ground under me trembled just a little and then I heard the diesels, oh so faintly.

The train passed near me but I could not see it from the woods. It was in front of me and not far. It was my ticket out and I'd come to it as I'd planned and as Mike had done before me.

And it brought the thought of Mike to me. He'd come around the swamp in one go with no boat or food. I wanted to talk to him when I got through That pushed me on, wanting to see Mike and to compare our stories.

In the dark, well after sunset, I put on my new clothes and even combed my hair again and put on the hat.

Skirting the green field, I found a two-rut dirt lane that headed up toward where I'd heard the train. Over a little crest I saw the farmhouse. It was all lit up so I skirted that too. I was absolutely cautious.

Then I came to a blacktop road that I knew had to run north and south, and just started walking north. I could not take the chance and wait for another train. I walked facing the traffic as far off the road as I could and still walk freely.

After the first few cars passed and continued on their way, I felt easier. The train plan went behind me. I had to move. When I came to a country gas station and general store I could not go in, as much as I wanted to eat. My nerves were far too tight.

I spent that whole night walking, and in the quiet I could hear the few cars long before they passed, and I hid from them.

There was no tiredness in me. I ate all of my remaining hard-tack and fruit and drank rainwater out of puddles. The air was cool and I moved ahead. Later I figured that I covered almost twenty miles.

All thoughts of the train had gone with the night. The town of Pascagoula, Mississippi, was up this road where it crossed State Highway 63. I'd be able to walk into town and not stand out.

The McDonald's at the edge of town was the best place I'd ever been. The mirror in the bathroom showed me a new face. This one had a good head of hair which I parted on the left and combed with water. I was clean and, except for a few bug bites, looked presentable. The clothes fit in well. I actually smiled at the sallow fellow in the glass.

There was a discarded newspaper on a table, so I took it with me to order breakfast. I was careful not to look nervous and only ordered enough for one.

There was nothing about me in the paper. Then I went into town and found the drugstore that sold bus tickets. At the little Trailways counter I bought a ticket on the nine-eighteen to New Orleans for fourteen dollars, and waited behind my newspaper.

In New Orleans I never left the terminal and paid twenty-three dollars to ride to Jackson, Mississippi, and as in Arlo Guthrie's song about Alice's Restaurant, I made an escape.

After spending the night in a homeless shelter in a church, I washed, shaved, and proceeded into the center of Jackson.

Life, you may have found, is filled with wonderful ironies. At first I laughed at it, but passing it again, I stopped short and went in. The sign said "Need Presser." It was in red crayon on a shirt cardboard in the window of a small Chinese laundry.

The little man was busy but smiled at his next customer: me.

"I'm a good presser. How much you payin'?" I said.

"You come show me press." This guy was all business.

So I showed him what six years of prison training can do and he said "Okay, seven dollars hour."

The fast trigger action has never left me. I answered, "Ten. I'm fast and I can start right now."

He said, "Eight," then I said, "Nine."

"Eight fifty—deal?" he offered and smiled.

"Deal."

We shook hands and he said, "Good, it's ten o'clock. Start now. Close at seven, okay?"

"Okay. My name's Bill."

"Me Mister Woo. Call me Woo, okay?"

"Sure." Then the dreaded question. "Do I need to sign up or anything?"

"No, no, not sign up. I hire every day, pay cash every night. Not do bullshit."

I could have kissed him.

"Where you live?" he asked.

"Just got into town this morning. I need to find a room."

"Plenty room in street behind. I know."

The pressing made me so happy I was singing back there in the heat all by myself, determined to be the best and fastest presser that Mr. Woo had ever seen.

He brought me a bowl of noodles and a Coke at one o'clock. "You do okay, Bill."

God, it was better than graduating from high school.

At seven sharp he shut down, and after he'd let the other two employees out, he took me out the back way.

"Here your money, I show room houses."

He passed me seventy-five dollars and set off briskly.

We went to his friend's home where I got a small clean room for sixty dollars a week, including breakfast and the use of the parlor. My room was at the back of the second floor. I had two windows, a double bed, and a small desk.

Mr. Woo warned me to be on time at eight o'clock. I saluted and he chuckled. We'd both found what we needed.

I sat in the parlor that night, a free man watching television with other free people. Later in bed, I read the local paper. If I never moved from there, I'd be happy.

Six days a week, eight hours a day (I went out for lunch), I worked for Mr. Woo and stayed very close to home for the next several months. I saved three hundred dollars a week while building up my possessions to resemble those of a normal man.

It was simply a time of freedom with myself. I couldn't even call Mitch; his phone was likely to be tapped.

And what of women, you ask? I can recall an appreciative waitress two doors away who must have thought I'd just gotten out of jail. Enough said, I think.

CHAPTER

When I found Mr. Woo, the decision to go to ground there came of its own volition. That there was no documentation of my employment or my room sealed it. All I could wonder was how it could be? Need a presser? Well, Mr. Woo got a hell of a presser. I can assure you of that.

The first days were strange to me, just walking out onto the street at noon and having lunch while reading a mystery book. Sometimes I'd walk a few blocks and after a while there would be faces seen again and nods or smiles.

Never a day slipped by without thinking of Mike and Mitch. They would be worried, but they'd know the backpack and bolt cutters were gone, so they must know I had a chance. Either I had made it or I had not. They must figure the odds were with me, for the equipment had been perfect and I knew the swamps.

After a few weeks I was going in the evenings to movies, sometimes with Emma, a middle-aged sad waitress who was tender beneath her crust.

In the house of Mrs. Young, there were four roomers. We were allowed to watch TV in the parlor in the evening. Believe me when I tell you I was grateful for the company.

We were all of us gaunt of history in that parlor and questions were not asked. Rather we bantered and were solicitous of the others' choices.

Mrs. Young weighed ninety pounds and ran a tight ship. The house was as immaculate as she was, and I tried to measure up.

But mostly I pressed and thought and read, and thought some more.

If you had your life returned to you, what would you do?

Leonard craved redemption. What I craved was revenge, and with that revenge, exposure of the guilty and punishment. In my case the guilty governed and enforced, but that did nothing but heat my ardor for their fucking blood.

I suppose that a regular seamless life proceeds, with its typical episodes, to its predictable effortless conclusion. Family is the core and the stages are obvious and inevitable. My family was Maynard, Eddie, Mitch, Mike, and Leonard, and it was Leonard who had made my decision for me. It had been made when he showed me how to get even, how to give back. While my giving back might be more aggressive than his, the motives and steps would be similar.

In that awful cage, Leonard had taught me to engage my mind. If not for him, I'd still be in there pumping iron, jerking off, and hiding from my soul.

Leonard would make a teacher out of his own twenty-six-year-old drunken murderer. Mike had made himself a Marine out of a misspent youth. Mitch would take the normal path and I blessed him for it. I would take the law into my own hands and I had one entire new lifetime in which to do it. On every day of my freedom I had visualized Maynard and Eddie slogging through the interminable time until they died, and I thought of our captors, Frank

Babcock and Ernie Collins. The injustice—the unfairness of it—constantly overwhelmed me.

At the public library, I reviewed the newspapers of Mobile and Montgomery and Meridian from the time of my escape. They were on microfiche, so no one could look over my shoulder and see what I was reading.

The headlines were bold and had lasted many days. The search had been enormous, using all police branches and the national guard. Even two weeks after my running into the swamp, there were road patrols and search parties going door-to-door throughout the whole area. It seemed a very fortunate thing that I'd decided to extend my camping trip.

I was assumed to have perished in the swamp, the victim of drowning, alligators, snakes, or mire. No one, they reasoned, could survive two weeks in that hot swamp in handcuffs.

So they had not found the tree house or connected it with me. Mitch was quoted as begging me to give myself up. I liked that.

I read about the sheriff charging the state trooper sergeant. His quote was to the effect that, while my escape was clever, I was very fortunate to have been delivered that numbskull as my accomplice.

And a big amen to that, brother.

I liked that sheriff.

CHAPTER

15

After six months I was finally ready to begin my revenge.

There were things to prepare and to prepare for.

First, I would salute my liberators. Carefully. How would John LeCarré do it? Or Agatha Christie? Nothing could ever point to Jackson, because I planned on staying there.

My plan prepared, I called the Marine Corps general listing number in Pensacola from a pay phone, five blocks from my room. Could I have a number where I might reach a Corporal Mike Nevens? She checked. She had a Sergeant Michael Nevens, gunnery instructor. That must be him. She gave me a daytime number at the gunnery school, saying I had to call early or late because of classes.

I called the next afternoon at four from another phone booth. No one could possibly expect me to call, but I was paranoid and proud of it.

A gruff man answered, or rather yelled, "Gunnery school, Corporal Edwards."

I was solicitous. "Yes, Corporal, could I speak with Sergeant Nevens, please?" I tried to sound important.

"Yes sir, he's here. I'll get him, sir." I must have sounded like an officer and my alter ego actor was satisfied enough to continue on his own.

"Sergeant Nevens here," came the authoritative voice of my old con-man pal.

"Yes, Sergeant Nevens, how are you today?"

"I'm good—who is this?"

"Sergeant Nevens, this is Colonel Sanders."

I waited.

"Colonel Sanders—?" Then he laughed, like he always had. "Sure, Colonel Sanders, what can I do for you?" He played along, but recognition had not arrived.

My actor adopted a Kentucky accent. "You alone, boy?"

Mike sighed. "Okay, who is it—Charlie?"

I took over myself. "Don't yell or make a fuss buddy, okay?"

Back when we lived together, I'd called everyone buddy.

Before he could answer I simply said, "Mike, it's me, Billy Ray. Can you talk?"

I could hear a big exhale, then he said, "Corporal, could you give me a couple of minutes here?—Thanks."

I heard a door close.

"Jesus, talk to me, boy. Talk to me."

"You off on Sunday?"

"Sure."

"Okay, me too. Do you have a car?"

"Sure."

"If you can drive up to Meridian on Saturday afternoon, I'll meet you at the bus terminal downtown about eight o'clock. That okay for you?"

"What about M—What about the other guy?"

"Not yet. We have to talk first. Can you come?"

"Absolutely! How'll I—"

"Drive by the entrance to the bus terminal at eight. I'll be on the sidewalk. What are you driving?"

"Green Mustang, old model."

"We can catch up and maybe stay over at a motel or something."

"What? You queer now?"

"You'll like it when you get used to it."

I hung up before he could answer.

When I'd last seen Mike Nevens he was Mike Andrews and we'd been part of a very stupid foursome of petty thieves, pot smokers, beer guzzlers, and skirt chasers. We'd had side burns, shades, and our hats prophetically on backwards. Mike had eluded terminal incarceration by sheer speed and some luck. My last recollection of him was flying out the back door of Mitch's house in his underwear with his wallet and shorts in one hand and his shoes in the other. We were twenty-three years old back then. Now we were almost thirty.

I was waiting for the Green Mustang to cruise up when a strong arm went around my shoulder and Mike said, "Who wants to meet in a fucking car? Give me a goddamned hug you smart son of a bitch."

He was taller than me and the Marines had made him thicker. We hugged there in the dead downtown Saturday night and slapped our backs just managing to breathe.

"Come on, hotshot, the car's over here."

We got in. It was February and cold. Mike said, "You want to go to a bar or what?"

"I don't drink anything stronger than Dr Pepper."

He laughed. "Well I'll be goddamned, me either. Afraid I'll tell."

"So let's eat and talk. You eaten yet?"

"Nope. Been here since five, wanting to take you to a rib joint. You game? I got us a motel nearby too if that's okay."

"Perfect. Let's go."

We were in a wooden booth at the back of the rib joint in ten minutes. It was private. We talked.

Mike's time in the swamp had been short but dreadful. He'd been treed by a nine-foot alligator for half a day and a night. He'd had to drink the swamp water and would have surrendered for a hot meal and a bed. But no one found him. He skirted the main swamp and came out near where I did almost four days later. He said he was deranged with fear and I believed him. The luck of a train slowing for a trestle saved him because he had only tattered shorts and his muddy wallet by then. He'd had to roll some drunk rummy for his clothes in Birmingham, but they were just the ticket to get him into a homeless shelter unchallenged.

Like me he hid for a long time before returning home to Texas and arranging his name change. He still feared that his Marine fingerprints would be matched to his Alabama ones. So far so good. He'd give them no reason to run them.

Mike loved my story. I told him about Leonard and finishing high school and about prison life and the escape, in detail.

We talked until two A.M. Mike had a girlfriend with two kids and he was thinking of marrying her and adopting them. He was a sergeant and was married to the Marines as well. He trained gunners now and felt proficient, a feeling he obviously cherished.

We talked about how I could get more information to Mitch and Leonard, and then I told Mike my plan.

He listened with big eyes and replied simply, "Well, they sure as hell won't see you coming."

"Mike," I said. "You came back and you got me out. Without

you I would never have had the nerve, believe me. Here we are, neither of us in the can, but the others are. You with me on this?"

"All the fucking way, pal, all the fucking way. What I can do, I do."

CHAPTER

16

Leonard told me later that he had decided to believe that I was free until they found my body. So he had continued to hope.

He bought his books from a school supply house in Montgomery. Mike went to that company's office and took an envelope and note pad with the company name on it. Then he sent a note to Leonard, all typed and efficient. The prison was used to Leonard's book correspondence. This one read:

Dear Mr. Mossgrove;

Schneiderman's essays on the history of spirits is out of print.

Sorry,

Mike had then scrawled unreadable initials.

I knew only Leonard would get it. When he schneidered me in gin rummy, he always called it a visit from Mr. Schneiderman.

Later, he told me that he was very happy to learn that my time spent reading mysteries had borne fruit.

I told Mitch myself. Mike still saw him every month or so in Mobile, so I had Mike bring him up to Birmingham using the ruse of a fishing trip.

It actually was a fishing trip, except I was there, too.

I never told either of them where I lived or what I did. They understood. Mitch said he would quit drinking, too, so as never to be tempted to talk about me.

Billy Ray Billings was dead. That's what everyone believed, he said.

I said that I would arrange to see them but it might not be frequent. We did not tell Mitch my plan. There was no point.

I was thrilled to be dead. How else to rise again?

CHAPTER

Getting the birth certificate of a person your age who died as a child is relatively easy. The mystery writers have it about right. Find the grave of some two or three or four-year-old who would probably have birth and baptism records and find out if his parents are alive. Once you have a dead kid with dead parents, you're in good shape.

The problem with new identities, however, is the fingerprints for drivers' licenses. But other than a driver's license, the rest would be possible, I thought.

I did not want a third party arranging this for me. So on Sundays, I hit the graveyards in and around Jackson, looking for an identity.

Families tend to bury together, so I was only a few weeks finding two candidates. Both were white families who'd lost a young son. One would have been four years older than me and the other three years younger. I chose the younger as more appropriate for my needs. Also this was an urban Jackson cemetery and I could more easily research and invent my assumed early years.

It's sort of like getting your first credit card. Fill out forms and sign papers until you're blue in the face—then everybody wants you to have their card as well.

Two months of assiduous preparation preceded my application for the birth certificate for Harry Phibbs Brown. My story was that I'd been living in Canada since I was two and had just come back. I'd bought an Ontario driver's license and a plastic social insurance card with a big red leaf on it from a Chinese man who specialized in such things. They were expensive, but authentic. And I'd read about Toronto and knew which schools I'd gone to and where I'd lived.

God, I was nervous. I went in person acting as dumb as I could. My two proofs of identity were accepted by the crisp black woman at the wicket. She asked me all about my parents and I knew the correct answers so she rewarded me with a plastic birth certificate. I signed my new signature and walked for a mile before looking at my new credential.

With these three credentials, getting a social security card took five minutes. Then I had four.

With the four, I sat for the SATs at Mississippi College, explaining that I'd gone to high school in Canada and had worked and traveled since. No problem, I was a potential paying student.

Six weeks later I started college and got my fifth I.D. This one was fancy with my photo and signature on it.

I told Mr. Woo that I'd had a little woman trouble and had not used my correct name. It took him a few weeks to get used to calling me Harry. He was good enough to let me flex my hours for classes. In general I studied early and pressed late. He got somebody else for Saturday when I had to catch up for the week.

That year I filed my income tax and paid like a good citizen. That's how they got Al Capone, tax evasion. Plus, I needed clean tracks.

I became Harry Brown, born in Jackson in 1967. My parents were dead and I had no siblings, not that anybody cared.

Harry Brown went to college.

Part 3

harry brown

CHAPTER

I went to class twelve months a year. A vacation never once occurred to me. It wasn't just my time I was playing with.

It was a good time and I will always remember it for its seclusion and learning. The work at the college was easy for me because I was totally dedicated to every word and concept. When you think you are stupid and discover that you are not, there is a thrill to learning. Anything.

I never took a loan or applied for help, but I did win a few small cash awards.

The room Mr. Woo had found for me was my home for all of those five years. Application forms usually ask for your address for the past three or five years. Stability would look good later on.

For a year or so I went out with a few women and then I met Gwen. She worked at the college in the registrar's office as the assistant head of admissions. She had a small daughter and lived in a neat little condo near the school. It was a small family but it was now my small family. After a while I would study at her home and stay over a couple of times a week. We are together to this day.

This story is not about Gwen or her daughter, Karen, it is about the law, so I shall concentrate on that aspect of the life of Harry Brown. I only bring her up at all to tell you that I was content in my family life as well as my academic life and lived rather normally. In my reason for life I could never be content, however, without vengeance.

Completing seven years in six, I graduated from the college with a degree in law. My specialty was criminal law. I was thirty-five years old. At the graduation I made sure Gwen took lots of pictures to add to my five-year-old identity. My picture was in the yearbook and I made the dean's list.

I never went on the round of interviews that new lawyers go on. The only job I wanted paid half what the top guys got and I just went downtown and applied in person.

In September of 1998, I passed the bar exam and became an assistant district attorney for the City of Jackson.

My plan was for two or three years, but there was little left to learn after one, so I left. Time was never my ally. Whenever I made up time, I deducted it from the three years of what I called my indecent incarceration. Although I'd spent seven and a half years in prison, I figured the twenty-two months on the road gang and three years in prison were just, and should have cured my stupidity. The last three years in prison, and what would have been the rest of my life there, needed to be canceled.

So I'd canceled two. One by finishing school early and one by getting through the prosecutor's office ahead of schedule.

All the time I'd been at school, I'd vacillated between two approaches to my problem. When you are pressing clothes on automatic pilot, there is ample time to contemplate. I'd work for weeks and months in my head, down one track and then head involuntarily down the other. Each, in the end, required an accomplice which I probably could never have.

Mike might have been a possibility, but he was a big-shot Marine out in San Diego by then, and I left him alone. He had come to my graduation with Mitch, but without their families. I had needed to show Gwen that I had old friends. Now we just talked on the phone every month or so using my new name.

Part of the construction of Harry Brown had been his looks. Billy Ray and TB18078, my prison number, had always been a bulked-up guy who liked to strut around like a stud. He had a full head of light hair that bleached easily in the sun. His lower teeth were crooked.

I paid cash for fixing my teeth, rather than having it on a dental plan, and I never went back to that dentist. I had him forward me my X-rays because I said I was moving to Canada. There would be no records of my changed mouth. He removed two teeth and I had to wear retainers for a year while the others took up their new position. He did a good job. He also fixed the rest of my mouth which had not been in good shape at all after years of neglect.

Harry Brown kept off the fifteen pounds he'd lost in the swamp, and on a five-foot-ten-inch frame, that is considerable. Thankfully, my hairline was receding and I kept it short and neat. Tortoiseshell glasses made me look smart, I hoped. I ran every day and stayed in excellent shape, but without obvious muscles. At school I'd worn jeans and a T-shirt like everybody else. Now I wore good suits and white shirts like everybody else.

Harry Brown looked like a merchant banker or a lawyer. Billy Ray would never have believed it was possible. I don't think he would recognize me.

While I was in the prosecutor's office I'd been able to access any criminal file I wanted. I'd been cleared for that after six months into the job. One night I had stayed late by myself and called up Billy Ray Billings on my screen.

There I was with my number and a prison haircut. Billy Ray Billings, Alabama State Penitentiary, life—no parole, felony A. Served seven years, five months, escaped, believed dead, body partially recovered, file deactivated.

For weeks I sniffed around, making phone calls pretending to be a law student. Finally a clerk in another jail in Alabama told me that they deactivated files when prisoners or criminals died. That was the law, he said.

All I could figure was that the prison system felt better thinking that I had died in that swamp. The clerk said it speeded up things to have these dead guys out of the system. Mitch told me that they'd pulled some human bones out of the swamp, but could not identify them. What did I care, they thought I was dead.

But that was not enough for me. I had to be certain. My odds were better now but not high enough. I had to take a chance to find out for sure, so I ran my own prints on a fictitious inquiry to the states around Alabama. They all came back negative. Believe me when I tell you that I was relieved. My bags had been packed and I had a plane ticket to New York.

Once I knew that Billy Ray was officially dead, things switched to my favor.

I took driving lessons and got a license, for which I was fingerprinted. Then I bought my first car, a four-year-old Chevrolet.

Gwen could never figure out why I wouldn't live with her and Karen. She never once bugged me to get married, though. All I could tell her was that I had something to do and then we'd see. In the meantime, I rented a condo near her and we were together a lot. I needed to come and go undetected and I couldn't be predictable. She didn't like it, but she knew I loved her and we had a good life together. She used to call me Harry Brown, Private Eye. Not so far from the truth.

The vacillation between courses of action ended one morning during my customary run. I'd take both. It was such a simple idea that it annoyed me to think I hadn't thought of it earlier.

I started a law office in a small storefront near the courthouse. I advertised, took any legal aid cases the prosecutor could give me.

When I didn't have a case, I started work on my other career. The by-line I used was "Harry P. Brown, Criminal Attorney." It was so simple. I'd go to court, take notes, interview some participants, and write up a feature on them. At first I got fifty or a hundred dollars for them from the newspaper. Later, I got as much as three hundred.

For two long hard years I built up both businesses. I got stiffed by clients, I lost some cases, but I became a pretty good defense attorney. I stuck to small stuff mostly, wanting lots of experience.

With the police, I was always friendly and correct and had drinks with them at any time to observe their practices. By and large they were decent people.

I established a relationship with a local newspaper: they bought my stories and issued me press credentials, even though I was not an employee.

Three years after graduation and eight years after my escape, I was ready to go back to the scene of the crime. Half way through a normal life span, and I'd never lived a normal day. Would I ever? I didn't pray to God. I promised Maynard and Eddie. It made me crazy that I couldn't even write to them.

CHAPTER

The night before my first trip back to Alabama, I remember laying awake beside Gwen, wondering if I was nuts. Why couldn't I just forget it and let sleeping dogs lie? Gwen and I could get married. We could have children. I was free.

Even while I was thinking this, it was also clear to me that my life could only have one purpose. If that could be satisfied, then Harry Brown could have his life. Not before. Revenge is stronger than love—for me, in any case. Besides, I loved my times with Maynard and Eddie, shooting pool and playing poker and watching television. They could never do that again, so any freedom I had was tainted.

Although I wanted to see my old haunts, I stayed well away from Grand Bay and Maynard's home in Mobile.

At first I'd only go to Mobile for a day or two at a time and then scurry back to Jackson, but soon I had a room in a rooming house that I used for more frequent visits and longer stays.

One Mobile paper liked my Jackson courtroom articles and they agreed to a similar deal. I was accredited by them and I reported on whatever felt to be a good story. They knew I was a lawyer and liked my hit on things.

I hired another lawyer in Jackson. He was not a young man and he drank too much, but he could follow instructions so I could travel even when I had cases going. We worked a lot by cellular phone.

CHAPTER

3

Frank Babcock and Ernie Collins were still on the Mobile Police Force. I brought up the roster on the newspaper computer. Frank was a detective lieutenant and Ernie was still a detective, first-class. They were both well under fifty with about twenty years on the force, so I didn't have to worry about them retiring or quitting on me. They were in it for the pension now.

The Mobile paper got good articles from me about three times a month. They were happy and I was becoming visible and credible. I let them do an article on me as an interesting fellow who had a successful law practice and liked to write as well. I told the interviewer that I might write a novel later if I could get enough real courtroom experience, both as a defense attorney and as a crime journalist. The picture they used was a very good one. It showed me in shirt sleeves and suspenders with a pencil in my mouth. Thinking. My smile had straight teeth and the tortoise-shell glasses made me thoughtful.

I let six months pass in Mobile before I made any move at all.

During that time my only focus was on the reporting of truth, showing a conservative law enforcement bias. It was important to establish that I only used correct information and that this reporter was no knee-jerk liberal. The police involved always got their proper rank and full name. They were never quoted out of context, and I chose occasionally to omit information that could have been used to color them less than true blue.

My newspaper writing was typically Southern and conservative, so I fit in and was welcome.

Similarly, I presented the prosecutors and judges in neutral or good lights while occasionally a defense attorney was mildly criticized if he or she was particularly obstreperous.

My experience with the law-enforcement people in Jackson had taught me that newspaper articles were read and saved by many, especially when police officers had made an arrest or secured a conviction. At first, I'd vented some of my hostility in Jackson, but I quickly learned that offended officers would not comment for the record on subsequent stories. In fact I'd been told by one to fuck off before he ran me in for loitering. His anger was real and it taught me to be less strident in my approach.

In Mobile, it was easier to swallow my rancor and toady up to the authorities. I was very careful not to go overboard, however, and become obvious. What I wanted was a carefully constructed reputation as a straight shooter who did not gratuitously trash the law-enforcement community. Generally, I did not annoy the defense attorneys, either. When they got it, it was quite obvious that they deserved it. What I did do was rail against the crimes and the criminals convicted. That was safe territory.

Occasionally people would ask me why I had two careers or why I didn't take cases in Mobile. I always treated those inquiries very lightly and said things just worked out the way they had with no planning and if one became more enjoyable than the other, then I'd drop one. Besides, I said, I needed all the material I could find if I was to be a successful novelist. I tried to sound off-hand but clever, so they'd think there was really some long-term goal to upstage John Grisham.

I became someone who had perhaps some promise and with no ax to grind with the police. In fact, I went out of my way to question police officers during trials and tried in other ways to get to know them.

The criminal docket in Mobile had seldom more than a few interesting cases a month, so I was able to cover all the good ones and schedule my attorney work in Jackson around them. Money was of no real interest to me then, except that I had to produce enough income from all of my activities to be free to move around as I wished. I had to work at least six days a week, usually saving Sunday for my family life. Ends met, but just.

Although I kept a room in a rooming house in Mobile, I didn't tell anyone there about it. In fact I always gave contacts my card with the business address and phone number in Jackson. There were to be no risks taken. I could be reached at my office, the newspaper, or on my cell phone.

When I was established as a known and friendly commodity, I asked the public affairs office of the Mobile Police Department for background information on all the senior police officials so that I'd know whom to call on specific questions, and I'd have their bios handy. Their front man was not very polite and told me I'd have to call them on every instance, and they would get the answer from the appropriate official. I remember the conversation well because it surprised me, after all my preparation, to be treated as a pain in the ass who needed to be dealt with in the usual controlling bureaucratic manner. I was standing at a counter, talking to a crabby middle-aged man in civilian clothes. He had a rather supercilious look, as if he was used to reporters flashing their IDs and trying to obtain things to which they were not entitled.

Sometimes in court or when negotiating a plea bargain, I'd revert to the actor's role I'd assumed often during my escape from prison. It would just occur that circumstances conspired to make me act in a manner quite different from my plan. This held risk, but seemed for some reason to be called for.

It would have been easy and even preferable to just back off and try another door. After all, the information must be public knowledge anyway. I had just come to this office because it had been logical. But a bureaucrat like this one probably had back up and it annoyed me. I did not wish to appear malleable in any way.

The man's name was Bridges. He had a name tag.

"So Mr. Bridges," I said. "It's your answer that I cannot have this information which I have asked for?"

He grew annoyed and pushed back from the counter. "What're you, a fucking lawyer? You got a question, you call me. That's what we do here."

"No Mr. Bridges, I am not a fucking lawyer. I'm a real lawyer and I will not call you, because you are arrogant with no apparent reason for that arrogance. Now I have asked you for a list of senior police officials and their bios. Either give them to me right now or call your supervisor to deal with me."

He started to reply with something like "Now look here pal—" but I cut him off.

"No more talk, smart guy. Get me your supervisor."

By then the whole office was quiet, watching us. Poor Mr. Bridges could not control himself. "Who the fuck do you think you are? This is the police department here!"

"Oh," I said, "are you a police officer?"

"Yes, I goddamned am." He puffed right up.

"Good," I said, " what is your service number?"

That slowed him down for the first time. He gave me a little conspiratorial grin. "You're not a lawyer, but nice try."

"Not just any kind of lawyer. I am a criminal defense lawyer and a newspaper reporter and I have asked you for your service number. You have identified yourself as a police officer. I am a citizen. We are arguing, and that is my right. Now give it to me at once."

My lawyerly talk had slowed him, but the sharp demand set him off again, probably against his own judgment.

"Fuck you, you're getting nothing here." He turned and went into his little glass office and slammed the door. I remember thinking that he must have been a treat at home.

By this time, I was enjoying myself. With my notebook on the counter, I quickly reconstructed our conversation, then introduced myself to the three ladies sitting at their desks and read them my notes for their corroboration.

Each desk had the occupant's name on a slot card, so identifying them was easy. They refused to answer my questions, but we shared a few laughs at Mr. Bridges's expense.

Mr. Bridges sat at his desk pretending to work, occasionally looking up to glare at me. I just stood there and wrote notes for the newspaper article.

When he could stand it no longer, Mr. Bridges came out of his office and up to the counter. He was now livid, apparently unaccustomed to insolence.

"You still here, jerkoff? I thought I told you to leave."

I smiled at him and wrote what he had said on my pad, smiling at the ladies as I did that.

He tried to grab my pad but he was too angry to be subtle and all he got was countertop.

"Give me that," he growled.

"Which way to the chief's office?" I asked the woman behind Mr. Bridges, knowing that would surely set him off again. He grabbed my lapels and I let him. He pulled me close and growled some threat or other. I just smiled and he pushed me away like a tough guy. It would have been easy to stay upright but I let myself fall back into the wall and to fall down, making a lot of noise as I did. And I didn't get right up.

Mr. Bridges by now was recovering from his angry outburst and he leaned over the counter to see if I was getting up.

I had never intended for any of this to happen and even when he had me by the lapels, all I had in mind was to write an article about police obfuscation and threaten a civil suit for impeding my constitutional rights. On the floor, where I had actually put myself, a whole new approach occurred to me.

Standing up quickly, my body language bristling with outrage, I put it to Mr. Bridges.

"Ladies," I said loudly. "You are all witnesses."

Mr. Bridges's anger flared again. "Witnesses to what, asshole? You tripped. You got nothing." He turned to survey his fellow employees. They looked away.

"Mr. Bridges," I said loudly enough to make it a proclamation. "I am placing you under citizen's arrest. You have assaulted an officer of the court and you have refused to identify yourself."

He just stared at me with a stupid smile as if I was nuts. But I continued. "Ladies, call the police." I waved for one of them to come and get the card I'd shown Mr. Bridges along with my reporter I.D. which sat beside it. Then I quietly told Mr. Bridges his Miranda rights while he yelled at all of us. Imagine that, and I had no idea if I had the right to arrest him or not!

Fortunately a uniformed officer next door heard the yelling and came in to investigate.

Poor fellow, he was obviously a rookie, so he was immediately out of his depth. He did, however, have the sense to know that, and told us all to shut up while he called for a more senior officer on the telephone.

What we got was the desk sergeant from the precinct on the main floor, to whom he apparently reported. It took them a few minutes to really understand what I was doing but I eventually convinced them enough for them to call for a prosecutor to come down and help them out.

I knew the prosecutor and he knew me. He had been the subject of some of my reporting. You never know when good preparation will pay off. Would that I had known that as a criminal.

We were able to speak civilly while I took him through my notes, emphasizing the assault. Everyone listened attentively except Mr. Bridges, who needed some restraining by the sergeant so he would not get into any further difficulty.

When I had finished, the prosecutor asked the women if what I had written was substantially true. They all nodded and Mr. Bridges glared at them.

That was how I came to be the friend of Assistant Chief of Police Joel Burroughs, when all I had asked for were some bios.

CHAPTER

Joel Burroughs was a tough old cop in his fifties with slicked back gray hair. He was tall, trim, and wore a meticulously pressed uniform. He knew enough to play it straight after the prosecutor had briefed him. When ushered in by a secretary, I asked immediately why I was there.

"So I can have a talk with you before we charge Officer Bridges."

"He's already charged," I said. "I did it."

"Well, I mean before things go any further then. Maybe when you calm down, you'll lighten up a little. You want to talk or has this gone too far for you?"

It's funny how words trigger reactions. His words were meant to save Bridges but they probably saved me from myself.

Over the next half hour, I let Chief Burroughs talk me out of my pique. He explained that Bridges was a problem and that he had only two years left to get his pension and that they had obviously put him in the wrong assignment.

That made us both smile. We agreed that any action against Officer Bridges would unnecessarily injure the whole department and that would be unfortunate.

When he told me the prosecutor had informed him of my reputation as a straight reporter (read pro authority), I knew the hook was well set.

We made an agreement, Chief Burroughs and me. Billy Ray was watching this one, and he was highly amused by the circumstances. Anyway, we agreed to have Officer Bridges reprimanded for his behavior and transferred to some job where he would not meet the public. I declined to hear Mr. Bridges's apology on the grounds that it would probably not be heartfelt. That brought a smile from Chief Burroughs.

The chief promised me not only the list of bios I had requested, but a meeting with any police official I wished, including the chief of police himself. It seemed we had averted quite a crisis here.

In the spirit of the moment, I gave Chief Burroughs what he really wanted but could not ask for.

"Chief," I said. "You have been very careful to concentrate on the lawyer part of this problem, and I know you can't ask me about the reporter part. Look, I have got more access than I ever hoped for and I'm not about to screw that up by writing an article about the information office."

For that I was thanked warmly. It had all been quite civil with poor old Bridges offered up as the sacrificial buffoon. I'm sure both Burroughs and I were satisfied.

The prosecutor was hovering outside the chief's office when I left and he was relieved to see us shake hands and part on good terms. Nonetheless, he escorted me to the elevator and then out of the building, all the while trying to find out what had happened. I told him the chief was a very persuasive fellow, and that he'd talked me out of any prosecution. Again I was thanked.

Outside, after my relief had passed, I had an overwhelming

urge to tell someone. There was no one to tell, but the light went on for some reason and I thought about Mike.

It had been a wild afternoon for me, and I suppose that my body chemistry was still pumped up. Things had progressed a year that day and I was much nearer any action than I'd expected to be.

Spur of the moment would be perhaps apt, but the sudden surfacing of a long-repressed need would be more to the point. Both perhaps, equally.

In any event, I walked to a pay phone with my little bundle of prepaid telephone cards and called Mike at Camp Pendleton, California. He was not there but they took a message for him.

By the time I went out for supper I had thought better of it and decided to tell Mike nothing except that I missed him.

CHAPTER

5

When I picked up my phone messages from Jackson that evening, there was one from Mike. I have one of those telephone company answering services which gives the time of each call in that annoying robot voice. This one said, 'Call number three, July 22, 2:34 P.M.' Then Mike's voice came on. "Hey Ace, it's me. Got some good news. Call me."

Mike started calling me Ace at Orville's pool room because I could shoot good pool. It wasn't until after I'd hung up that the time struck me. After hearing the message again, it was clear that he'd called me before I'd called him. That was a coincidence. We only talked about once every four or six weeks.

Mike's wife answered and didn't ask who I was. She put Mike on right away.

"Hello."

"Ace here, how're they hangin', General? Don't answer, I

know you can't talk. Do you know we both called each other today? I got your message after I called you at the base."

"We can talk Ace, I'm outside now. I've got a portable phone."

"Good, what's up?"

"We're moving back to Pensacola. I thought you'd maybe want to go fishing or something, you know."

"That's unbelievable! Jesus, would I ever? What's happening? You get promoted or what?"

"Sure did. Warrant Officer. I'm going to be the ranking N.C.O. at the gunnery school there."

"Wow, that's terrific. When will you be here? I have something to tell you too—about—well, when will you be here?"

"Movers are coming the day after tomorrow. I start in two weeks. Can it wait till then?"

"Absolutely. I'll call you over there in two weeks. You pretty happy with the promotion?"

"Only you would appreciate how much."

"And maybe a couple of other guys too."

"Amen to that. That what we're going to talk about?"

"Yes."

"What, you been watching too much TV? What do we need? Three or four choppers and assault teams?"

"Oh much more than that."

"Okay Ace, I'll have a battle plan drawn up."

"Good. I'll call you. See you back here. Jesus, this is good news. I'm getting lonely here."

"Hey, I thought you were all set with Gwen. You on the loose again?"

"Oh no. She's great. It's my other life I'm lonely in."

"Well, save me some of whatever you're drinking, okay?"

"Never touch the stuff."

"See you soon, Ace."

CHAPTER

6

I had checked out Orville's pool room one night when I felt invisible under a baseball cap and behind heavy glasses. I needn't have worried. Orville had died and a small black man ran it now.

When Mike arrived, we had waited until we could get the back table where we could talk. I hadn't played any pool for years, but Mike had and it took a few games for me to win one.

Neither of us drank anything stronger than Diet Coke. We had only each other in this whole world who really knew everything and it felt good to relax in a normal environment.

While I had occasionally alluded to trying to help Maynard and Eddie, Mike had assumed this meant asking for a new trial or a mistrial on the grounds of police scams. He never took it all that seriously, however—being who we had been, the risks were too great.

We shot pool for a couple of hours and then went to the all night burger joint the four of us had frequented. It was almost empty so we could talk easily in a corner booth. Over pool I had said I might need some help from Mike and I was glad the Marines had moved him back to Pensacola.

We were each thirty-seven years old, fourteen years removed from that morning in Grand Bay when Mike had run into the swampy woods.

"So tell me about your new post," I said to him.

Even in a T-shirt and jeans, Mike was a Marine. There were flecks of gray in his tight crew cut and muscles filled out his blue T-shirt.

"Well, I'm finally the man. I'm a warrant officer, which is someplace between an N.C.O. and an officer, and I run the day-to-day operation of the school. There's a colonel in charge. He does the politics and sets the standards and I do the work. I even have a colonel I was with when he was a major and I was a staff sergeant. We operate well together."

"Jesus, you sound like a business executive."

"You know that's what the colonel says. I have to tell you, Harry I have a damn good life."

"I do too, Mike, and I owe it to you. If you hadn't made it through the swamp and come back to check up on me, I'd still be in there, you know."

"Strange how things work out, isn't it? Remember what we were like? I always remember that day. The only reason I got out was that I woke up early. I just grabbed what I could and ran. I had no idea what was going on at all. And then you got out, for Christ's sake, Billy Ray—oh sorry—Harry. You busted out of the toughest prison down here. How incredible is that? Man, how lucky are we?"

"Do you still communicate with Maynard and Eddie?" I asked.

"Oh sure. I send them both a package every month right after pay day. Never missed a one. I have to drive to San Diego or L.A. or wherever so the postmark is from a big city and I never sign the note, but I think they can figure it out. You know, books, cartoons, little stuff I pick up. I wish they could write to me, but that's much too risky. That's all I can do and I even wrap them at the office so my wife can't ask me anything. It's not much but it's the best I can do. You?"

"I do three," I answered, and then told Mike more about Leonard who would be out soon in all likelihood.

We talked about Maynard and Eddie and the fence scam quietly for a while. Finally Mike looked straight into my face and asked, "You have a plan to get them out, don't you, Harry?"

"Yes I do, but it's a long shot. Could be very risky."

"Good. I'm in the risk business."

"You sure you want to know any of this?"

"You need a partner, right?"

"It would be better that way. Yes."

"Good. I'm your partner."

"Don't you want to hear the plan first?"

"Harry, I'd go in there with fucking tanks if I thought we had half a chance."

"We might get caught. It's a possibility."

"Not if I know you, Harry. Let's get to work. Those guys are getting old in there. We have to try and I haven't got a clue about how to help them, but I am a very good Marine and that ought to be worth something, don't you think?"

"Well, I'll say this, you have the best cover imaginable."

"Don't I though."

CHAPTER

Mike attacked his assignment in the way he'd been taught as a Marine. He read everything available on surveillance and took a part-time security job to familiarize himself with the equipment. I told him he had about six months to prepare. He assured me he would be ready.

The part-time job, Mike told his wife, was preparation for civilian life in a few years. He gave her an extra paycheck to prove it. Giving up some downtime with his wife and boys was a small price for him, compared to our goal, he said.

He compartmentalized his life so that the only one who suffered was himself. The Marines got their money's worth, and he quit watching TV and reading at home anymore, instead just being with his family. His discipline was perfect.

We agreed to limit calls to pay phones as much as possible for the duration. I would call him at the base, or he would call my cell.

Mike had his mission and he was launched.

I set about mine by calling on Joel Burroughs, the assistant chief of police. The grapevine said that Assistant Chief Burroughs ran the department while the police chief, Chief Ross, dealt with the politicians, charities, and special interest groups. It sounded like Mike's description of the Marines to me.

As he had promised, Burroughs sent a memo for me, asking all lieutenants and above to give me a few minutes for a get-acquainted session.

Working down from the top, I'd left the lieutenants until last. It took me three weeks to get to Frank Babcock.

With each man I'd been professional, respectful and, for a lawyer, friendly. It was important that Frank be conditioned to be receptive.

Everything I had done since leaving the swamp almost nine years earlier was on the line when I went to meet Frank Babcock. The first vague outlines of a plan had come to me at the pressing machine in Mr. Woo's laundry. Hardly a day went by in which Frank, Ernie, and their scam did not surface to remind me of the reason for my work. Perhaps I could have settled for just being a good student and normal lawyer, but a life sentence with no possibility of parole as the result of police entrapment, however, is not something easy to ignore, especially when you are one of the victims.

It had occurred to me on many, many occasions that I could simply kill these two miscreants and send the obituaries to Maynard and Eddie, but that would accomplish only physical retribution. Even though I was no longer a criminal and had assumed the role of officer of the court, I could end their lives in a heartbeat the same as they'd ended ours. And perhaps, I thought at the time, I would kill them anyway. First, however, I had to see if they were still at it or if anyone else was. There had been only two three-time losers sentenced in the past six months and both looked like normal cases to me. One was a known pedophile and the other had held up a 7-Eleven on his fourth day out of prison.

All of the other officers I'd interviewed were at headquarters or in a precinct. Frank Babcock was listed as the lieutenant in charge of special operations and his secretary gave me some unusual directions for our meeting.

Frank's office was in a big beige double-wide trailer on a concrete pad beside a scruffy suburban park. There were four single trailers lined up like a school around it, two at the back and one at each side. Surrounding all of this was a high chain-link fence covered with opaque green plastic mesh. There were no signs, no police cars, nothing to say this was anything at all. It could easily have been a satellite office for an insurance company. In fact, that's what it looked like to me.

I parked in the visitor spot and went through the small gate to the big trailer. No one had told me what special operations' role was, nor had I inquired.

What I did know was that Roberts Electrical Repairs was still in business and in the same building where we had been photographed, videotaped, and railroaded. I'd checked it out. The upstairs was rented out to a finance company and the whole main floor looked like it was used for the electrical repair business. The owners were Frank Babcock and Ernie Collins. That had surprised me. They had bought it the year after Maynard, Eddie, and I had been convicted for life. The place looked legit as did the building purchase documents, which I had also checked. Not wishing to attract attention, I had left it at one quick perusal of the premises and a review of the deed.

Frank was expecting me. In fact, he greeted me the second I came up the metal steps and opened the door. He had the same self-assurance and ready smile which had sucked us into his web in the first place. He was still trim and hard-looking, even though his hair was graying. He was taller than I had remembered, and very well dressed in a suit and tie.

"You Harry Brown?" he asked with a smile, appearing pleased to see me.

"Guilty," I responded, matching his seemingly good mood.

"Good. Frank Babcock. Come on in."

I took his extended hand and we continued our smiling and regarding. He'd never seen me before. That was obvious.

We sat in a rather spacious office, given we were in a trailer. For a split second I stepped outside myself, regarding this bizarre scene, but I'd promised myself a particular performance and came quickly back as Frank was halfway through a sentence. Fortunately, it was more banality.

Immediately, it became clear that Frank was either a good actor or he was actually happy to have me there, because he seemed relaxed and in good spirits. Some of the others had not been anything more than civil, but the assistant chief got what he wanted and they had put up with me. On those occasions I had been brief and got out before anyone got a bad impression.

By the time I got to Frank, my opening remarks were set and I delivered them quickly. I was there for two reasons: to gather a short bio on each officer to be used if they appeared in one of my articles, and to get a deeper knowledge of police organization and methods.

Frank listened and then said, "Chief says you're a lawyer too. That right?"

"Yes, it is. At the moment I'm about sixty percent lawyer and forty percent journalist."

"Chief wants to know if he can trust you. Says you're pretty smooth."

The smile was still there but the words were less friendly. Not unfriendly, mind you, but their insertion was planned. That was obvious to me. I believed at once that he had been asked to check me out.

"Lieutenant Babcock, I'm a criminal attorney and a crime reporter. How devious could I be? I'll take the smooth part as a compliment. Thank the assistant chief for me."

Frank liked a little sass and he laughed out loud. "Gotcha. I see what you mean."

Then he surprised me by opening a folder on his desk. I recognized one of my articles on top.

"I read all your stuff and I read it all from Jackson, too." Then he went deeper in the file and said. "You are a very smart fellow, Harry. You got great marks at law school and they tell me you're a pretty good lawyer. How come you don't do it all in Jackson? This must be some pain in the ass coming down here all the time."

My actor came out at once to help me now that it was clear I'd been checked out, and was being challenged. My actor was never defensive. The real me would have been, but not him.

"Two reasons, Lieutenant. One is that the crime life of a port city is more interesting, the other is that it's a much more interesting place to set a novel."

"What novel?"

"You're looking at the next John Grisham."

"Who?—oh the writer-lawyer guy from Mississippi. That what you're up to?"

"Hopefully, but I need experience first."

"Why not move here then?"

"My lady friend is married to Jackson and my practice is already pretty good there. I even have employees now. So Lieutenant, I'm probably just like you. I'm doing something a little different and it makes people curious."

Frank folded the file. "Fair enough, it sure is different, but what the hell, who ever got ahead on normal?"

"Precisely. Now why are you out here by yourself, cleverly disguised as a school annex?"

Frank was quick. "Because we do not wish to be recognized." He was no longer smiling.

"And why is that?"

"Ground rules, okay? Burroughs owes you—told a few of us about your run-in with Bridges. Chief's a stand up guy. He owes, he pays. But what we have here is not for public consumption. I'm going to tell you some of what we do here, but only if it's background and not for attribution at all. We clear on that?"

I would have agreed to anything, of course, but I parried for a minute or two before acquiescing to his terms.

"Good," he said and got up. "Come on, I'll give you the tour." I believed by his demeanor that we had reached a good place where he believed there was mutual respect among professionals. I followed him down the narrow hall and out onto the gray concrete pad.

One trailer was for electronic surveillance. There were TV monitors and some audiotape recorders which were voice activated. There was one monitor used to track people under house arrest with ankle-cuff transmitters.

Another trailer was for surveillance teams to be briefed and debriefed.

A third trailer was locked and we passed it by, and went on to the last one, which essentially consisted of three interview rooms. Frank said they used it for questioning suspects and witnesses.

The double-wide trailer was mainly administration, the largest room being set up like a mini-theater with six chairs in front of a large TV. Frank called it his pride and joy.

"How's that?" I asked.

"Well just let's say it's my specialty."

"What, watching TV?"

"No, watching stupid assholes on TV."

"Oh. I see. Surveillance tapes and things like that?" I said it in such a manner as to convey a mild whiff of impropriety.

"All on the up and up, counselor. Don't forget, what I give the prosecutor has to get by smart guys like you."

"Touché, Frank, very impressive. What's in the locked trailer?"

"Oh that? Just storage. Old equipment and files."

I let it go. Frank felt good when he felt in charge. My challenges of him had been delivered in the spirit of friendly banter, never confronting him directly.

We did his bio in his office over coffee. He was forty-three, had a college degree in criminology, had been married to the same woman for fifteen years, and had two daughters. He coached soccer and was on the board of two local charities. His police experience was all with the Mobile police force, but he'd taken several courses, including three with the FBI.

"Frank," I said. "Do you realize you've probably got the best background of anybody I've talked to? Are you that good?"

Now, that he liked.

"I'm like you Harry. I've got my own agenda." He gave me the wide eyes that said 'You figure it out!'

"Oh sorry, I guess I'm slow. Moving up are we?"

"I certainly hope so. I'd hate to think I'd spent twenty years to end up a lieutenant."

Then I got serious, like a good citizen. "God, it's great to meet someone in the force with that kind of ambition. It's hard to find in government jobs usually. Are they able to pay a man like you enough? I mean you could probably get a lot more in the private sector."

He was dead serious now. I thought for a second I'd gone too far and he'd inferred that I was probing about kickbacks. Fortunately, he had not, because he was proud of something else. It seemed Frank liked to preen.

"That's probably true, Harry, but I happen to like police work, and I'm pretty good at it too. I looked after the money part years ago. We've got some commercial real estate and a little business on the side, which my wife supervises, and she likes to keep active so she works mornings for a vet near where we live."

"I'll be damned," I said. "It's certainly good to meet a man who's in control of his life." I was kissing his ass. Maybe that's how he felt when he was sucking us in.

We solidified our new friendship for a few more minutes, during which Frank alluded to Assistant Chief Burroughs with enough familiarity to let me know that his connections up the chain of command were first-rate.

As I was leaving, Ernie Collins came through the gate and took the path to one of the side trailers. Still the junior sidekick, Ernie had aged less gracefully and started a paunch and receding hairline. He said "Hey, Frank, we got 'em—" and stopped when he did not recognize me.

Frank just said, "Good, come over in a few minutes."

Ernie nodded, glanced again at me, smiled, and went on his way.

Tempted though I was to ask who they had got, I did not wish to disturb our parting, so I let it pass.

After a hearty handshake, I walked back to my car, grinning inwardly. It had been the most important hour of my new life and it had gone well.

CHAPTER

Mike had a part-time job working for a security company that handled residential and commercial accounts. He worked as a fill-in man so he got to see a lot. They trained him on the job, usually by having him call a hot line when he couldn't figure out the equipment. By the time I had finished my round of senior police officer interviews, Mike was fairly well along in his new specialty. He'd learned enough to know that the money was in sales, and he'd taken that as yet another sideline. His wife liked the extra money, so he gave it all to her. He and I were like-minded now. All we wanted was revenge and we made whatever concessions were required. Both Gwen and Mike's wife, Leslie, got more presents than they were used to and when we were with them, we were one hundred percent theirs.

Mike's other assignment was to look for cops on the make and their likely prey. So he had slowly integrated himself into the seamier side of life, getting to know some of the petty thieves and hustlers who hung out in the bars by the docks. He could still talk the talk and was never pushy, always smooth. They all drank too much, so information came to him after not too many nights. He said it was not amusing—watching what we had been.

When Mike made his sales call at Roberts Electrical Repair, he was told they didn't need any more protection. They had their own system hooked up with the local precinct. He had a little look around anyway and found nothing that interested us. All the business there seemed to be on the up and up.

Then he started to tail Ernie Collins whenever he could. It was very haphazard and, at first, fruitless. What we needed—a surveillance team—we could not get.

We were frustrated but there was more we had to learn, so we talked ourselves into patience. All the while I continued to report crime stories accurately and had achieved a mild notoriety as a nonconformist.

Our break came from a completely unexpected source. I'd become somewhat friendly with the prosecutor who'd taken me to see Chief Burroughs that day I'd had the problem with Officer Bridges. We had a coffee sometimes at court recess, and once we sat together in the cafeteria for lunch.

The prosecutor's name was Hal Lyman. He was tight with everybody. To the judges he was the correct friend, to the cops he was an ally, and to the defendants he was the tough D.A. He had it wired.

We were having a Coke one afternoon during a court recess when his cellular phone rang. He answered, scowled, punched the end button and said, "Shit."

"Bad news?" I asked.

"Oh—not so bad. Just a guy we usually—hey, do you play poker?"

"Not very well. Why?"

"Good, we need fresh meat. You busy tonight?"

"Not very. For what?"

"We have a poker game once a month and one of the guys just wimped out. You want to fill in?"

"I'm really not very good."

"Even better. Don't worry, it's only a quarter limit. The most anybody ever lost was a hundred bucks."

I had intended to drive back to Jackson that evening but I was always ready to get closer to anybody of use in Mobile, so I accepted. My assumption was that the group would be his friends or other prosecutors, but I didn't ask. I must add, in all candor, that I felt in need of human contact. I always felt lonely in Mobile.

CHAPTER

The poker game was so surreal that, for a time at least, I could not focus on my cards.

I had been welcomed by all, as one who would naturally be there with the insiders. Never having been an insider, I could only emulate the behavior I observed.

We sat at a round catering table in an unused banquet room behind a local grill. A waiter brought us food and drinks.

There were colored chips and new cards. As new meat, I was greeted cheerfully. These men obviously had played poker together for years and considered themselves good.

At times like this, Billy Ray would always surface for a look from his particular perspective. TB18078 also regarded the scene. Both were amused. I was nervous.

A judge, Assistant Chief Burroughs, two prosecutors, Lieutenant Frank Babcock, and Harry Brown. The second prosecutor was the same man who had worked so well with Frank on our first trial. Here we were playing poker.

We bantered regarding my poker abilities. While I professed rank amateur status, they had heard all that before and judged me a charlatan. The truth was that since my days with Leonard I had kept a good sense of cards and had played poker on several occasions.

When the drink orders were taken, their banter expanded to include my sobriety.

Soon, however, they were all relaxed and eating their burgers as if I'd always been there.

Strangely, I felt at home with them. There was no need for the actor tonight. I was a lawyer and I was a journalist and I knew these men professionally. At once my focus went to extending my friendship with each of them.

Fortunately, they were good poker players so I didn't have to manipulate the game. In fact, I had to play as well as I could to stay with them.

There was no shop talk. That surprised me and I wondered if I was the reason. But the evening was not strained and I came to enjoy what they enjoyed, a good game of poker.

I saved my big bluff until near the end. Up until then, I had not bluffed at all that they knew of. I threw in poor hands early with regularity, and raised conservatively except for once when I had a killer hand. I took a huge pot after very aggressive raises had forced everyone to fold. It was seven-card stud and I had two Jacks and an Ace showing. Everyone assumed I had a full house. I had two pair. They wanted to see my hand but I refused. They liked that, the possibility that I had bluffed them all out. I played it down so they would think the opposite. It seemed to bring them closer to me; they admired a little audacity.

As we broke up, the judge told me they met the second Tuesday of each month. They wanted their money back so I had to join them.

I'd made fifty dollars and the judge had made sixty. The others had all lost.

We ended with handshakes and said we'd see one another next time.

As I drove through the night to Gwen, I wondered how to use this access. It was the invisibility it gave me that finally overtook any desire to somehow overtly use the access I now had to the men at the poker table. They assumed I was one of them. They were ambitious so I must be. They were establishment, so I must be. I would use my access to become one of them.

In the ensuing days I learned that there was no public knowledge of the poker game, and I told no one. Our meetings in public were always professional and friendly. That was how insiders acted.

In another life they might have been friends.

Mike and I met after the first game and had a good laugh at the absurdity of it all.

Mike finally hit pay dirt with Ernie Collins. He'd followed him twice in a ten-day period from the little trailer park where I'd met with Frank Babcock to a small warehouse near the old train station. Each time, Ernie had changed his clothes in the locked trailer and emerged in a black sweater and slacks. He drove a faded blue van, which was usually parked at the back. On his second trip, Frank Babcock had gone with him, also informally attired.

That was enough for Mike, who was itching for some action. He called me to talk it over, and we decided to check it out. I was itchy as well.

Since we couldn't know if the building was under electronic or any other kind of surveillance, we used one of the service trucks from Mike's security company. He got me a company shirt and repairman's cap, and I wore sunglasses, too. If anyone was looking, we had a good cover.

The warehouse was somewhat isolated, with a high wire fence

around the property and a padlocked gate. The building itself was one tall story with a row of opaque white windows high on each side. There were two big loading doors at one end and a rusted steel door at the side. The old lettering of peeled red paint said that it had once been the home of the Peerless Freight Company.

A check of the surrounding building exteriors showed no apparent surveillance. There was, however, one small TV camera just behind an old floodlight over the loading doors of the warehouse Ernie and Frank had entered. I would never have seen it, even if I'd looked straight at it. It was small and had been strapped to the neck of the light fixture with heavy matte black tape. It looked like an electrical component. With binoculars, I could just make out the small lens.

Mike said he had a good eye from his Marine training and his new security experience told him what to look for. He believed the camera to be off, but could not tell from a distance. To him it was behind the light for night filming. It was certainly not to deter thieves because they would never see it.

We had gone as far as we could for the moment, but were excited by the possibilities.

CHAPTER

10

We really had no solid indication that any undercover fence scam was still operating. Nothing had told me it could be until Mike had followed Ernie and then Frank to the warehouse.

The camera behind the light was instructive but we needed to get inside or at least see some activity before we took more direct action.

I'd only really known Mike as a thief and a friend in the old days. He'd been thorough and organized as a thief and he had used those same skills to succeed in the Marines. He was used to planning.

We talked out our options over breakfast in a diner and then took our first overt steps. Mike laughed and said this must be how cops feel when they think they're on to something. We were cops, in a way. At least we were trying to catch criminals. That's what we thought of Frank and Ernie.

Mike installed a surveillance camera on a lamp pole in the property adjacent to the warehouse. The lightbulb was broken and the fixture corroded and rotten. It had not operated for years, Mike said. It did, however, still have live electricity, and Mike installed the camera inside the broken glass housing. He said it was undetectable and I believed him.

The camera was the standard kind used at banks and other commercial establishments to deter criminals by recording their activities. It shot a frame every few seconds. The result was jerky but intelligible. The date and time were on each frame. We could let it run for a week. We did just that.

Mike had installed it at three in the morning using a security company truck and equipment, which he sometimes took home if he was working the next day.

In the meantime, two more things happened which amplified our interest considerably. First, in reviewing the deed to the warehouse, I found it had reverted to the city for taxes and was for sale. There were no real estate signs on it, however.

The second clue came inadvertently from Frank himself at a subsequent poker game, my third with my new friends. By then I'd heard a couple of things I could have used in a story but had refrained. While I couldn't know if this was noticed or not, it at least made me feel more trustworthy and my demeanor reflected that. That was how it felt, anyway.

We were finishing up the last couple of hands around eleven o'clock. They had all had a few beers, but no one ever seemed to be affected by the alcohol.

No one but me would have understood what was being said.

One of the prosecutors looked over at Frank as a thought came to him and asked. "Hey Frank, how are you guys coming on that thing we talked about last week?"

Frank was slow on the uptake. "What thing? Oh that. Good. One down, one to go. Whose deal is it, anyway?"

It was mine so I said so and took the cards. Taking as long as

I could to organize my chips and shuffle, before dealing, I waited for more.

The prosecutor obliged. "The next one all set?"

Frank gave him a rather stern look and said, "Yeah. Now let's play cards. Okay?"

The prosecutor got it. "Sure. What's the game, Harry?"

"Five stud, jacks or better, progressive. Ante up, boys, I need an infusion."

Mike retrieved the videotape from the light pole across from the warehouse. We watched it in fast time on a monitor in the service truck at one in the morning, feeling like cops and crooks at the same time.

I still have that tape, hidden away with our other treasures from that operation. I understood how fishermen must feel when the net is, for once, full.

Ernie was on the tape first, entering on Monday in mid-morning. He arrived with another man in the van Mike had seen before. Both carried dark canvas bags with shoulder straps. We watched on the monitor as they opened the fence gate, drove in, and locked it behind them. They even looked around carefully, which came through as jerkily furtive. It was really comic, in itself, while the circumstances were certainly not.

Mike noticed that the fence lock and the padlock on one of the loading doors were identical.

They came out a half hour later and backed the van up to the big door then went back inside. In fifteen minutes, they reappeared and drove off after locking up.

That night, Ernie had been back at nine o'clock with the same man, who we took to be his partner, as well as Frank Babcock. They went in quickly and left the gate unlocked.

Less than an hour later a pickup truck with a closed back unit had driven up and a man got out of the passenger side and swung open the gate. The truck then went over to the loading door and backed up to it. The passenger closed the gate and walked quickly to the truck.

We felt like we were watching true crime on TV. It was just like that. Jerky black-and-white images of crooks performing their act.

The floodlight over the door was a godsend. It worked well for their camera and for ours as well. In one frame we had the two visitors plus Ernie Collins and the truck license plate. We couldn't read the numbers but Mike said he could bring them up on his computer at home. For some reason it had not occurred to me that Mike would be able to operate a computer, much less own one.

The great thing about watching surveillance videos is that you can stop the show at any time to ask dumb questions. That's what I did. I expressed surprise that Mike had a computer at home.

Well, it seemed that modern gunnery uses computers and that Mike had very advanced knowledge of much more sophisticated equipment than was available commercially. He took it in good spirits that I had assumed he was perhaps capable but not brilliant, and asked me to reserve judgment on his technical skills until later.

I'd always liked Mike and he had always been a stand-up guy. I guess I had just assumed that in this operation I'd be the officer and he the N.C.O. From the tone of his voice during our little aside regarding his computer skills, I got the impression that he was running his end without my input and had not told me all the details. I got the impression also that Marines acted rather than talked. It made me feel good. When I told him that, he said he was happy for me and went back to watching the tape.

The men from the truck were young. Neither of them wore hats or had facial hair, so a blow up of their images would be useful. They went inside and we could see some activity at the back of the truck, but nothing definite. The loading door closed and the light went off.

The truck drove off an hour later.

Twenty minutes after that, the cops had left, carrying nothing.

That was it for the first week. Our camera was reloaded for another week.

We checked our time and dates and saw that Frank's comments about one down and one to go had come the night after the activity on our surveillance camera. It appeared to us that those two guys in the truck were probably more than halfway to life with no parole. We were the only ones who could have guessed that.

We were ready with a basic strategy to implement if we found a hot situation. For us, this was it. All the signs were there.

My schedule was always flexible and changed on whim, so no one would remark on the fact that I stayed in Mobile longer than usual. Outside of the poker game, I had no friends and kept completely to myself. Mike was on a less flexible schedule, especially when new courses were starting at the base. We were fortunate with our timing. A course had just ended and there was a two-week hiatus until the next one. The colonel took off for a week to visit relatives and Mike took a week's vacation. He told his wife he would be working at the security company and, in fact, he was able to get steady work that week on a service truck. We could not have planned it better except for the fact that he actually had to work on legitimate calls. But he said he was quick and could fit our work in without showing unusual time off the job. He could finish a job well before lunch and start another well after. Best of all, however, he would take the service truck home every night. We could use it at will.

CHAPTER

Mike watched Frank's house from the service truck and I watched Ernie's from my car.

The light in the upstairs front window of Ernie's house went out at eleven-thirty and I called Mike on the cell phone. Frank's had gone out at eleven. We had seen them both return home for supper and their cars had not moved since. We'd checked them out every hour with a driveby.

Just in case there were surveillance cameras which we had not detected, we wore baseball hats and had neckerchiefs around our faces like bank robbers in a bad western. We wore plain blue coveralls from the service truck and rubber kitchen gloves.

Mike was sure of his plan and I fell into doing what I was told. He was very focused, to say the least.

We parked the van behind another property that gave onto a different street and walked the two hundred yards to the warehouse, each carrying a tote bag full of Mike's equipment.

He'd seen the make of the padlock and produced a big ring with dozens of keys on it and started trying them in the lock. His company kept such things to help customers out. He'd taken them without signing them out.

The big padlock snapped open halfway through the ring and we closed and locked it before proceeding to the pull-down door at the loading dock. The same key opened the padlock that held it down. We went inside at once.

Not daring to turn on the lights, we used flashlights to check out the warehouse.

There were rows of high shelves, filled with TVs and radios and microwaves, some in boxes and some open. There were other things as well, like guitars and rugs. There was also a big metal safe in a corner along with some old chairs and a coffee table. We walked back through the shelves finding that after the first three rows, they were empty except for fifteen or twenty skids of large appliance cartons at the back in an open area.

It was a very simple setup. Mike found the first video camera in an air vent running along a rafter above the little seating area. He went right to it after sitting in one of the chairs and looking up. The camera could not be seen but he knew that was the best place to hide it. There was a ladder beside the shelves and he climbed that to take the cover off the vent and locate the camera. He got very excited when he found a cassette still inside.

The second camera was behind a light fixture, also on the ceiling. It was similarly loaded with a cassette.

We could find no other cameras—video or still—in the area.

Mike had hoped the cassettes would still be there and he showed me quickly how to make tapes of them using equipment he had in one of the bags. While I did that, he installed our own camera on the top stock shelf closest to the seating area. There were old dusty boxes up there that had not been moved for months, so he placed a small matte black video camera between two of them, well out of view and well away from the other cameras.

He found the remote that activated their cameras and adjusted our camera so that it would activate with theirs. We tested ours manually before we left, but not theirs because the date and time would probably be recorded.

We were out in an hour and I must admit that it had all been quite calm and controlled. Mike had been very well prepared indeed.

CHAPTER

12

The next day Mike magnified the license number on the pickup truck on his computer and someone in his security company ran it for us. It was stolen. Not the truck, the plate. We drove around downtown Mobile in the security company's truck and sure enough, there was the truck, parked under a streetlamp outside a bar. We laughed when we saw it. And we thought we'd been stupid. At least Mike and Maynard had hidden the vehicles they used to steal in and used legitimate plates.

Mike was in the bar for a half hour. When he came out, he just got in and shook his head. "Jesus, what a couple of dumb buggers. I almost told them to just get in the truck and drive to Mexico. They're sitting at a table with two women and all four of them are so stoned it's ridiculous. I just sat at a table and listened. Joshua and Joseph. They bought me a beer, asked me if I was a soldier. Said they could tell by the haircut. We toasted the Marines. Know what they claimed to be? Ladykillers. Poor dumb fuckers."

I asked Mike if they resembled anyone we'd known. He said we were never that bad.

"Not a care in the world," he said. "Gonna get laid. How sweet it is," Mike said, but he was not smiling.

Mike and I let Joshua and Joseph carry on their part of the seedy little criminal drama which was unfolding. We had considered telling them, but that one meeting warned us off. They were on drugs and they were loud. They'd go down whether we were watching or without. In that respect, our consciences were lightened.

These guys were not at all cool. But our mission was not about Joshua and Joseph. It was about police entrapment and men in prison for life for stealing radios and rugs. And, if we were really truthful, they reminded us of our younger selves. We were not impressed. We concentrated instead on following the developing case using our camera in the warehouse. In war, there are casualties.

They say the biggest sucker for a pitch is a salesman. Well, the police in this instance had no security whatsoever in their warehouse. I guess when you're a cop, you don't expect anyone to be watching you. Who would be?

On our first visit to the warehouse we'd missed the obvious. Our camera was activated with theirs. We would probably miss the police-only conversations which preceded and followed the visits of our felons. So we installed a voice-activated camera with a three-hour tape. Every week thereafter we harvested their tapes and our own, making copies of theirs and leaving the originals as they had been. I say 'we,' but Mike usually did it himself when he had a good opportunity deep in the night. He preferred rain.

Our perps lived up to police expectations and presented them with three separate hauls, all recorded for the courtroom. Included were some details of their crimes, provided by a boastful Joshua and Joseph, who were well pleased with the whole setup. They were pros now. Like we'd been. I felt stupid all over again, just watching these two fools act important.

They were busted in their truck outside a bar near the docks. I'm sure they were easy to find. You can imagine their shock. We remember ours.

We allowed the first trial to proceed without intervention. It needed to go just as the prosecution expected it would go to set up our plan.

Joshua and Joseph had a local lawyer of modest talent who went through the motions but could do little in the face of video-taped confessions. The trial lasted less than a day and resulted in an eleven-year sentence for each offender.

Of course I covered that trial and Mike sat back with a few others on the other side of the courtroom.

Wham, bam, thank you ma'am—and the felons were sent up the river.

My article was a little longer than usual and concentrated on the great police work involved. I mentioned that the felons had been videotaped fencing their goods, but not that the cops had set them up.

All was normal. Frank was very upbeat at our next poker game. I did not ask why.

When their second trial was announced, I wrote a follow up piece saying how dumb these felons must be to commit yet another crime while out on bail, pending appeal. Of course this was incorrect, and when I feigned discovery of my mistake, the paper published a correction of my error. These men had not been out on bail. They had been in the county jail all the time. The obvious question was, "How could they commit a crime while locked up?" That was the question my following article posed.

I questioned the police, talking to officers other than Frank and Ernie, and found out that the second crime had just then come to light, after the first trial was over. I said thank you and wrote an article to that effect. I told my readers that I'd never heard of indictments being piggy-backed previously, but that the police had told me it was not all that unusual. The police even assured me that, had they known about the second crime earlier, it might have been combined with the first. I reported all these shenanigans as something logical and part of regular police policy.

Part 4

the trial

CHAPTER

Mike and I had gone to the A.C.L.U. in Atlanta directly after the first trial of Joshua and Joseph. We figured from our own experience that we had about two or three weeks before a second trial. They agreed to see us with no idea as to why, simply because I was a lawyer and said I had a case that might interest them. Mike and I drove together to Atlanta.

We asked for, and received, lawyer-client privilege and told the director of that office our entire story. He never asked a question until we had finished. Then it took us a good hour to convince him not to turn me in for escaping. He said that as an officer of the court it was his duty. I agreed that normally that would be the correct action, but I had been wrongly convicted and had good proof and needed to be free a while longer to help all the others. I agreed to surrender myself when it was over, if he still wanted me to.

Then he took our case, and he took it personally. His name is Abe Nordhoff. Abe is a short, slight man in his forties with curly gray hair. He is a veteran litigator and he could not have been more pleased. He agreed not to inform his staff, in case of leaks. I would be his unseen assistant. He would take no other staff with him.

Abe contacted the attorney who represented Joshua and Joseph and got him to agree to his help, saying he was being paid by friends. Joshua and Joseph then officially engaged Abraham Nord-hoff as their counselor of record. His A.C.L.U. affiliation was not mentioned to the court or the two felons.

CHAPTER

The second trial of Joseph and Joshua started just as their first had and our two had. The prosecutor stated his case to the judge.

It was expected that the defendants would submit to normal procedure and agree to trial by judge.

Abe stood and tersely demanded a trial by jury. The judge asked him why he wanted to waste all that time and money when the case seemed simple enough for him to handle on his own. He was close to condescension.

Abe quietly said that he wanted the judge to excuse himself at once because of his obvious bias and that he did not have to explain to anyone why he wanted a jury. The judge grew very angry and asked Abe who the devil he was coming into his court and accusing him of bias.

Abe said he was the southeastern director of the American Civil Liberties Union and that he further demanded a change of venue because of the prejudicial conduct of this court.

None of the witnesses were present, only the lawyers, the defendants, a handful of spectators and me, of course, as a journalist.

The judge had no experience with a lawyer like Abe, who had absolutely no fear of anyone and who had fought Southern judges for a living for a very long time.

Abe listened attentively while he was further admonished to stop being so insolent, and then he quietly informed the court that if the judge did not excuse himself at once, he would be immediately reported to the state attorney general.

"Your Honor," he said. "You have called this a simple matter, which means that you know the outcome, and you have not granted us a jury. Now I know you didn't expect the A.C.L.U. here this morning, but here we are. Think about it a moment. You will be removed from this case and we will have a jury. That I can guarantee you. We will also request a change of venue for obvious reasons. Now please do as I ask before this whole thing gets any bigger. Could I suggest you call a recess to consult with your colleagues?"

After a staring match during which Abe actually smiled at the red-hot judge, he slammed his gavel and called a recess. A half hour later the clerk announced that the trial would start in two days with a different judge and a jury.

We never wanted a change of venue, just a good story. We had one now. I ran a big article, wondering why the A.C.L.U. would defend two convicted felons. Why would the director himself come to try this case? Why had the judge been so sure of the outcome and why had he resisted a jury? What was going on here? The radio talk shows and the news media all picked up on my article. Interest soared.

The new judge was younger and seemed very serious. He was junior in tenure and experience. We assumed that older peers had seen the potential danger and thrown him into the ring. His name was Calvin Simms. He had a professional, somewhat lofty appearance and pursed his lips compulsively. He reminded me of a Baptist insurance salesman I'd known in Grand Bay. It seemed so natural for a Baptist to sell insurance.

Jury selection was easy. Abe wanted anyone at all except right-wing men. Since the prosecutor didn't know what was afoot, he simply went through the traditional motions looking for people who favored law and order.

The jury was empaneled by noon of the first day. It was two-thirds black and seven were women. Abe was pleased. The other lawyer at Abe's table had not uttered a sound. He was getting a hundred fifty dollars an hour for just being there, and he was thrilled. His check would come from the A.C.L.U.

The small courtroom was packed, many people left standing in the hall.

Abe suggested to Judge Simms that precedents suggested that this trial should be moved to the largest courtroom available to accommodate the citizens who wished to watch the justice system in action. Abe then so moved.

Judge Simms responded that he had not heard of any such precedents and that he would hear the prosecutor on the subject. Abe waited.

The prosecutor argued that this was a trial of common criminals and that there was no need of theater.

The jury was sitting there, watching attentively. The small courtroom held about seventy-five people. All were quiet, watching closely as the legal drama unfolded. Judge Simms said he was inclined to agree with the prosecutor. He said it in a way that implied they'd won, two to one, and that Abe could drop it now. Judge Simms made no ruling, just went on to the next phase, which would be opening arguments. He started his comments to the jury but was interrupted by Abe.

"If it please the court, what's your ruling, Your Honor?"

"Ruling? Ruling on what?" Judge Simms seemed mystified by the interruption.

"A larger courtroom. I have a motion before the court to move this trial to a larger venue in order to accommodate the citizens who wish to watch."

"Well, Mr. Nordhoff, I think we've handled that. We see no reason for a change."

"We? Is that the court or you and the prosecutor, Your Honor?"

Simms was annoyed. "Mr. Nordhoff, you are getting very close to sanctions here. I have ruled!"

"With respect, Your Honor, you have not. There is a motion before you and you have not ruled."

"Oh, I see, Mr. Nordhoff." Now Simms was falsely condescending. "You wish to play this by the book. Very well then, you shall have it. Motion denied."

"Thank you, Your Honor. The defense moves for a mistrial. The citizens have demonstrated a desire to view these proceedings. You have denied them. And on their behalf, I move for a mistrial and the appointment of another judge."

The judge was livid now. "Into my chambers, all of you." He stormed out, followed by two prosecutors and the two defense attorneys.

Abe told me on the phone that night what happened.

Judge Simms cursed out Abe as a showboater trying to get a few cheap points from the jury. When the judge had finished, and felt better after this venting, Abe explained three recent cases in Alabama where courtrooms had been changed to accommodate larger audiences. The Judge, now in high dudgeon, replied that it was not the law and he wouldn't move. Then Abe gave him an out.

"Judge, I don't want to sandbag you here. I'm on this case because it will be a huge one, and in a week or so, there may be national media here. If you move now into the larger courtroom,

I'll withdraw my mistrial motion. Believe me, Judge Simms, when I tell you that this will be a big trial."

"What the devil are you talking about? These are two convicted felons. What's so important about them?"

"Their civil rights have been violated," answered Abe.

"What civil rights, for God's sake?" The judge had heard the dreaded words *civil rights* and was veering a little from anger and toward apprehension.

"Judge, I cannot try my case in here. Just please believe me that the A.C.L.U. is on a serious mission in your courtroom. Moving to a larger venue is easy for you to do. The main courtroom is vacant. This is not worth making an issue of."

"I'll be out in a few minutes. Please resume your places in the courtroom."

A half hour later, Judge Simms reappeared. It was two-thirty. He announced that court would be adjourned once Mr. Nordhoff had withdrawn his motion, and then he addressed the jury. He informed them that the ensuing proceedings would take place in Courtroom A on the second floor. It sounded like a small procedural matter. Abe withdrew his motion and the jury then got the standard instructions from Judge Simms and went home early.

Abe was all over the evening news being questioned, but he gave them nothing more than "turn up and see."

Why was the director of the A.C.L.U. trying a case in Mobile? My article, among others, asked the same question.

In a criminal trial the prosecution addresses the jury first, as the trial starts and last, as it ends. They have the burden of proof.

In his opening address to the jury, Wes Wentworth, the prosecutor, did a workmanlike job of degrading these two felons, and felons in general. He pooh-poohed as a smoke screen any defense allusions to the violation of the civil rights of these admitted criminals. He told the jury that the good citizens of Mobile sure didn't need any fancy A.C.L.U. lawyer coming down to help them administer justice. A couple of jurors nodded and Abe Nordhoff made a note on his yellow pad. The whole thing took only a few minutes. We were surprised to hear the words *civil rights* come from his lips. I suppose he was attempting a put-down before Abe could make his own remarks.

Wes sat down quickly, looking cool and mildly amused. He looked like the winner.

Abe stood in front of the jury and regarded them calmly. He had no notes and his hands were clasped behind his back. He took off his glasses and put them in his jacket pocket and waited for absolute silence.

"Citizens of this jury, we need your assistance. There is what is popularly termed a three-strike law in Alabama. I am not permitted to ask each of you if you fully understand that law, so I am obliged to explain it so that I can be certain that you do.

"The law says that if a person has been convicted of three separate felonies, no matter their severity, then that person shall be imprisoned for the rest of his life with no possibility of being paroled upon his conviction for a fourth. That means, simply, that a man or woman who steals three cars or an armed robber who wounds police officers three times, all get the same punishment, if they are convicted of a fourth crime. The law was passed in the hope of stopping habitual felons from continuing their criminal activities after two or three tastes of imprisonment. I will not comment on the law. One can like it or not. It is the law.

"Politicians passed the law and politicians brag that the law has reduced crime. I shall not comment on that either. One can agree or disagree. There are ample statistics on both sides of the question.

"The spirit of this law presumes the serving of three terms before the three-strike law is invoked. It assumes that the serving of three sentences will stop felons from continuing in their old manner, because a fourth conviction will result in life in prison, with no hope of parole. The letter of this law says simply that a felon must be convicted thrice before it is invoked.

"What we have in this case is very clear and simple. I will state three facts for you and then I will prove them. When we are finished, you must make a decision for all the citizens of Alabama. The decision will be either for our continuing liberty or for a police state. This case is that important."

Abe paused for them to look at him to see that he was serious. He was.

He continued. "I said there were three facts. The first is that my clients committed the robberies they are charged with." Abe smiled as the courtroom buzzed. The judge gaveled silence and Abe continued.

"The second is that the Mobile Police Department systematically and deliberately encouraged additional felonies so that arrests could be made, and the third is that the Mobile Police Department set these men up for multiple crimes so that strikes three and four could be accomplished in a matter of weeks and the statistics of the three-strike enforcement would be enhanced for political gain. This has been going on for years. We will prove all this for you. All I ask is your attention."

He certainly had that, and the courtroom's as well. Abe sat down.

Judge Simms let the buzz go on for a couple of moments, then he asked the prosecutor for his opening presentation to the jury, before he brought his witnesses.

The prosecutor, Wes Wentworth, was a midlevel career prosecutor, and was accustomed to less powerful adversaries. He had not anticipated the defense which was to be mounted, nor had he anticipated the brevity of Abe Nordhoff's opening remarks.

"If Your Honor pleases," Wes said. "Could we recess a little early so that I can have the lunch break to—er—ah—to better prepare the state's presentation. You know—getting witnesses here, and all."

"It's only ten-thirty. Aren't you ready?"

"Oh—certainly Your Honor, only—well—We thought the defendants' attorney would take the morning, that's all."

The judge looked out over the two hundred faces looking up at him. They had come for a trial.

"Fifteen minute recess," said the judge.

CHAPTER

During many trials, I was the only reporter in the court-room. Occasionally, one more would join me. Abe had nicely whetted the local-news appetite and there were now six reporters there with me in a cordoned-off area marked PRESS. I talked to them as little as possible for fear I'd let something slip. Reporters have very good antennae.

Wes had a slam dunk but he also had an audience. It is a rare lawyer who does not like a full courtroom. He took his time with his first witness, Detective Ernie Collins. We were given his years on the force, his exemplary record, his virtues as a family man, and his community involvement. When there were no objections from Abe, Wes pressed on with Ernie's military and religious history, and finally his son's Little League.

The judge at last interrupted to ask if Wes would soon be finished introducing his first witness. As an aside he asked Abe if he might object to the length of the introduction. Abe stood po-

litely and said quite seriously, "He sounds like an ideal law enforcement officer and citizen to me, Your Honor. I have no objections, thank you."

There were a few smiles from the jury and the audience but
no laughter. Abe had not played to the crowd at all, but a few of
them got it anyway.

The judge did not. He reminded Abe of his rights to object
and he asked Wes to finish up his introduction.

Wes was amused but not suspicious. He was focused on the
introduction of the surveillance tapes, the defense strategy being
so clear to him because there could be no other.

He then led Ernie on a tour of police procedures, concentrating
on surveillance techniques. It was an artful job. Ernie showed his
accumulated knowledge of the increasingly sophisticated methods
which the police employed in the detection of crimes. The use of
surveillance cameras was just a modern refinement of the classic
methods and was right up there with the eye-witness. In fact, Ernie
answered that they were even more reliable because electronic
memory was perfect and incorruptible by time or manipulation.

The next tour was through the world of police undercover practices, which were also time honored and universally accepted.
How better to detect criminals than by operating in their own mi-
lieu? A hint of danger was introduced to underscore the dedication
of the Mobile Police Department, and its brave detectives.

Ernie described the fencing operation as "pro-active police
work." He had to work late at night and operate in the presence of
criminals, but what the heck, that was his job.

Since Abe never once objected, Ernie's beatification continued well into the afternoon to the accompaniment of universal
boredom.

The judge inquired of Wes, following the afternoon bathroom break, when he would be through with that witness. Wes

replied that it would be before the end of the day. The jury visibly brightened.

Ernie told of the chance discovery of the second felony while the perpetrators were still in custody in Mobile. Then he described the crime itself.

In a show of strength, Wes asked about the other crimes for which these two felons had been recently convicted. Ernie dutifully fully replied as to the nature and severity of the previous offense.

Then Wes asked. "Why do you not just lump these felonies with the others? They were detected in the same manner, were they not?"

Ernie said sadly that the law was quite specific about that, and once criminals were convicted in a trial, that conviction must stand on its own and any new crimes must be prosecuted toward a new and separate conviction.

The videotape was not introduced that afternoon, although Wes alluded to it, as did Ernie, on many occasions.

Wes kept an eye on the clock and turned the witness over to the defense for cross-examination at 4:10, leaving Abe only twenty minutes until the regular adjournment time. This, of course, would normally disrupt the defense as they would have to hurry or split the cross-examination.

Abe looked up when told it was his turn to cross-examine, and said softly that he had no questions at this time for this witness but reserved the right to question him later.

That was his perfect right. The judge quickly instructed Wes to produce his next witness. Wes was not prepared, he said, and smiling, referred to the late hour.

The judge smiled at Wes as if all was normal, but said, "Is your next witness in the building?"

"He is, Your Honor."

"Then produce him please."

"But Your Honor, we hadn't anticipated—"

The judge cut him off. "The prosecution was prepared to let the defense operate late in the day. We have twenty minutes left. Produce your next witness."

Wes said, "It will take ten minutes to find him, Your Honor."

"Then I shall add ten minutes to our day, counselor, now stop sparring with me and produce your witness, please."

Wes produced a lawyer employed by the city to inform the court about the laws concerning convictions, and how they add up to three or four strikes. At ten to five, the judge asked Abe if he wished to cross-examine this witness then or in the morning.

Abe thanked the judge for his thoughtfulness and said that the lawyer had summarized the facts perfectly and that, as he had with Ernie, he passed for now but reserved the right to a future cross-examination of this witness.

Judge Simms shook his head as if to indicate the defense's strategy was beyond him, but was happy to end the day's proceedings nonetheless.

CHAPTER

The next morning the prosecution presented witnesses who identified their stolen property. Their testimony was well rehearsed and formulaic. Abe then used his cross-examination to apologize to these witnesses on behalf of his clients and to thank them for their time and effort in coming to court and testifying.

That brought Wes to his feet with a big objection. "I object, Your Honor."

"Yes?"

Wes stood there wondering what "Yes" meant. The judge helped him. "What is your objection, counselor?"

"Well—he's—. The defense is playing to the jury. This is out of line, Your Honor."

"Mr. Nordhoff?" asked the judge.

"Your Honor," Abe replied. "I have stated in my opening remarks that my clients committed these thefts. I was simply being courteous with their victims on their behalf."

"There!" Wes said. "He's doing it again. If they did it, why doesn't he just plead them guilty and save us all this." He gestured at the full courtroom. "This—this time and money."

Judge Simms smiled as if he had gotten his fondest wish. "That seems like a legitimate question. Mr. Nordhoff, would you care to answer him?"

"Not at this time, thank you, Your Honor."

Wes continued. "He just wants a plea bargain." It was said just loud enough to be retracted as a vocal thought if the judge didn't like it. But the judge heard it well and hoped aloud that that was not the case, because if it was, he would not be at all amused by the use of his good courtroom for that end.

The judge looked down at Abe Nordhoff to emphasize this hope as he spoke. Abe remained standing and inscrutable. He did not reply and the judge stopped short of actually questioning him further.

Abe used the ensuing awkward silence to request that Wes's objection be withdrawn. Both Wes and the judge had forgotten about the motion. When it registered, the judge said, "Objection overruled." The witness was excused.

Wes filled the afternoon with two more detectives who showed some slides of still photos taken during the selling of stolen property to undercover cops. Some of the photos showed Ernie or Frank with Joshua and Joseph. All normal police practices.

On the phone that night, both Abe and I were very fearful that Wes would be smart enough to rest his case right there. He easily could have, and thereby denied us discussion of the videotapes. In a trial, you never know the game quickly enough. Perhaps Wes had been playing possum with his talk of plea bargains. Perhaps he thought we'd fight the introduction of the tapes on the grounds of entrapment or civil rights. You could never tell.

CHAPTER

5

We needn't have worried. In the morning, Wes was all business as he called Detective Lieutenant Frank Babcock to the stand. Frank sported a fresh haircut, blue suit, white shirt, and a red power tie. He spoke clearly and looked often at the jury. He was the very model of a modern police executive.

Wes took him down the same road as Ernie, but more rapidly. By ten o'clock, we were all well aware of Babcock's excellent credentials and record. By eleven we had again heard the sad story of our two felons, with their latest crime having come to light only recently.

By twelve, we had been shown more photos of the transactions in the warehouse. The pickup truck was identified. The felons were identified and the goods were identified again by Frank.

Over the lunch break I worried again that Wes would rest his case now without the tapes, relying instead on the still photos.

At one-fifteen Frank resumed the stand, and to my immense relief, Wes asked him about the video surveillance. As I sat and listened to Frank justify his sting operation, I had the reflection that in the future I'd always ask myself twice a day, that if I would rest my case at that moment, what would happen. Wes could easily have rested his case without the video. But in his mind, I suppose, even if we fought it, and had them disallowed, the jury could still visualize the videos based on the still photographs and testimony.

I could see Abe relaxing a little now and setting to work recording Frank's remarks on his yellow legal pad.

Wes wasn't a good lawyer but he did have one thing down cold. That was his timing. All through his preparation for introducing the tapes he kept looking at Abe and up at the big clock above the judge. Abe just sat quietly taking his notes and looking concerned.

Finally, at three o'clock, after the break, Wes asked Frank if he had the tapes ready to play for the jurors. Frank said there were three monitors wired so that the jury and the courtroom could view the tapes simultaneously.

The judge asked Abe if that was going to be all right with him.

"Yes, Your Honor," was Abe's answer. Nothing more. Wes held back his smile and in two moments, after the lights were dimmed, we all watched the scam on TV.

Everyone seemed to be impressed with the police work.

Abe was asked at four-thirty if he'd like to cross-examine the witness. He said not yet, but he'd like to see the last tape again.

We did and that rounded out the day.

In the morning, the judge asked Abe if he would cross-examine Lieutenant Frank Babcock. That's when our trial started.

"I would, Your Honor, and I ask that Detective Ernie Collins and Detective Lieutenant Frank Babcock be kept apart for the duration of this trial. They are both witnesses for the state. It is the right of the defense, Your Honor."

"Well, I know, but they are police officers who work together. I think they can be trusted," answered Judge Simms.

"I do not," replied Abe, "and I ask the court to restrain them from any contact whatsoever until this trial is completed."

"But counselor, how can we do that? They work together."

"If you order it, they must comply or be held in contempt of court. We will watch them closely, Your Honor."

The judge was not at all pleased and turned to Wes for any help he might offer.

Wes shook his head in mock disgust. "It's their call, Your Honor. I think it's insulting to two fine police officers."

"Very well. So ordered," said the unhappy judge. "Mr. Nord-hoff, this can't make these witnesses more cooperative with you, you know."

"I'm not expecting them to cooperate with me, Your Honor. I'm trying to stop them from cooperating with each other."

Judge Simms ordered Wes to take a few minutes to inform the two police witnesses of his ruling and to be firm that there was to be absolutely no contact.

"Tell them if they violate the order, I shall hold them in contempt of court and defense counsel could move for a mistrial. I won't tolerate a mistrial caused by collaborating witnesses."

Judge Simms cast a grim smile at Abe to show he had seen the gambit and warned against it. Abe nodded as if he'd been found out.

Frank Babcock was called and ushered by a bailiff to the witness stand. Abe let Frank wait while he went through his notes for several long minutes. Then without looking up, he asked quietly, "Lieutenant Babcock, do you consider the clandestine use of video-taping equipment to be good investigative procedure?"

Frank looked at Wes. Abe sat quietly, waiting. Wes nodded once.

"Yes." Frank answered. "I do."

"And do you use it often in your work?"

"When it's appropriate."

"And when is it appropriate?"

"Well—eh—when the situation calls for it."

"I see, and who usually makes those judgments?"

"Well—I do. My unit specializes in surveillance."

"So you are an expert at surveillance, then?"

"Yes. That is my job."

"Have you taken courses in surveillance?"

"Yes, I have, several of them."

"So you understand the laws pertaining to surveillance, do you?"

"Of course." Frank was mildly offended.

"Good. Would you be kind enough to inform the jury of the laws pertaining to clandestine surveillance, both personally and remotely controlled?"

Frank fidgeted and looked to Wes and then looked up to the judge. "Is this my job? Why can't he—?"

Abe was on his feet at once. For the first time in the trial he was loud. "I move to strike that as unresponsive and combative, Your Honor. He said he knows the laws. We wish to hear them. Please instruct the witness, Your Honor."

The courtroom was dead quiet now, while Frank looked around for help and the judge sized up the situation.

"The record will show the witness as unresponsive and the witness is ordered to comply with counsel's request." The judge did not look at Frank as he spoke in a low monotone.

But Frank kept looking at him. "But I'd need time to put it together. I can't just reel it off the top of my head."

Abe just stood there with his arms folded. Judge Simms said, "Counselor, will you grant the witness time to collect his thoughts?"

"Certainly Your Honor. I'll give him a pad and pencil and a few minutes right here and now. We can wait until he organizes his thoughts." Abe went to his table, took a new legal pad and pencil, walked over to Frank, and laid them on the rail.

"I meant to go to my office," Frank said to Abe's back as he returned to his chair.

"Please inform the witness that he is only to respond to questions, Your Honor. He has not been excused, we have just shown him the unusual courtesy of allowing him time to prepare his answer."

"I don't need some smart-ass—" Frank stopped himself, but the damage was done.

Abe said, "Let the record show that those remarks were directed at defense counsel." Then he went to his chair and proceeded to make notes.

Frank looked at the judge, who looked away.

Frank wrote nothing on the pad until Wes coughed and made a writing motion for Frank. There were a few nervous laughs.

Abe stood a few tense moments later and asked the judge if he could continue. The judge said, "Please," to a few smiles.

"Alright, Lieutenant Babcock, please inform the jury regarding the laws pertaining to clandestine surveillance and the use of videotapes."

A more composed but still tight-lipped Frank regarded his few notes, then the jury.

"Well I can't give you all the legal words, but I can give you our working definitions in the department. We can use any technique of surveillance we like if we have good reason to believe that there is a strong possibility of criminal activity. That's it in a nutshell."

"What about phone taps, Lieutenant?" Abe asked.

"We never tapped their phones," Frank responded quickly.

"Oh, I'm not suggesting you did. I only wanted the jury to know the distinction."

Frank was angry again and could or would not hide it. But he did respond. Only the police could tap phones and only with a court order after showing cause.

"So you can videotape and sound-record a suspect, but you can't tap his phone without court permission?"

"That's correct."

"Now you said that only the police could tap phones. What about video surveillance? Can only the police do that?"

Frank thought for a few seconds, then answered. "No, private investigators do it and security companies and banks. All the time."

"And they are not police. So can the jury assume that anyone can videotape anyone else?"

"Well I suppose so, but not anything private—like—well sexual or personal."

"Yes, I see. So it's pretty loose, the law on videotaping unknowing subjects, is it?"

Frank looked at Wes who nodded once.

"Yes," said Frank, "it is loose, but in the Mobile Police Department we keep it under tight control."

"I'm sure you do. So, Lieutenant, your clandestine videotaping of my clients was conducted by your unit but could have been done by the warehouse owner if he saw fit. Would that be a true statement, in your opinion?"

"Yes, but as I said, we only do it where we have good reason to believe there is criminal activity."

"I see. Let me ask you a hypothetical question, Lieutenant. Suppose a private company or even a citizen, thought there was criminal activity afoot, could they put video cameras where they thought the activity was, on their own initiative?"

"Absolutely."

"Good, thank you, Lieutenant. Now let me ask you about this particular case."

CHAPTER

6

The clandestine video discussion had taken an hour and Judge Simms took advantage of the natural break for a fifteen-minute recess. Frank left the stand and glared at Abe Nordhoff as he walked toward him on his way out of the courtroom. As he strode past Abe, he growled, "You still lose, asshole." Abe looked up but said nothing and then continued writing on his legal pad.

When Frank returned to the courtroom ten minutes later, he slumped down in the seat beside me before the court was called to order.

"Do you believe that guy?"

"Who? The lawyer?" I answered with no apparent interest.

"Yeah. Who the fuck is he, anyway? A.C.L.U. Big fucking deal. What's he gonna do, try to get these jack-offs off on an entrapment deal? No fucking way! We have precedents up the wazoo on that. It's procedure, for Christ's sake. What's he think he's gonna do, swing public opinion? Give me a fucking break. No way. The only shot he had, he just blew."

That got my interest. "How's that?"

"Fuck. There's no firm law either way on videotaping like there is on phones. We figured he'd fight on that one and if it looked like he had a chance, he'd want a deal."

"Would you have given him one?"

Frank looked at me closely, and hesitated before saying, "Off the record?"

"Sure, of course, off the record." I'd have donated a kidney for that answer.

"Well, understand Harry, this is just me talking, not the prosecutor and we're definitely off the record here, okay?"

My little risk taker clicked right in on cue, and I answered. "Look Frank, if this is making you uncomfortable, just forget I asked."

But my little risk taker had a good nose for these things and he just put Frank at ease.

"No. Sorry, Harry. I'm just still a little pissed, I guess. Look, we might have done a deal if we thought the jury would be tough. We want to keep the laws like they are. We're doin' good work here. A plea bargain is not a decision. Nothing would change."

"Could it still happen?"

"No way! It was like he was making our case. All he's got now is entrapment and believe me, we have that nailed down solid. We even got a professor helping us on that. We're solid."

"That off the record too?"

Frank thought and then smiled. "Yeah, thanks for reminding me, Harry, but I'll ask Wes if it's okay to use it. How's that?"

"Great, no problem. Hey what's the deal with them keeping you and your partner apart?"

"Oh, that." Frank smiled his understanding. "They're just trying to catch us in anything that they can use to get a mistrial. That's just lawyer bullshit."

"Will you do it?"

"Do what?"

"Not talk to him?"

"We still off the record?"

"Until you say we're on. Okay? This is fascinating stuff. It's great background for me."

"I'm not saying we would talk. But it wouldn't be too hard for a cop, you know what I mean?"

"What? You'd use police radios?"

"Nah, too many ears. Can you spell cell phone?"

"Ah." I said. "Of course. No wires, right?"

"I never said it."

"And I never heard it."

We laughed about our little complicity but were interrupted by the clerk's call that the court would be again in session.

Frank retook the stand and Judge Simms told Abe to resume his cross-examination of the witness.

"Lieutenant." Abe stood close to Frank now and looked directly at him. "I'd like you to repeat for the jury and the court what you said to defense counsel as you were exiting for the break."

Frank was obviously puzzled for a few seconds and then understood what was being asked. He glared at Abe but said nothing.

Silence ensued, and a staring match between Abe and Frank. The judge didn't like this strange turn of events, so he asked Frank if he had said anything.

Frank saw his way out and smiled at the judge. "Maybe I asked him how he was doing or something. I don't remember exactly. It was no big deal." He shrugged it off as nothing. All the while he had addressed only Judge Simms.

Then the judge asked Abe, "Counselor, you all right with that?"

"Your Honor, there is a question to this witness. It requires his answer. Would you please instruct him to answer."

The judge did not want this to go any further. "Look counselor, a little sarcasm in the heat of the moment isn't going to hurt anybody. Can you please resume with your cross?"

Now Abe moved to his left two paces so that he faced the judge frontally.

"Your Honor, you leave me no choice but to move for a mistrial on the grounds that the judge has encouraged an important prosecution witness, who is a police officer, not to answer a proper question posed by the defense. Your Honor, the answer to that question is critical to our defense. We move for a mistrial." He did not wait for an answer but turned on his heel and went to his table where he sat and waited.

Judge Simms rose and growled for the lawyers to come to his chambers. There he bluntly told Abe to withdraw his motion and stop trying to upset the court with his disruptive tactics. Abe waited quietly while the judge scolded him, to the delight of Wes and his associate.

"Your Honor," answered Abe. "While I have the highest regard for you and this court, I have only one duty here and that is to obtain justice for my clients. Their civil rights have been violated by the City of Mobile. One of its senior police officers has said offensive things to their defense counsel in the midst of his cross-examination. Now either you instruct him to answer the question or the motion for mistrial stands. The appellate court would grant it in a heartbeat."

"Are you threatening me?" demanded Judge Simms.

"No, Your Honor, I'm not, but you were threatening me a few minutes ago and it didn't work. I don't threaten people. I act."

Abe said later that it was like the air had left the room. He said he guessed threats to lawyers in chambers usually worked in Mobile, but he was from Atlanta and didn't give a shit.

"We'll see," said the judge finally, working hard on composure. "Please leave now. I'll be there in a few minutes."

The minutes went to forty before the judge returned and

called the lawyers for a sidebar. He said to Abe, "Counselor, I just called a colleague in Atlanta on the Federal Court. He said you had an excellent reputation there and that your motion was in order. Perhaps I misunderstood your motive. Please withdraw your motion and I will instruct the witness to respond."

"I appreciate that, Your Honor. Thank you very much."

Now everybody was happy except Wes and he was soon to be even more unhappy.

Abe asked that his motion be removed from the record. The judge instructed the jury not be distracted by these little legal skirmishes, saying that they were all part and parcel of their wonderful system of justice.

He asked the court reporter to read Abe's last question for the court and told Frank to answer it.

"Your Honor," said Frank, quite sincerely. "It was nothing. Just something offhand on the spur of the moment. I didn't mean anything by it."

Abe was on him in the next breath.

"The judge did not ask you the question, Lieutenant, I did. You were instructed to answer me. Now please do so."

Now Wes was on his feet. "Objection, Your Honor, he's badgering the witness."

"I certainly am badgering him, Your Honor," said Abe. "And I shall continue to do so until he answers my question."

Judge Simms had, it seemed, finally realized that Abe was not an ordinary attorney. This time he was crisp and businesslike. "The objection is technically accurate but in this instance it is overruled. The witness is again instructed to respond directly to the question."

Wes heard the tone change and stood for a moment, apparently thinking of a challenge. He sat finally, and nodded to Frank, who was now decidedly uncomfortable in his exposure.

Abe waited, directly in front of Frank. He seldom changed

his quiet demeanor, and even now there was little threat in his stance. He told me once that he always tried to think like a curious juror, not a combatant. It kept him centered.

Frank asked for the question to be reread. It was, and by this third reading, encased as it was in all the drama, had become an important question. The courtroom waited for his response.

"Well, like I said, it was just a throw away. Something off-hand. I don't remember exactly. Anyway it's not worth all this."

"All this what?" asked Abe.

"All this fuss!" said Frank, with something between annoyance and frustration.

"I see," said Abe. "If you know it is unimportant, then how is it you don't know what you said?"

"Because if it was important, I'd remember it, wouldn't I?" Frank answered in a mildly sarcastic tone.

"Answers phrased as rhetorical questions are evasive, Lieutenant. If you cannot or will not recall your words, I shall. I wrote them down at once when they were said to me. My co-counsel did the same. May I, Your Honor?" he asked the judge.

"Have you any objections, counselor?" he asked Wes.

"Yes, Your Honor, it's just his word against the lieutenant's."

"Your Honor," Abe said, "It's two defense counsels and the two women sitting in the front row there behind our table. They heard it as well. We asked them."

Wes just shook his head at Frank's predicament and sat down. "Go ahead. No objection, Your Honor."

"Go ahead," ordered the judge.

Abe read loudly from his notes. "You still lose, asshole."

The court let out a collective gasp, many short laughs, and some throat clearings.

Abe pressed on, still in his louder voice. "Does that ring a bell, Lieutenant?"

"I don't remember."

"Your Honor, this behavior by a senior police officer is an affront to the court, it shows that this witness's testimony is prejudiced and that he has disdain for the defendants and their counsel. I move that the witness be reprimanded and instructed to behave in a more civil and respectful manner."

"Your motion is under consideration. I will rule on it after the lunch break. Court is adjourned until one-thirty." The judge rose.

"All rise," yelled the clerk. Frank rose and stormed out of the courtroom using the door at the side where the prosecutor had an office.

I was dying to talk to Abe to tell him about Frank's off-the-record remarks to me, but I did not. Abe had warned me off any daytime calls unless they were urgent. He said he felt sorry for boxers between rounds because when they most needed rest and relaxation they were bombarded with advice from people who weren't in the fight. Only the fighters know what's going on, he said. Telling a guy who's getting hammered with left hooks to take a step in and lead with his right only invites acute consternation and uses up energy best saved for combat. The analogy was not lost on me.

Abe read the paper and had a sandwich and a coke out of his briefcase in a corner he had found somewhere on the fifth floor. He said it was the best hour of his day. Besides he was the most able litigator I'd ever seen up close and I didn't want to annoy him or distract him.

Mike and I did talk, and he was excited to hear that Frank and Ernie might try to communicate.

"Is there any way we can find out if they talk?" I asked.

"Sure, phone company records, but you need a subpoena for that. Let me think about it, okay?" The techie in Mike was rising to the bait.

To start the afternoon session, Judge Simms read a prepared

statement admonishing Frank Babcock for speaking rudely to the defense counsel and gave him a mild lecture on his responsibilities as a senior police officer. He hoped this slip would not recur. The jury was informed that the witness's behavior was uncalled for and off color, but asked them to remember the adversarial relationship inherent in trials.

It was the mildest rebuke possible. The courtroom was quiet as it waited for the expected argument from Abe for the judge to be more severe, and I was concerned that any more on that subject would be counterproductive and annoy the jury.

I could not see a way for Abe to just back off though, and let the judge diffuse the thing and let Frank off the hook with so slight a reprimand.

Abe smiled that little smile we see when one is in a good contest and the opponent makes a good point one had not anticipated. He gave the judge a little nod that said "touché" and then his smile widened. "I bow to Your Honor's wisdom. I'm sure we have all heard enough on this subject."

"Well, thank you, counselor," the judge replied, himself smiling in satisfaction. "Can we proceed with the cross now?"

"If Your Honor pleases, in light of the morning's contentious atmosphere with this witness, defense requests an interruption in his testimony until later in the trial. We would like to cross-examine other prosecution witnesses now. Please understand, Your Honor, though we are prepared to continue at once with Lieutenant Babcock, it just might be better to let a little time pass before we resume. It's entirely up to you, Judge."

Instead of walking into the judge's enticement to overplay his hand, Abe had deftly turned the situation to his advantage by stroking the judge. What he really wanted, of course, was a fresh day for Frank.

It seemed the judge was a pretty intelligent fellow and enjoyed the clever repartee in which he was currently engaged.

"I think it's a good idea, counselor. This witness is reminded that he will be recalled for further cross-examination and that he is still under oath. The witness may step down."

Abe spent the afternoon cross-examining the lawyer from the prosecutor's office regarding the laws on surveillance. This guy was fully primed with the prosecution's intent to have their tapes kept in evidence. Normally, a defense counsel would have had this witness barred as prejudicial on the grounds that he worked for the prosecutor's office. Abe had reluctantly admitted to his expertise and had seemed somewhat unhappy when he had earlier agreed to his inclusion.

The lawyer explained to the jury the lack of either legislation or pertinent case law in the regulation of video surveillance. It would seem to anyone watching that Abe was prodding for a soft spot in the testimony where he could introduce questions that might cast a poorer light on clandestine video recording.

Finally after two hours of Abe asking and the prosecution lawyer parrying, the judge asked when this cross-examination might come to a conclusion. Abe looked up as if from a dream, amazed that the judge or anyone else was not as rapt as he was by the proceedings.

"Oh," he said. "Oh. I see. Yes, Your Honor, I'll try to finish up today. Would that be satisfactory?"

"Were you planning on more?"

"Well, frankly, yes. I'm looking for something here—and—" He smiled a little self-consciously.

"And you can't find it?" asked the judge.

"Not yet, Your Honor. But I will."

"Proceed."

"Thank you."

I was sure everyone in the courtroom, except me, thought that Abe was not looking good on this and that the judge was being kind to him. The prosecution lawyers were having an afternoon off while one of their own made their case as a witness.

Abe kept up his questioning for another hour. They were really the same basic questions, phrased differently or with different hypotheses. The witness was expansive in his replies, thus facilitating Abe's job. For his part, Abe's apparent mood shifted slowly toward a controlled frustration. He seemed to be trying to extract doubt about the legality of clandestine video recording, but was met at every turn by positive responses to his negatively phrased questions. It was, of course, all meticulously planned by Abe. He wanted the prosecution to overstate their case because they would expect him to bring his own expert witness. In fact, Abe had listed another A.C.L.U. lawyer as an expert witness for that purpose, and he had been deposed by the prosecution.

At four-fifteen the judge coughed and pointed to his watch. Abe smiled and shrugged like he had fought the good fight on this one but had been frustrated.

"Okay, let's finish up here for the time being, sir," he said to his witness. "Is it your testimony that it is the lack of pertinent legislation and decisions in the courts which permits just about any use whatever of video cameras in clandestine surveillance?"

The lawyer, sensing a trap, went for the bait of another trap. "I'd say it's more that practice has established precedent here, and that many courts have ruled for inclusion of videotapes because they are so clear in establishing the true facts of a case."

Abe cringed a little as if to say "ouch!" and slapped his pad against his leg.

"The way you make it sound," he said, "is that anybody can do it anywhere. Why—" and he looked about, searching for his next phrase. Then he had it. "Why, could someone come into this building, or your office, or any public building and put in a camera?"

"Well"—now the lawyer had to think about this sweeping definition—"they sure could. If they had good reason to suspect a crime."

"Just like the police?"

"Exactly."

"But how could a private citizen suspect a—oh, never mind."

Abe turned to the lawyer and thanked him for remaining polite in the face of all his questions. Then he told a relieved Judge Simms that he was finished with this witness.

"For good?" asked the judge. Everyone smiled or laughed.

Abe answered, with chagrin. "For good, Your Honor."

"The witness is excused," said the judge grandly. "And this court stands in recess until Monday at 9:30 A.M.

"All rise."

CHAPTER

I was with the other journalists who tried to corner Abe after the Friday session. He was courteous but firm. We could interpret things for ourselves. That wasn't his job, he said.

"Look, folks," he continued. "It's our policy not to make public comments during a trial. I'll give you all the time you want when it's over."

As he left, one of the reporters yelled, "Hey Abe, what if I write you're getting your ass kicked by a real good police force? What if I write you blew your wad? You got nothing left? What about that?"

Abe turned and smiled. "It's fortunately a free country. Knock yourself out." And he was through the doors and gone.

The reporters milled and chatted for a few minutes to see if anyone had anything unusual. None had, so we all went to file our stories.

My article concentrated on the testimony regarding video surveillance and the lack of control. I didn't mention the blow-up over Frank's intemperate remarks to Abe.

On Saturday I read all the other reporters' pieces or watched them on the TV news shows. Most wondered what the big deal was. Some speculated, correctly, that Abe was not finished because he had not presented his case yet. He was still cross-examining the prosecution's witnesses.

Abe's wife had flown down for the weekend and they had taken a room at the Hilton on the coast, east of Mobile. under her name. Mike and I knew about it, of course, and had expected to go out to meet them on Saturday. We called Abe on Saturday morning and told him we wouldn't come unless he wanted us to, and that maybe it would be better for him to just relax and enjoy himself.

He quickly agreed and thanked us for understanding. There was one question he had, and it made us smile. We were in Mike's truck on a speaker phone.

"Hey, Mike," Abe said, "there's no way a smart guy like you could find out if those two cops are talking to each other, like on police frequencies or anything like that, is there?"

Mike said, "You know you sound just like this other lawyer here, except he asked me a couple of days ago."

"And?"

"And I have it covered."

"Say no more. Just let me know if they talk and we can prove it. Okay?"

"My pleasure."

"I'm sure. All right guys, see you Monday."

"Oh," I added. "How are our boys holding up? You talk to them?"

"Yeah. Yesterday before I left. They think I'm some liberal do-gooder and they give me no chance whatsoever, but they are behaving well and are doing what we tell them."

"Which is?"

"Look like clean-cut victims."

"They pull that off and it's Hollywood for them." Mike said. "How are you doing with those two?"

"Actually they are very polite, not all that dumb, and scared shitless,"Abe said evenly. "Given the circumstances, they come off good in my books. I like them."

CHAPTER

On Monday morning, Abe appeared with a healthy-looking tan, a white shirt, and snazzy yellow tie.

After the call to order, Judge Simms asked Abe if he was ready to resume his cross-examination of Lieutenant Babcock.

"Your Honor, I'd like to call Detective Ernest Collins at this time. As you will recall, I passed on him but reserved the right."

The judge seemed mildly surprised, but asked Wes if the detective could be quickly located.

"Yes, Your Honor, he's in the building."

Detective First-class Ernie Collins took the stand and waited for Abe to start. Abe stood and went to the lectern he seldom used and placed a pile of notes on it. Then he organized those notes for a few minutes, making sure that Ernie saw that there were scores of pages with writing on them. When he finally looked up, Ernie was shifting on his chair, waiting.

"Good morning, Detective Collins."

"Good morning, Mr. Nordhoff," Ernie answered for the audience.

"Did you have occasion to discuss this case with Lieutenant Babcock this past weekend?"

"No sir, I didn't."

"And why is that?"

"The judge instructed us not to talk."

"And why is that?"

"Because we are both witnesses in this trial."

"And?"

"And we shouldn't collude."

"Collude? That's a twenty-five-cent word. Would you mind defining it for the jury? In your own words, of course. Just what it means to you."

Ernie thought about that and glanced over to Wes and got nothing but a blank face.

"It means we can't get together so we can tell each other what we said so the other guy isn't tripped up."

"Good. That's exactly what it means. Thank you."

"My pleasure." Ernie looked over Abe's head at his greater audience.

"Detective Collins, did anyone else tell you about the testimony of Lieutenant Babcock last week?"

"Yes sir. The prosecutor told me and I read some things in the paper. Oh yeah, I saw some on the news, too, on TV."

"Do you think that's fair?"

"Absolutely. The prosecutor can tell me anything he likes."

"Including what to testify?"

Ernie smiled. "No sir. He just gives me information and I make up my own mind."

"When was the first time you met the defendants, Detective Collins?"

"About six months ago. It was in the winter. I can get the date out of my book if you like."

"Just the month will do."

"January."

"Where did you meet them?"

"In a bar by the docks."

"Were you dressed as you are now?"

"Oh no, I was working undercover. I probably had old clothes on and I had a beard then." He smile. "They just cleaned me up for the trial. Usually I look like a crook." He glanced out at the courtroom for approval and got a few smiles.

Abe, of course, saw this and smiled as well.

"Were you in that bar for a specific reason?"

"Just trollin'. Looking for information. Doing my job, looking for crooks."

"I see, and you found some?"

"Those two over there." He pointed to the defendants.

"Oh, you knew that they were crooks? How did you know? Did they tell you?"

"Yeah, in so many words."

"For instance?"

"Well, we had a few beers and they told me they just got out of prison."

"Did you have a few beers too?"

"Sure. I have to, to keep up appearances."

"Sounds like a pretty good job to me."

"It has its moments."

"I'm sure. Wouldn't telling you they just got out of prison denote that they were former crooks?"

"No. They were looking to score."

"What does that mean, 'looking to score'?"

Again Ernie played to the audience with his eyebrows raised.

"Well, in this case, it meant they were looking for something to steal so they could sell it and make some money."

"Is that how they came to use you and the fencing scam set up by the Mobile Police Department?"

"Well, I wouldn't call it a scam."

"Really?" Abe looked up surprised. "What would you call it?"

"An undercover police operation."

"Oh, I see, if the police do it it's not a scam. What if—" he thought for a moment. "Okay, Detective Collins, what if you or anyone else, me for instance—what if someone set up a phony fencing operation and videotaped thieves selling their stolen goods and then used the tapes for blackmail. What would that be? Same building, same camera, same crooks."

"Now that would be a scam. That would be criminal behavior. Blackmail is a crime. See we set it up to catch crooks, just the opposite."

"But the prosecutor's office has a lawyer who testified that anybody can tape anything, just about. Couldn't anybody just tape like the police do?"

"It's all about intent," Ernie answered with certainty. "Our intent is to catch crooks. If the intent is criminal, then it's an entirely different matter."

"Okay," he said, nodding his head in understanding. "I see that. It's all about intent. Your intent was to catch crooks in the act of selling the goods. Is that correct?"

Ernie answered "Yes sir" firmly.

"Did you have any other intent, Detective Collins?"

There it was. That was a huge question for us and I held my breath as Ernie looked a little unsure of his response. Then his face cleared and he asked. "What other intent could there be?" He had returned the ball.

But it came quickly back. "I'm the one asking the question, Detective." Abe had a great knack for turning things to his favor. He didn't demand an answer or repeat the question, which left Ernie as the center of attention, unsure of his position.

Ernie sat there, seeming to think, but he finally looked up and said to Abe, "Yeah. Give me the question again. Okay?"

Abe prolonged the moment by looking at the judge and saying "Your Honor, would you please ask the court recorder to repeat my question for this witness?"

Now it was a much bigger question, thanks to Ernie. The judge instructed the clerk and he read the question, and the few lines before it so that context was clear. The clerk read loudly for all to hear:

> DETECTIVE COLLINS: 'It's all about intent. Our intent is to catch crooks. If the intent is criminal, then it's an entirely different matter.'
>
> MR. NORDHOFF: 'Okay. I see that. It's all about intent. Your intent was to catch crooks in the act of selling the goods. Is that correct?'
>
> DETECTIVE COLLINS: 'Yes, sir.'
>
> MR. NORDHOFF: 'Did you have any other intent, Detective Collins?'
>
> DETECTIVE COLLINS: 'What other intent could there be?'
>
> MR. NORDHOFF: 'I'm the one asking the question, Detective.'

The reporter stopped and the courtroom waited.

"No," Eddie said.

"No what?" Abe asked. "No, you won't answer, or no, you had no other intent?"

Ernie was obviously nonplussed by his sudden isolation before so cold a question.

Wes tried to help him out by objecting.

"Objection, Your Honor. The witness answered the question."

"Yes he did," said Abe, "but not to my satisfaction. Shall I rephrase it, Your Honor?"

It was a good out for the judge. Everybody wins. "Objection sustained. Counselor please rephrase the question and Detective Collins please answer it with a complete sentence." He looked like he wanted to add something but resisted.

Abe asked, "Detective Collins, when you ran your police undercover fence operation, was there any intent on your part or on the part of the Mobile Police Department to do anything other than apprehend criminals, including the defendants?"

Ernie was finally tuned in to the correct channel, but he overreacted, reaching for a little help from the audience.

"No sir, neither myself or the Mobile Police Department had any intent with the undercover fence operation other than to catch crooks. That okay?"

"Thank you, Detective. That was perfect." Abe had taken Ernie's forced levity and made it lighter as if they were in this little thing together and there were no hard feelings.

Ernie said, "Whew!" and wiped his forehead for effect.

After the morning break, Abe took another tack. "How many undercover fence houses do you operate, Detective Collins?"

"None now. This one's blown with all this publicity."

"Oh, I see, I've ruined it, have I?" Abe was lighthearted.

"You sure have. I'll probably have to dress like a woman or get plastic surgery after this."

"Please send me pictures."

Ernie laughed along with everyone else.

"How long did you have the warehouse which was used to catch my clients?"

"About six months."

"Oh. Just about the same length of time that you knew my clients? Is that a coincidence or did you just acquire the warehouse in order to videotape my clients?"

"We never acquired it; it belongs to the city, for back taxes I think. We just used it."

"I see. Did you use it specifically to tape my clients?"

"Well—not exactly. We'd use it for anybody else we found too, you know."

"Did you use it for anybody else?"

"No, just this one. We never caught on to any other operations during that time."

"I see. So it was used only during the six months you were working with my clients and only for them, is that correct, Detective?"

"Well, if you put it that way, I suppose so, but we'd have used it for other operations, too."

"Is that a yes and a maybe? I do not understand your answer. Let me rephrase it. Was the publicly owned warehouse where you installed the video surveillance equipment only used after you met the defendants and exclusively to catch them in the act of selling stolen goods? Yes or no, Detective. No editorial."

"Yes."

"Thank you."

"You're welcome." Ernie loved the last word. Abe let him have it.

In the afternoon, Abe stayed with the warehouse. "Did you lease the warehouse, Detective Collins?"

"Not officially, but they knew we were using it."

"They?"

"City property office."

"Who paid the utilities?"

"They did."

"No rent?"

"No, we borrowed it."

"Was any other use made of the warehouse, Detective Collins?"

"Like what?" Ernie answered in a voice that had a hint of something in it.

Abe kept on. "Like anything other than videotaping my clients?"

Abe had no idea where this was going, but he knew about the repair shop from our case so his antennae went up at once.

"We stored some stuff there," Ernie said, with a resigned shrug, as if it was of no consequence.

"Really?" What kind of stuff?" Now Abe was interested.

Ernie looked exasperated by the whole thing, and Wes stood to express his own sentiments. "We object, Your Honor. This line of questioning is not at all relevant. What does it matter if the police store something in a public warehouse? This is not germane to this case and we ask that defense counsel stay on the track and stop wasting our time with totally extraneous questions." Wes had gone a little further than he should have, but he didn't seem to care. He seemed frustrated by the defense digging where he knew nothing existed.

The judge looked to Abe. "Counselor?"

Abe answered. "Your Honor, the witness did not say the police stored things in the warehouse, he said 'we.' I'd like to know who 'we' are, and I appreciate that the prosecutor is annoyed with me, but that's the nature of a trial, Your Honor. Perhaps the witness can help us out here by telling us whose goods are in the warehouse."

The judge nodded. "Objection overruled. The witness will answer the question."

Ernie sat, obviously thinking hard. Abe asked again, "For the record, Detective Collins, whose goods were or are in that publicly owned warehouse?"

Ernie let out a short sigh and looked up unhappily. "They're mine. I'm storing some personal stuff there."

Abe was great. He'd been on a fishing expedition, actually killing a little time so he'd have all the next day for Frank. Now he'd caught on to something and he went right on as if he'd known all along.

"And did you pay any rent to the city for the space you used, Detective Collins?"

"No. It was empty. There's no harm in that." Ernie tried to make his answer definitive but came up short.

"Oh, I see, if a publicly held property is empty, you can store your things there, is that it?" Abe asked. "Is that because you are a police officer? Is that a usual perk?"

Ernie became testy. "No. Look, there was all this space we weren't using and we put a few things in there for a couple of months. It's no big deal."

"We? I thought you said it was your stuff. Does some of the stuff belong to someone else or perhaps more than one person?"

Wes objected again and the judge overruled him without taking his eyes off the witness. "I'd like to know the answer myself, Detective."

"Frank Babcock and me. We stored a little personal stuff there."

"I see," said Abe. "Did you and Lieutenant Babcock have permission to store your stuff there?"

Wes was upset now and on his feet. "Objection, Your Honor, these detectives are not on trial here. He's just fishing for anything at all to stay off the subject."

"Overruled," said the judge.

"But judge, don't you see what he's trying to do?" Wes continued with some pleading in his voice.

"I'll forget you addressed the court in such a disrespectful way, counselor, but I will answer your question. Defense counsel is attempting to discredit your witness. That is his right. Now keep quiet before I lose my patience. Detective Collins, please answer the question. Did you and Lieutenant Babcock have permission or not?"

"No, Your Honor." Ernie said, looking up at Judge Simms.

"May I continue Your Honor?" asked Abe.

"Yes, but let's step it up a little, shall we?"

"Certainly. Detective Collins, please describe the goods, or stuff, that you and Lieutenant Babcock store at the public warehouse. Give us the type of goods and quantity and duration of storage."

Ernie was quick in his response for once. "Okay. There's a few old radios and a few old TV sets, some old washers and dryers, and about twenty or thirty boxes of odds and ends."

"Are they still there?"

"Yes."

"Judge, could you order an inventory?"

"If I think it's germane. But go ahead for now. I'll let you know."

"Thank you. Detective Collins, how do you and Lieutenant Babcock come to have so much electrical stuff?"

"We own a repair shop. These are just unclaimed pieces. We— we just stored them there because we got tight on space."

"Instead of renting space on the open market?"

"Sure. Why not? It was empty."

"How do two active police officers come to own an electrical repair shop?"

"We've had it for years. Maybe nine or ten. We started it for extra income. We never work there. It's run by a manager. Our wives are involved, too, to supervise it."

"Yes, I see. That sounds reasonable, but I'd suggest that you remove your commercial goods from a crime scene."

"Absolutely," said a relieved Ernie. "Right away."

"No inventory?" asked the judge.

"No, thank you, Your Honor. I'm prepared to move on to another subject."

Ernie Collins sat back, relieved to be off the hot seat.

"Could you wait until we have a break?" the judge asked Abe.

"By all means. I could use one myself," Abe answered, in good spirits, like he and the judge were pals.

CHAPTER

In some trials there is one moment when it becomes clear that things are no longer as they originally appeared. Abe provided that moment at three-thirty that afternoon with his first question following the break.

Ernie had fended him off before the break and looked relaxed as he went into what he believed to be the homestretch of his testimony.

"Detective Collins, I want you to take your time and consider your answer to my next question very carefully." He looked up at Ernie who nodded that he would.

"Detective Collins, how many times have you been involved in a prosecution for a fourth felony, where the defendants were still in your custody following their third felony conviction?"

Ernie straightened and could not stop himself from looking at the prosecutor. Wes could do nothing and looked down at his notes and picked up his pen.

"I'd have no idea about that," said Ernie. "I'm not even sure they keep those statistics."

"They normally do not," answered Abe. "But guess if you have to, just approximate it for us please." Abe sounded like he was asking the price of tomatoes.

"I don't know. Maybe once. Maybe none. I never thought about it." Ernie shrugged it off as if it were not worth his breath.

"I have, Detective. I've thought a lot about it. Would it surprise you to know that it has happened several times?" Abe asked, not altering his calm delivery. Abe stopped. Ernie expected more. There was no more. Then Abe asked again, very courteously. "Would that surprise you, Detective?"

"Nah, not really. I guess it can happen. I never thought much about it. We got a case, we go with it. If the perps are here, so much the better."

"Perps?" Abe asked.

"Perpetrators. The guys that did it. The crooks."

"Yes. I see. But I have a problem with your response, you see, Detective Collins."

Abe looked to the judge. "Your Honor, defense counsel have researched the statistics in question and we have them here, but since we are not yet in the defense phase of the trial, I cannot introduce them."

"Where did you get the statistics?" asked the judge.

"From the Mobile Police Department's public information section. We inquired in writing and have their written response."

"If it please the court," Wes was up again. "This is highly irregular. We were never advised of this evidence."

"Oh," said Abe in mild surprise. "This isn't being offered as evidence. We had no intention of introducing it now. It's just part of our usual research. I'm only trying to help the witness answer a question. If you'd rather wait on this until the defense phase, I understand completely. I'd do the same thing. By then, Detective

Collins will have done his own research and will have had his memory refreshed and can properly answer the question. We can recall him then."

"May I have that report?" asked Wes.

The judge looked to Abe who thought before he responded. "No, Your Honor, I'm sorry, but he cannot. That would make it evidence, which it is not, and the prosecution is not entitled to our working notes and research. If it wasn't for that I'd give it to you. I'm sure the Police Information Office has copies of the correspondence."

Judge Simms held up his hand. "See if this will help. What you have is, basically, public information. I could get it or the prosecutor could get it in five minutes by fax. Here, counselor, give it to me. It is not offered in evidence. I'll have the clerk make two copies, one for the prosecution and one for the witness. Then the witness can tell us if he agrees or not. Is it in detail, Mr. Nordhoff?"

"It is, Your Honor," Abe said as he walked forward and handed up the file to Judge Simms.

Wes studied the documents for a good five minutes. There were three pages. During that time the audience looked from him to Ernie Collins, who was similarly engaged. The judge had read his copy more quickly, and sat back waiting. Finally, he said, "Well, Detective, does that jog your memory?"

"Yes sir."

"Do you think the information is accurate?" Judge Simms asked.

"Yes sir, but it requires explanation."

"Counselor?" he inquired of Abe, "Could you restate your question please?"

"If it please the court, Your Honor, could the clerk read it back?"

"So ordered," said the judge.

The clerk read: "Detective Collins, how many times have you been involved in a prosecution for a fourth felony, when the defendants were still in your custody, following a third felony conviction?"

Ernie answered "It says seven here."

"Do you recall each case, Detective?" Abe asked.

"Vaguely," said Ernie, not looking at Abe, but looking out to the audience.

"It's okay, Detective, if you wish to wait for the defense presentation, I will understand. Answers like 'it says seven here' and 'vaguely' are not acceptable. It's your choice. Tell us now or tell us later." Abe was still very deliberate, his voice not raised in challenge. He was, if anything, resigned.

Wes's voice covered Ernie's as they both spoke loudly at once. Wes heard Ernie well enough, however, to resume his seat and say, "Nothing, Your Honor," when the judge asked him to repeat himself.

"Detective Collins, did you respond?" asked the judge. "I didn't hear your response."

"Seven," Said Ernie.

Abe quickly followed up. "Can I take it that your response is that seven cases were as described—where three-time losers with fresh convictions were charged with a fourth felony while waiting transportation to state prison?"

"Yes."

"Thank you, Detective Collins," Abe continued, "How many convictions were involved?"

Ernie looked a little confused, but answered. "Seven—we got—seven."

"That was the number of cases. There were as many convictions as there were people—defendants? How many convictions, Detective? Review your notes if you wish."

"They're not my notes."

"They are now," Abe answered curtly. "Please answer the question."

Ernie's head shot up. "They're your notes."

"Well," conceded Abe, "let's say they're our notes now, and they come from your police department. That is not the issue. How many people were convicted in this manner?"

"What manner? What do you mean by manner?"

"I mean the manner of getting multiple convictions while the defendants remain in your custody."

Ernie sighed and made a show of opening his file and adding the totals.

"Seventeen," he said quietly.

"Speak up for the jury to hear you, please," Abe said.

Ernie shook his head and looked to the judge who nodded to comply.

"Seventeen!"

"Thank you, Detective Collins. What is the time usually spent in the county jail for convicted prisoners awaiting transportation to a state penitentiary?"

"It varies."

"With what?"

"With when they come to get them."

"I see. What's an average then?"

"I suppose two or three weeks, sometimes less, sometimes more."

"Could we say one to four weeks would that be fair?"

"I'd say two to four."

"Thank you. What was the average stay of the seventeen men listed in our notes, Detective Collins?"

This time Ernie just figured it out using a pen and then replied, "I make it three point five weeks."

"Me too. In fact they were all charged during the fourth week, isn't that a fact?"

"That's what it says here."

"So it does. Thank you, Detective. Were all seven cases developed using hidden video cameras?"

"I'd have to review the cases."

Abe went to his table and took out another file. "Would you like some more help?"

Wes objected that Abe was going beyond the bounds of inquiries initiated by the prosecution in its direct examination of this witness.

Judge Simms was quick to respond. "We're too late for that now, counselor. Objection overruled. I might have agreed with you a few minutes ago, but we are well along with this line of questioning now and we require a response. Detective Collins, do you need time or additional material to answer the question?"

When Ernie did not respond, the judge added, "Can you answer his question?"

Wes was nodding no but Ernie was looking at Abe with a sullen stare. Abe never even seemed to notice it. He just went to his chair and looked at his watch. It was four-fifteen. He waited.

"Yes," Ernie finally said, looking still at Abe.

"Good," Abe said, as if Ernie was a child who had done well. "How many of them involved fence houses?" Abe had that technique down cold. Whenever he let a witness delay for a second, he came right back with a tough question.

Ernie only hesitated long enough to give Abe another hard look. "All of them," he said.

"Oh!" Abe said, as if surprised. "Were all the premises engaged like the warehouse in this case, once the suspected perpetrators were identified?"

"I can't remember."

"Take a guess."

"No."

Abe stood and addressed the judge. "Thank you, Your Honor,

the defense is finished with this witness for the prosecutorial phase of this trial."

"Hey," said Ernie, "I want to explain a few things. He said I could explain."

The judge said. "You will get your chance later during recross. The witness will step down. Court is adjourned until tomorrow at nine-thirty."

"ALL RISE."

Ernie did rise, but he just stood there, visibly angry. I noticed several jurors looking at him curiously.

CHAPTER

10

Lieutenant Frank Babcock was recalled to the stand on Tuesday morning. Again he appeared serene and gave a snappy "Good morning, Your Honor" to Judge Simms, who replied in kind. Frank carried a file folder with white papers in it. He placed the file on the rail as if offering up his preparedness. I suppose he expected to have to repeat Ernie Collins's admissions and had been prepped for that by the prosecutor.

Abe said good morning as well, but in a remote, afterthought manner. Frank was obliged to reply, but did it curtly.

"Is it a fact, Lieutenant Babcock, that you and Detective Collins used the public warehouse for two reasons?"

"Sorry? I don't understand the question."

"Very well. You used it to store your company's merchandise. Is that correct?"

"Well, we did put a few things in there—but that—"

Abe cut him off with a slightly raised voice. "Yes or no will do,

Lieutenant. Did you or did you not store your company's merchandise in the public warehouse in question?"

"It's not a public warehouse."

"Really? I take it then you would rather debate the definition of the warehouse than answer my very direct and simple question. Very well, please define the status of the warehouse for the court and then perhaps we can get back to my question." Abe turned and went to his chair and sat, waiting for the response.

Frank was visibly upset and looked up at the judge. "Your Honor, all he's trying to do is make me mad."

"And he is succeeding. Answer his question." Judge Simms was neither flippant nor piqued. He was, rather, thoroughly detached in demeanor.

Frank looked to Wes and got a stare in return. Frank was on his own here. He took a snarly snort of audible breath through his nose and looked straight at Abe.

"The warehouse is city property which we had on loan."

"Officially? In writing?" asked Abe.

"No, just verbally. We do it all the time. It's quite normal."

"Did you store your own private company's merchandise there?"

"Yes."

"How much merchandise? How many cases?"

Frank opened his file with a little flicker of satisfaction. He was prepared for this question. "Right now, there's a hundred and twelve," he answered quietly, not too pleased with his admission.

"Were there more before?"

"Maybe up to two hundred."

"What were in the largest cartons?"

"Refrigerators."

"Was there a fork lift at the warehouse?"

"Yes."

"Is it still there?"

"We borrowed it to move some stuff around in our own warehouse to make room to bring this stuff back."

"I see." Abe never played to the jury. He always gave them the courtesy of unembellished information. He just went to the lectern to resume reading his notes. The jury could think about the fork lift.

"And what was the other use to which you put the warehouse, Lieutenant?" Abe resumed after a couple of very quiet moments.

"You mean the main reason?"

"No, Lieutenant, I do not. Your Honor, please instruct this witness that it is his function to answer my questions, not to attempt to rephrase them to suit his own purposes."

Before the judge could respond, Frank said, "Your Honor, he's just trying to give the jury the wrong impression. I should be—"

"That's enough!" snapped the judge. "I'm sure the jury can make up their own minds, and I remind the witness to answer the questions as asked unless prosecution objects."

Everyone looked to Wes, who, I suppose, felt he had been invited to object, so he did.

"Yes, Your Honor, we object to—to—an argumentative question."

"Which was?" asked the judge.

Wes could not quickly recall the last question so he asked for it to be reread.

The clerk read: "Mr. Nordhoff: 'And what was the other use to which you put the warehouse, Lieutenant?'"

"Where is the argument in that?" asked the judge.

"Well, Your Honor, it's not literally argumentative—it's potentially misleading."

"You think he's trying to mislead Lieutenant Babcock with that question?"

"No, Your Honor, the jury."

"Well, I think this jury is astute enough not be mislead, Mr. Wentworth. Objection overruled. The witness will answer the question as posed."

Frank said, "We used it as an undercover fence operation to apprehend criminals."

"Which criminals, Lieutenant?"

"Those two."

"Let the record show that the witness has indicated the defendants," the judge said.

"Anybody else?"

"Not yet."

"Oh, are the cameras still there?"

"No, but we'd put them back if we needed to."

"I see. Has your private company used space before in public buildings, at no cost to you?"

Wes stood abruptly, knocking over his chair. His voice was an exclamation of its own. "I object to this line of questioning, Your Honor. This is just another fishing expedition. The lieutenant is not on trial here. This stuff is totally irrelevant."

Judge Simms considered that and then turned to Abe. "Counselor, I am inclined to agree. Unless you have specific, pertinent information that is germane to this trial, I'm going to have you move on to something else."

"I have that information, Your Honor. May I continue?" Abe moved again to the lectern ready to resume the questioning.

"Not so fast, Mr. Nordhoff," said the judge. "What is your information?"

"I'd prefer to extract that information in the normal manner, Your Honor."

Wes spoke up. "Your Honor, I think he owes us an answer. He says he has information. I think we should hear it here and now."

"I am not a witness, Your Honor, but I'd be happy to oblige

with a statement of fact, phrased as a question and this witness can answer yes or no. Would that be acceptable?"

"Mr. Prosecutor?"

"Perfectly," said Wes and resumed his seat, seemingly satisfied.

Abe made a show of leafing through many pages before extracting one from near the bottom.

"All right, here we are. Lieutenant, I am going to make a statement and then ask you if it is true or false. Your private company, the Roberts Electrical Repair Service started as a front for one of your first undercover fence operations. After the thieves in that case were apprehended, you and your then-partner, Ernie Collins ran that service as your own company for profit using city-held property at no cost for over one year. Then you bought it at less than half of market value without the usual public auction. Since then your company has repeatedly used city properties to store goods at no cost." Abe looked up at a consternated Frank Babcock. "Yes or no, Lieutenant?"

"Well yes—but I can explain—"

Abe cut him off. "Your Honor, may I resume my questioning?"

Wes was on his feet again. "Objection, Your Honor, defense is attempting to—to try the police here. This is not material to the matter at hand. This whole line of questioning is way off the mark."

"Counselor?" asked the judge.

"Your Honor, I would say that it is precisely on the mark."

"Which is?"

"That this witness and his former police partner and long-time business partner, Detective Collins, have not been totally honest in their dealings with the city. That leads me to believe that they may not have been totally honest in their case work, and that, Your Honor, is very germane to this trial."

All noise ceased in the courtroom except for the air conditioning hum. No one moved until the judge said, "Objection overruled. Please continue, counselor."

Abe had succeeded in introducing our case from fifteen years before without even mentioning it. We had considered it very likely that this line of questioning would be blocked. Once Abe had seen his chance, he went for it all in an instant and his information was so accurate that Frank had no choice in his response.

Not wishing to tip his hand, Abe went quickly to another matter.

"Lieutenant Babcock, is it normal Mobile Police Department procedure to collect information on more than one crime by the same perpetrators and then try them separately to get two convictions where one could have done?"

"Absolutely not. We didn't know until after the first."

"After the first what?"

"Conviction."

"I see. So if you do know of—say—multiple thefts by a thief, you put them together to make a stronger case and get an easier conviction and perhaps a longer sentence. Is that it?"

"Yes sir. That's how it works, usually."

"So my defendants were just unlucky that you uncovered the theft upon which this trial is based, after their other—their third—conviction?"

"Exactly."

"And you were lucky that they were still in your custody at the time?"

"I'd say unlucky for them."

"Just so. How many times has this happened?"

"What? Has what happened?"

"That you and Detective Collins set up an undercover fence operation with hidden video cameras to nail one group of suspected criminals, got a felony conviction and then, about four weeks later, while they are still in your custody, got new information on another crime and obtained another conviction and sent those men to prison for life with no possibility of parole? I want a number from you,

270 • Len Williams

Lieutenant. One word. I would guess that the prosecutor has told you about previous testimony so I would presume you are prepared for this question. What is your answer, Lieutenant Babcock?"

Frank wanted Wes to object but he could not.

"Seven," Frank finally said.

"And how many men were convicted in that manner?"

"What manner?" demanded Frank, now highly incensed and flushed with anger.

"Your Honor, I think the witness has forgotten my original question. Could the clerk read it back for him?"

Judge Simms asked Frank if that was what he wanted.

"Seventeen," said Frank. "Seventeen convicted criminals. That's what we do here, we convict criminals." His chin was out and his eyes flashed defiance.

"That has never been at issue, Lieutenant. The issue is how," Abe said, with emphasis on the "how," looking with hard eyes at Frank Babcock.

Frank started to respond but Abe cut him off coldly. "That was not a question, Lieutenant, and you are not to respond."

Before Frank could think of a reply, Abe asked. "Lieutenant, how would you feel if someone surreptitiously videotaped you— say at work—yes, at your work?"

Frank smiled. "No problem." Then he grinned for the audience and cocked his head, giving them wide eyes. The inference was there was no problem because it wouldn't happen.

"Good, so if someone did, hypothetically, videotape you or your men, you would come off okay? Is that it?"

"Sure. Yes, probably. You know, maybe—yes."

"So can I take your answer as 'yes'?"

"Yes."

"Your Honor, I'm going to start a new line of cross-examination now and perhaps this would be a good time for the morning break," Abe said, ignoring Frank, and speaking in a friendly manner to Judge Simms.

"Coffee time," said the judge thankfully. "Court is in recess for twenty minutes."

When Frank was back in the witness stand after the coffee break, Abe went to the lectern with only one piece of paper. Without looking up, he read his question much more slowly than anything he had previously said. It was in that slow motion that the audience and Frank received it.

"Lieutenant Babcock, describe fully your participation in the apprehension of my clients from the time you first heard of them until today. Please supply all the detail you can. I shall not interrupt you. Take as long as you wish."

Frank looked to Wes immediately and made a face of questioning. Getting no reaction from Wes, he pursed his lips in thought and looked up to the judge. Again, no help. Frank sat still, in thought, and said nothing.

Abe walked to the defense table, took his seat, and watched Frank.

Wes finally stood. "We object, Your Honor, the witness has already testified to that. This is a cross-examination. The Lieutenant is not his witness."

Judge Simms thought for a moment and then said, "Overruled. The witness can answer the question and should."

"But Your Honor," continued Wes. "We've been over this all before. And the question is too broad. It goes beyond this case and—" Wes stopped, waiting.

"Oh? How so?" The judge was interested now. "How does it go beyond this case?"

Wes answered at once. "His question goes back to when Lieutenant Babcock first heard of the defendants. This trial is limited to the offenses charged in this case only. Your Honor, please reconsider."

Abe just watched as if a passive spectator to it all, sitting back in his chair, with his arms folded.

Judge Simms finally turned to him and asked his reply to Wes's objection.

"Your Honor," Abe answered. "I want to know how the Mobile Police Department apprehends suspects, and in particular, these defendants. It's a simple question that bears very directly on this trial."

Wes spoke out again, without being asked. "Your Honor, it's just a maneuver to try to connect the two crimes."

"Two crimes?" asked the judge.

"Yes, Your Honor, the crimes of this trial and the latest previous conviction of these defendants. That is not permissible, Your Honor. That trial is separate. That is completely clear in law."

"Counselor?" asked the judge, turning to Abe.

"Your Honor, the Mobile Police Department must have continued the entrapment of my clients after they had enough evidence for the first conviction. Otherwise, we would not be here. The prosecution cannot slice this up surgically to suit their case. My clients were allowed or encouraged to continue after their first crime. I want to hear of the entire relationship between the Mobile Police Department and my clients, and with respect, Your Honor, we have every right to that information."

Wes looked to Frank who stared hard at him encouraging him to carry on. Wes tried to, but his first words were cut off by Judge Simms.

"That's enough, thank you, Mr. Wentworth. The point is clearly stated by the defense counsel. He does have the right to the entire scenario of the operation which—which—resulted in the arrest of the defendants. It goes to the heart of his defense, if I am not mistaken; their right to have been stopped by the police.

Objection overruled. The witness will answer the question fully."

"Judge, can I have a few minutes to make some notes and— and confer with the prosecutor?" Frank asked.

"You may take a few minutes to make notes, but you may not leave the stand. Do you have paper and a pen?"

"But Your Honor—"

Judge Simms cut him off sharply. "Look here, Lieutenant, I am being very lenient with you. Now stop complaining and make your notes. You have five minutes." The judge looked up. "This court is still in session and there will be no change in the demeanor of those in attendance while the witness prepares his answer."

Frank was ready when the judge asked if he was. "Detective Collins met the defendants in a bar. They told him they had stolen goods which they wished to sell. He came to me and we got the warehouse and set up the cameras. He told the defendants that he had a fence operation and they brought us stolen goods. We taped everything. We prepared our case against them. Later they brought us more stolen goods and we thought it was just more from their first haul. We taped it but never used it because we felt it was redundant. After we had those two tried and convicted, we received complaints about other thefts and we realized that we had those goods in our warehouse. We had no choice but to charge them again since we had the evidence and their confession on tape. The law says so. It's not our fault those guys are thieves. Our job is to catch them and that's what we did." Frank paused to see if Abe would stop him or object, but Abe wasn't even looking at him, so he continued. "We found them, we got good evidence and we convicted them. We can't help it if they didn't stop. The law's the law. They were already convicted. We had to charge them again."

Frank stopped when he had nothing more to say. He seemed pleased and sat straight and confident.

"Oh my," Abe said with surprise. "That won't do at all Lieutenant, we were looking for a continuum of contact and impressions between you and my clients, not a facile justification of your action. Oh, no, not at all. Would you like another go at it, or shall I take you through it step by step?"

Wes objected that the witness had answered the question. Judge Simms sustained the objection but said he agreed with defense counsel that he could ask follow-up questions.

The judge looked at his watch. It was eleven thirty. "How long might this take, counselor?"

"Probably a day or two, Your Honor. Perhaps more. It depends on the witness."

Wes was on his feet again. "Objection, Your Honor! How can he know it will take two days? Two days! This is absurd. He's not on trial here."

"If I may respond, Your Honor?" asked Abe.

The judge was growing weary of the debate. "Please do."

"Our research indicates that this witness has left out many details from his response to my question. I intend to ask scores of detailed questions to help me ferret out the information which I seek. Either the witness will honestly and completely respond or he will not. We shall see. It is our right to do so, and if the prosecution continues its tactics to prevent this witness from fully and truthfully testifying, I trust Your Honor will stop them. This witness has not told the whole story. It's as simple as that."

Abe had injected a stridency into his style that was new to this trial. He was not angry, but he was absolutely resolute. No one had any doubts that he was going to grill Lieutenant Frank Babcock for days and days.

The judge overruled Wes, recessed early for lunch, and called all attorneys into his chambers for a conference.

At the conference he told Wes to knock off his objections unless he had a clear point of law and he told Abe to speed it up. Then, without asking for replies, he told them to enjoy their lunch and got up and walked out.

Wes then asked Abe if he was enjoying the little show he was putting on, wasting everyone's time. Abe answered that he was very much enjoying it and asked Wes if he was. Wes strode out and slammed the door. Abe said later he was pleased to have both the witness and the prosecutor so pissed off at him.

For the next day and a half, Abe quizzed Frank Babcock meticulously and chronologically about his dealings with Detective Collins, other police officers involved, and the defendants.

What had been presented by Frank in his first short answer as a distinct division between the two crimes, ran together more seamlessly under Abe's close cross-examination.

Frank had good recall and was adept at coloring information or leaving it out. He was clever enough to seemingly frustrate Abe in his apparent aim to obtain an admission or at least a probability of a choice made by the police to separate the two crimes in order to obtain separate convictions.

Abe was winding down with Frank on Wednesday at three-forty-five. He said he had but two final questions.

"Lieutenant Babcock, can you say unequivocally that the Mobile Police Department, represented in this case by yourself and Detective Collins, did not arbitrarily decide to prosecute two separate cases concerning my clients, when you could have arrested them earlier and had but one?"

Frank knew he'd won. "Absolutely!"

"Thank you, Lieutenant, you've been very patient with me."

"My pleasure." Frank said with some relish, feeling that his time on the stand was over.

"Oh, one more thing, Lieutenant."

"Yes." Frank answered, as he was picking up his file.

"Have you had any communication with Detective Collins during this trial? As you will recall you were instructed not to?"

Frank lost his smile. "No, I have not." He seemed insulted.

"Are you certain, Lieutenant? I believe that you have, and an admission would be less damning than—"

Wes was bellowing his objections. Abe stopped in mid-sentence and waited for Judge Simms, who was quickly on him as well.

"You'd better have some very good information, counselor. You have just accused this witness of lying."

"Yes, I have, Your Honor. Shall I present it here?"

"Counsel to my chambers please. Court is still in session." The judge stood and left.

In his chambers, Judge Simms was quick to ask for Abe's explanation and said it had better be damn good or he would think seriously of a reprimand and punishment in front of the jury.

"Of course, Your Honor, I'd expect nothing less. Let me be brief here. The defense has an investigator who overheard Lieutenant Babcock talking on his cell phone to Detective Collins. In order to be certain that he had, we had a subpoena issued to the cellular phone company. Their records show four calls between the parties; three from Collins to Babcock and one the other way. Here are the records." He put two pages of phone calls on the judge's desk.

"Hey!" said Wes. "How the hell did you get a subpoena without me knowing? Judge, what's going on here?"

"We asked for it this morning. It was granted at twelve thirty. We obtained these lists at two o'clock and I got them during the afternoon break. Your copy was delivered to your office at two-fifteen."

"Fuck!" said Wes. "Judge, this is bullshit. He can't just come in here and pull this kind of—well, he can't do it."

"May I see the subpoena?" asked Judge Simms.

Abe pulled it out of his file and handed it over.

Wes reached for it too, but the judge told him to relax for a minute. Then the judge read it and handed it to Wes, adding "It's signed by Judge Toms."

"Shit!" was Wes's first comment, after he had read it. "Who is this Western Security Service listed as the witness here?" Wes asked after rereading it.

"A large, professional security company. Would you like to see the copy of their invoices?" Abe inquired.

"No, never mind." Wes was very upset, but he'd been had. His witnesses had talked to each other.

"Well," said Judge Simms. "What would you like to do about this, Mr. Nordhoff?"

"I want Detective Babcock charged with perjury, Your Honor."

"Isn't that a little rough? I can admonish him in front of the jury and hold him in contempt of court. That might be enough, don't you think?"

"I'll take your advice on this matter, Your Honor. But I am very disturbed by this blatant affront to the court."

"Good. Thank you, counselor. No point in overdoing it. I appreciate your help on this and I'm sure Lieutenant Babcock will too when he learns of it. Thank you, gentlemen. I shall handle Lieutenant Babcock." Judge Simms then scowled, raised his eyebrows and let out a sigh. "Will you move for a mistrial? Was that the plan, after all, Mr. Nordhoff?"

"No sir," Abe answered. "That is the last thing we want."

"Good, thank you, counselor."

Back in court, the judge addressed the jury. "Ladies and gentlemen. It has come to the court's attention that this witness, Lieutenant Babcock, has had communications with Detective Collins at least four times by cellular telephone in direct and flagrant contradiction to this court's specific order." The judge then turned to Frank. "Lieutenant, we have a witness who overheard you speaking with Collins on your cell phone and telephone company records showing four calls. I ask you now if you spoke to Collins during the past four or five days. Yes or no."

Frank shot a glance at Wes who nodded sadly. Then he glared at Abe, who was looking at the jury.

"Yes," Frank said to the judge.

"That's better. This witness is admonished for answering falsely under oath and is held in contempt of court. Punishment is thirty days in the county jail or three hundred hours of supervised community service. And you're lucky at that." He was speaking coldly to Frank. "Defense counsel would be within his rights to have you charged with perjury."

Frank was shaken, but he could do nothing but squirm.

"Anything further, Mr. Nordhoff?" asked the judge.

"One question and I'm finished with this witness, Your Honor."

"Go ahead, please."

"Lieutenant Babcock, what did you and Detective Collins talk about on the phone?"

Frank thought for a few seconds and replied. "I don't recall exactly, just things in general."

Abe made a little "I give up" gesture by raising his hands and smiling sardonically at Frank. Then he said to the judge, "That's all, Your Honor. I'm through with this witness. Shall I recall Detective Collins or would Your Honor prefer to handle that separately?"

The judge was quick. He excused Frank and told Wes to produce Ernie Collins at once.

Ten minutes later Wes walked back in with a white-faced Detective Collins.

Ernie took the stand, quickly admitted his faux pas and was held in contempt of court and given thirty days or three hundred hours of community service. Then he was coldly dismissed by Judge Simms.

The following day, Thursday, Wes tried to rehabilitate Ernie and Frank by taking them through their stories again and trying to make light of the phone calls as the natural action of old friends.

Each testified that they couldn't get any more information from each other than they got routinely from the prosecutor and they had suffered a lapse of judgment for which they had been appropriately punished.

The prosecution rested at noon.

CHAPTER

The problem had always been how to introduce our tapes into evidence and show them to the jury. That we had gotten this far was a testament to the prosecution's certainty of the police evidence and the outcome of the trial. This was not their first time at slam-dunk life sentences. Their statistics were perfect and their strategy was simple. Even after all the damage Abe had done to Frank and Ernie, the case was still theirs because we couldn't actually prove they had conspired to have two separate trials. That is, not without our own videotapes being admitted into evidence.

We had debated several scenarios and in the end let Abe make the call. We all knew the risks, but the other schemes to get the tapes admitted depended on a certain amount of trickery, and Judge Simms had shown he could be quite impartial and could go either way on closely contested issues.

When Abe began his defense presentation, he spent Thursday afternoon and all day Friday questioning Joseph and then Joshua.

He led one and then the other through the details of their contacts with Detective Collins in the bar, the commission of their crimes, the loot, and going to the warehouse to fence the goods. Both Joshua and Joseph were clear and straightforward. They had done a lot of drugs and been criminals for several years.

Abe sounded like a prosecutor as he made his clients continually admit to their previous life, or perhaps like a headmaster exacting the truth before he meted out punishment. But his clients were well rehearsed and gave it all up to him. It was not pretty, but it rang true.

I felt that the jury must believe them, and I hoped they felt some sympathy for their predicament.

Wes could hardly wait for his turn, and soon had the two felons admitting their crimes again. Abe sat quietly, never objecting. The defendants answered all Wes's questions fully and clearly. They were repentant thieves. That had been their instruction from Abe—to look repentant and tell the whole truth. He had not told them about the tapes, but he did say that he had more to show the jury later, and the jury had to believe that they were now truthful and repentant for them to have any chance at all of having the two felonies combined or getting an outright acquittal on the current charge.

We prepared all that next weekend at a motel in Pensacola near the military base so that Mike could be home at night.

CHAPTER

We had added Mike's name to the defense witness list on Thursday, presenting him as Michael Nevens, Marine Warrant Officer and a part-time employee of the Western Security Company. We hoped he'd be presumed to be a witness to the cell phone conversations between Frank and Ernie. If that was the case he would probably not be closely deposed by the prosecution. Why should he be? The prosecution could simply stipulate that their witnesses had talked, as was already on the record and be rid of him in a few minutes. They knew from the subpoena that Mike, as a security agent, had followed Frank in the street and overheard him say loudly into his cell phone, "Yo, Collins, where are you? We need to talk."

In fact, they had deposed him late on Friday, but it was only a perfunctory deposition conducted by one of Wes's juniors and he had merely inquired how he happened to witness the phone call in question and had not asked about anything else.

"Why should he have?" I asked Abe later, as we prepared Mike.

"If he worked for me, I'd have him drawn and quartered. You always ask if there is anything else. Always. Even if it's not specific. Don't you?"

"I do now," I answered. "I'm glad I don't work for you."

"You might yet. So pay attention."

I left it at that and paid attention.

Mike took the stand first thing Monday morning. We were in the third week of trial and the audience was still full and attentive. The press had swelled by two or three for the long anticipated defense.

The clerk swore Mike in and Abe started.

"You are in the United States Marines, is that so, Mr. Nevens?" Mike answered, "Yes sir."

Wes said half aloud. "What?"

"Would you repeat your answer for the prosecutor?" Abe said.

"Yes, I am a member of the United States Marines Corps," Mike said loudly and with pride.

"I object, Your Honor. What have the Marines got to do here? We were told he worked for this security company"—he checked his notes—"here, Western Security."

Judge Simms looked to Abe, who responded at once.

"Your Honor, we gave notice of this witness's appearance on Thursday afternoon. He was deposed by the prosecution on Friday. We gave his name as Warrant Officer Michael Nevens, USMC, and he was listed as a part-time employee of Western Security. What's the problem here? I'm simply qualifying my witness. Perhaps the prosecutor has forgotten. He could check the notice we sent him."

Wes's assistant handed him a paper and Wes read it, looking angrier as he went. There followed a brief unpleasant whispered encounter with the assistant and then Wes said he'd missed it and withdrew his objection.

Abe looked into space and raised his eyebrows in mild consternation at the behavior of the prosecutor.

"All right, Mr. Nevens, you are a Warrant Officer in the Marine Corps. What are your duties there?"

"I am the course director at the advanced gunnery school at Pensacola, Florida."

"Is that highly technical work?"

"About half technical and half Marine Corps motivation," Mike answered.

The audience and the jury laughed politely.

"And you work part-time as a security officer?"

Wes could not help himself. He was pissed off at everybody and objected that Abe was leading the witness.

Judge Simms looked sharply over at Wes and said, "Into what? Admitting he's a part-time security officer? Overruled and the prosecution is cautioned not to be disruptive. Is that clear?"

"Yes, Your Honor." Wes sat down.

"What is your relationship with defense counsel, Mr. Nevens?"

"I engaged you on behalf of the defendants and you have engaged Western Security on one assignment."

Wes was either not listening or had not processed Mike's statement. The judge had. His head shot up as if he might have misheard. He looked from Abe to Mike, but neither looked at him. Some of the jury had picked it up and my fellow journalists had obviously all heard it.

Abe continued while Wes's assistant urgently whispered to him.

"And why did you engage the A.C.L.U. in this case, Mr. Nevens?"

Wes was now standing and shouting. "Objection, Your Honor! He's listed as a witness in the cell phone thing, not as a—a—client."

"Mr. Nordhoff, what's going on here?" the judge asked warily.

"To the best of my knowledge, Your Honor, I'd say that the prosecution is being deliberately disruptive. We gave him proper notice, and he or someone on his staff has deposed the witness. If he cares to read the notice, he will see that Mr. Nevens is a Marine Warrant Officer and a part-time employee of Western Security. We are not obliged to tell the prosecution who our clients are. I was simply asking Mr. Nevens to be forthcoming to ensure that the court is aware that this witness is also our client so that his testimony can be interpreted from that standpoint. I am obliged to name my witnesses. The prosecutor may depose them and he may cross-examine them when I have finished. Nowhere on our notice to him or the court is there any mention whatever of what this witness may or may not be questioned about. Certainly we did not say he would testify concerning the telephone debacle. I think we've had all we need on that subject. Now, Your Honor, I respectfully suggest that the prosecutor be given a few minutes to review our notice and then withdraw his objection. I have been interrupted three times in succession and it isn't ten o'clock yet. If he does not withdraw his motion, I will move for censure. My patience is at an end."

Abe's delivery had been rapid fire and louder than usual. Even the judge would not interrupt until it had run its course.

Judge Simms considered Abe's statement for a moment and looked to Wes. "Show me the notice."

"But Your Honor, that's not the point here."

"Oh, isn't it?" The judge played a surprised look across his face. "What is the point then? Help me out here, please."

"He—he sandbagged us, Your Honor. He's going to question his own client."

"Then we agree. Objection is overruled."

No one stirred. Wes didn't get it. "We agree? Then why is it overruled?" he asked.

The judge spoke slowly and clearly. "You have indeed been sandbagged, but you had ample chance to depose this witness, and you apparently did not do a very thorough job of it. That's not my fault or the fault of the defense. That's how it works. We also agree that Mr. Nordhoff is going to question his client. That is his right and I, for one, am very interested to hear it. Now please resume your seat. You may cross-examine the witness when defense counsel has finished. I will tolerate no more interruptions because you are poorly prepared. Mr. Nordhoff, please proceed with this witness."

"Thank you, Your Honor. Mr. Nevens, why did you come to the A.C.L.U. in Atlanta for help?"

"We felt that there was criminal activity afoot in the Mobile Police Department in that they have consistently conspired to, and in fact have, systematically denied the civil rights of many individuals, including some who were once known to me personally. We went to Atlanta because it's in another state and is the southeastern headquarters of the A.C.L.U."

Mike had spoken in his clearest Marine Corps instructor's voice. It was a canned statement, delivered coldly as fact. The courtroom was alive with all senses concentrated on the unfolding drama. There were only two players now, and it was riveting.

Abe asked. "What is the nature of this alleged criminal conspiracy, Mr. Nevens?"

"The Mobile Police Department set these defendants up to be convicted of multiple felonies quickly, so that the police can have a good record of convicting three-time felons to life in prison with no parole. They did this with forethought and planning as they have for at least fifteen years, by allowing the felons to continue to commit crimes, when they should have been arrested."

The court was stone still. Wes was shaking his head involuntarily. Abe milked the silence before continuing.

"And how is it that you know this to be true, sir?"

"I videotaped their videotaping of these defendants."

There it was. Said from the witness box in open court by a U.S. Marine.

A rustle of gasps and comments forced the judge to bang his gavel for silence.

Wes seemed unable to decide whether to object or not. Then he did. How could he not?

"If it please the court, I'd like a sidebar on this. We had no prior notice of such a tape, if it exists."

"Mr. Nordhoff?" asked the judge, obviously perturbed by this dramatic turn of events.

"Yes, Your Honor, how can I help?" Abe was the soul of civility.

"Was the prosecution given notice of the videotapes?"

"Absolutely. Ten days before trial. Perhaps the prosecutor has forgotten. Perhaps he can check his notices again, but Your Honor, this pattern of interruption is becoming worrisome in that it could be construed as—well—I'll be liberal—deliberate interference to disrupt the defense."

The judge knew he needed to be sharp here. "Check your notices, Mr. Prosecutor, and then bring them up to me so that the court may also review them."

"What about the sidebar, Your Honor?" Wes asked.

"We'll review the notices now, please."

Wes heard the warning and huddled with his assistant as they thumbed through two files until they found the notice.

"Here it is, Your Honor. It says—"

"Bring it here. Do not say another word until I have read it."

Wes brought it up and started to talk again, but the judge told him to sit and wait.

A moment later, the judge excused the jury so they would not be influenced by the upcoming squabble between lawyers.

With the jury gone, the judge asked Wes what the problem was. The notice said that the defense would review videotapes taken at the warehouse. Wes said he thought they were the police tapes and the defense was just going to try to pick them apart.

"Did you ask to see them?"

"No. We thought they were our tapes."

"Mr. Nordhoff, what have you to say?"

"Your Honor, the police were taped in the same way that they have taped our clients. We gave notice that we would show tapes just like the prosecution gave notice that they would show tapes. Our tapes were made in a public building after my clients had very good reason to suspect the police of criminal behavior. We had every right to make those tapes, as was amply testified to by the police officers in this case and the prosecution's own attorney who specializes in surveillance law. What's sauce for the goose is sauce for the gander. They have edited their tape. We have not. We have copies of their unedited tapes as well and they will also be offered into evidence."

Wes was quick to respond. "But the building was—was locked. How did he get in?"

"The same way the police did. With a key. It's a public building that the police were in illegally to start with. We have checked the statutes and it's quite clear that publicly held buildings can only be occupied by those who apply in writing, make a public declaration, and pay appropriate market rent. The police were there illegally, not to mention the storing of private merchandise there by the police. We are on better legal ground than the police here, at least we did not profit financially. Your Honor, I have many precedents for your perusal. This is not at all unusual. If the prosecution is not attentive or prepared, it is not our problem. These defendants are facing life in prison with no parole, for a total of four unarmed thefts. My clients and I are here to see justice done and we have the same right to show our tapes as they did."

Wes started to speak but the judge put up his hand. "Stop!" he said. "Mr. Nordhoff, what are your precedents?"

Abe went to his table and read summaries of six cases regarding various instances where the police were shown by either personal, audio, or audio-visual means to be committing criminal acts when they were not aware they were being watched. Two were inside police stations.

The judge called a recess until one o'clock so he could study the matter. He took a copy of Abe's precedents with him.

At one o'clock he overruled the prosecution, saying that he could not stop the defense from showing its tapes. It was a terse comment, I suppose because he already suspected the outcome, which would not be good for his city.

In later conversations with journalists, Judge Simms said he was most swayed by the last of Abe Nordhoff's list of precedents. A vagrant had been sleeping off a drunk in a public building after breaking a window to get in. He overheard and then saw two policemen taking a payoff from two prostitutes and then receiving oral sex from them. Judge Simms said he knew then that any court would admit our videotapes. We reporters pressed him on the matter, but he would not admit that he had allowed the tapes because he was sure that any other decision would be overturned by higher courts, but we understood that influence clearly enough. Even after the trial he was not happy with the way we got our tapes and what was on them.

For his part, Abe Nordhoff told Mike and me that he'd given us odds at one-in-three without Mike and two-in-three with him. He did emphasize, however, that if he'd been the prosecutor, the tapes never would have been admitted. We believed him.

"He's a lazy, passed-over, municipal employee. He had no reason to prepare well and was never interested enough to try to figure out what was really going on. If I was a prosecutor, and an A.C.L.U. director appeared to try a case and used the words civil liberties, I'd have gotten the judge to put the trial off a couple of weeks and called in some more talent. I suppose the irony is there for us, however. He and those two cops had done this before, without a blip."

Abe told me that he had deviated from our planned sequence for showing the tapes because he still feared some interruption or delay when Wes's superiors or the police hierarchy heard what was happening. Originally, we had agreed to first present the edited police tapes already seen by the jury, followed by the undoctored police tapes, and then our tapes.

He asked Mike to present our tape as evidence right after the court had ruled in our favor. Mike looked surprised and Abe said, "We will question this witness on the details of this surveillance once this tape has been put into evidence and shown to the jury."

Mike looked confused for only a second and then did as he was asked. No one said a word as Mike pulled many tapes out of his case and handed two to Abe.

Abe asked all the correct questions concerning the validity of the tapes and then put the first tape in the machine, which had been left in place after the prosecution's presentation.

Abe then asked Mike to explain the tapes as they proceeded if it would help the court understand what it was looking at.

Wes objected woodenly that the tapes should be viewed without comment and that Mike was obviously biased.

Judge Simms knew he had a point, but asked Abe if he had a good reason why he should not sustain the objection.

Abe looked surprised. "Detective Collins and the prosecutor commented liberally while they showed an edited tape, which, by the way, was not mentioned. We are obviously entitled to the same courtesy."

"Your Honor," Wes continued. "They probably let us comment so they could." It was out before Wes knew how lame it was.

Judge Simms looked at Wes with condescension. "That, I would have thought, was obvious. Overruled."

The first tape started with voices in the dark, and then lights came on to show Ernie Collins and another man climbing a stepladder and checking their hidden cameras. There were a few comments about when the stupid assholes would be coming. Then the two men sat at the table and Ernie got them two beers from a bag at his feet and they toasted the assholes. Then they talked about sports until Frank Babcock turned up. He took a beer as well and asked if they were all set.

There ensued twenty minutes of small talk, but no one in the courtroom reacted with anything less than their full attention. They were watching their police at work.

Just before Joshua and Joseph came in, Frank said very clearly, "Okay lads, here we go. Now keep this separate from the first stuff. This has to stand on its own. We got enough on the first one. That's in the bag. We do this right and these two dickheads are gone, and I mean gone."

There followed the actual fencing of goods as seen on the police tapes, and the felons departed.

When they had gone, Frank said "Nice work boys. Ernie, you'll take off that first part before they get here, okay?"

"Sure thing, boss. These little babies will be just about perfect. When should we bust them?"

Frank said, "You ready on the first one? The prosecutor all set to go?"

"Hundred percent."

"How long you guys need on the stuff from tonight?"

"One day, it's already been reported stolen. We can check the owners out tomorrow."

"Perfect. These assholes just keep getting dumber and dumber. Do them whenever you like, just give me time to go with you. I love to see their faces when they see us with the badges."

Then, almost incredibly, as if it had been rehearsed, Ernie Collins sang loudly, "One, two, three strikes you're out at the old ball game."

They all laughed and gave each other high fives.

After a celebratory beer, they set to work tagging evidence and taking fingerprints off some cartons. Then they walked off camera and came back pushing two dollies filled with other cartons.

"Okay," Ernie said. "This bunch is number one and tonight's is number two. We'll take the first stuff over tomorrow and I'll come back in a week or so for the rest."

They turned out the lights and left.

Abe had Mike put in the second tape which, he explained by the date and time seen on the screen, was one day after the defendant's first conviction.

Ernie and the other cops were seen carrying the cartons out and were heard commenting on the dumb crooks now about to be charged for number two. They were jubilant.

The court broke for coffee at three o'clock. At three-fifteen, Abe came back with Mike. I had seen them leave together and return together, so I figured they were now in sync.

Mike took the stand again. Everyone was ready for more tapes and testimony from Mike.

Abe said to the judge. "Your Honor, I think we have all seen enough tapes." He turned to the prosecution table. "Your witness," he said softly and went to sit at the defense table. The defendants were full of life now. They had been truly surprised by the tapes and the jury had certainly noted their reactions.

Abe had made a swift tactical decision to make the prosecution act when unprepared.

Wes rubbed his chin and then stood slowly to ask for time before he cross-examined Mike. Judge Simms glanced at Abe, who did not react except for a hard stare. The judge was forced to ask Abe if he would agree to Wes's request.

Abe shot to his feet. "Your Honor, at the very least, the prosecutor here is an unwilling part of this awful charade. This awful misuse of power by the police. I would not agree to one minute's delay. He has objected continuously to interrupt the defense. Let him cross-examine our witness. We are ready even if he says he is not."

Abe did not sit down. The judge had been clearly challenged, but it was couched in contempt for the law establishment—embodied by the prosecutor and the police. Judge Simms must choose to join them if he allowed Wes time to prepare his cross-examination.

He sighed deeply and told Wes that the witness was his and he had as long as he wished, up to one hour beyond normal time if that would help him.

Wes again complained that he needed time to prepare.

Judge Simms grew visibly angry. "I have ruled. Proceed with your cross, counselor!"

Wes saw a way out and sat down. "We have no questions for this witness at this time."

Abe's head shot up and then he looked from the prosecutor to Mike to the judge and then to the jury. Everyone expected a rocket to be launched at the prosecutor.

Instead, Abe sat quite still for a moment, then he rose slowly to clearly state, "Your Honor, the defense rests."

Abe had previously submitted several names of witnesses. They included the defendants' families and friends and they had been deposed all in one morning by Wes and his assistant. He had seen them in the witness room and had expected days of defense aimed at convincing the jury to take it easy on the defendants. He also expected to see more tapes and other defense witnesses.

"Thank you," said a very formal Judge Simms, who was likely grateful to finally see an end to this trial. "Does the prosecution wish to cross-examine this witness at this time?"

Either Wes misunderstood the question or he took the opportunity to cut his discomfort. He stayed seated and said, "Not at this time, Your Honor."

"The defense has rested, counselor. There will be no other opportunity to question this witness."

Wes looked at Abe who sat with his arms folded, a look of anticipation on his face, and then he looked up at the judge and said, "No questions, Your Honor."

The judge went into his boilerplate instructions to the jury and opposing counsel regarding summation. I heard his voice, but not the words. Wes, that fool, had missed the only opportunity he would get.

Mike got out of his seat and out of the courtroom as quickly as he could without running.

I heard the gavel bang down and the clerk shout "All Rise." I rose and finally tuned into the turmoil in the courtroom. Abe was talking to the defendants, who were standing with the bailiffs ready to take them back to the county jail. Abe was animated and they were fully attentive. Finally, they nodded and were led away.

Abe sat at his table until only a few journalists were left in the courtroom, clambering for his comments.

He rose and gave the time-out signal to quiet us.

"Write what you saw and heard. This is important stuff. See you tomorrow. You know the deal. When it's over, I'll talk. Right now I have a summation to prepare."

We had to call him that evening. We had prepared Mike for a tough cross-examination and he had been steeled for long days of testimony, bitter wrangling over questions, and most of all, he was prepared to take the Fifth Amendment if cornered.

Abe was just as surprised as we were when Wes had given up. He said he'd gone to our tapes first for fear that Wes would move for a mistrial which, he said, had a chance of succeeding. Then he said he just felt the prosecution was on its heels, and it was a good time to unsettle them further by forcing a cross-examination on them when they were still pissed off about Mike and the tapes. When Abe saw that the prosecution was desperate for time and the judge had been forced to refuse them, he went for the jugular on the spur of the moment and rested his case. He had fully expected Wes to finish out the day with meaningless questions, so that he could take the night to prepare his next move. The fact that Wes backed off totally at the end, Abe said, could only come from his lack of meaningful questions. He had obviously been so stunned by the rapid-fire crushing of his case that he just gave up. He'd lost and quit.

"He'd make a piss-poor soldier," Mike said.

"Well he's a piss-poor lawyer," answered Abe.

"And thanks be to heaven for that," I said. "You ready for tomorrow, counselor?" I asked Abe. "Your summation taking shape?"

"That's the first thing I do on a case, Harry. I spend the trial getting to it. Tonight I'm going to a movie and then get a good night's sleep. I just read over my summation and it's set. See you in the morning."

CHAPTER

13

The prosecution goes first when they address the jury at the beginning of a trial, and again when they sum up at the end. In fact they go twice at the end so that they have the last word after the defense finishes its summation.

Wes had not had a pleasant evening. We learned subsequently that his boss, the district attorney, had been livid that he had not been kept fully abreast of this case and demanded an explanation as to how such an obviously illegal videotape could have been allowed into evidence and then its owner not cross-examined. When he had exhausted his anger, the D.A. had put together a team of lawyers to help Wes prepare his summation.

Reactions within the police department were no less severe. No one rushed to help Ernie and Frank, however. This had been Frank's ticket up the line and it was gone. With their screw-up coming to light so obviously, they were on their own. There was some commiseration but no offers of help.

Wes's summation was actually quite cogent and had it been delivered by its writer, and in a more lawyerly manner, it might have had better impact.

He said essentially that the defendants had admitted guilt and therefore should be condemned regardless of the defense strategy, which he said was mounted solely to deflect the jury from its rightful path to conviction. The police had been shown to perhaps be too zealous in their work, but it was justifiable work against known criminals. Would the jury find for their police force who protected them or for these thrice convicted felons who preyed on them? That was the question he asked to begin and end his summation. He started at nine-fifteen and finished at ten-fifteen.

Abe stood in front of the jury at ten-forty that morning to sum up everything I had worked for since I had met Leonard those many years ago in the state penitentiary. I wished that he could have been there to witness it. And I thought about Maynard and Eddie and Frank and Ernie's other fourteen victims.

"Fellows citizens," Abe said, looking into the eyes of the jurors. "Your work will soon be over and you will have been very fortunate to have participated in this important trial. My work has only started. I must try to free all those who were convicted of a fourth offense by dishonest, criminal police subterfuge. There are seven cases to unravel and perhaps more. I will guarantee you this. I will work at it until it is done or I am unable to continue. I give you my solemn word on that. I am committed to the overturn of every one of those convictions. Nothing less. When those seventeen men are all free, I will take up other work. If I have to quit the A.C.L.U. to accomplish this, I will ask my wife to support me."

He paused and looked around the courtroom, his eyes met mine for an instant, then Mike's, then they returned to the jury.

"I am in the company of exceptional clients. They deserve no less an effort from me. Now"—here Abe gestured with his arms out to the jury—"it is your time to express your reactions to what you have seen in this courtroom. I will not insult your intelligence by recalling my version of what has been uncovered here. My clients are guilty of, and have been convicted for, their third felony. An attempt was made to put them in state prison for *all of the rest of their lives* with no possibility of parole, by police officers who acted illegally by denying them their civil rights to have been arrested after the first crime was discovered. They were set up for the second, to fatten the conviction statistics of the Mobile Police Department and the politicians on whom they depend for funding. You have the opportunity to tell them who is ultimately in charge in our society. Please, my fellow citizens, find my clients not guilty of this trumped up charge so that they may serve their sentences and get on with the rest of their lives. I hope they have learned their lesson. They say they have. Only time will tell, but that is not the issue, is it? The decision is yours, ladies and gentlemen. You represent all of the citizens of Mobile here. I thank you for your time and for your efforts."

Abe slowly returned to his seat and sat facing the judge. His summation had taken less than five minutes, and for that it was not easily forgotten. He had made the case huge by promising to personally follow through on all the other convictions. He had given the jury seventeen additional fates to consider.

The prosecutor then rose to demand a guilty verdict for known felons who had admitted their guilt. Nothing could be clearer. He was emphatic.

Judge Simms charged the jury and asked the foreman if the jury would start deliberations at once or in the morning. They said at once.

After all my years of travail, and all the years of the seventeen four-time losers in prison, a group of ordinary citizens had heard our case and would soon make a judgment.

I knew how fickle juries could be and so did Abe. You win or lose when you least expect it. It's sometimes like a boxing match where you are sure your guy has won handily, and all the judges see it the other way.

Frank and Ernie had not come to the courthouse that morning. I would have loved to watch their reactions to it all.

All I could do was walk around by myself, waiting for my cell phone to ring. All the journalists had made a deal with one of the bailiffs to call us. Actually, we had promised him a bottle of Scotch.

The call came at three-thirty that same afternoon. The jury had a verdict.

As I sat with the other reporters, the jury filed in looking very solemn.

Judge Simms called the half-full courtroom to order and asked if the jury had reached a verdict.

"Yes, we have, Your Honor," said the foreman, a tall black man whom we knew to be a retired schoolteacher.

"And is it unanimous?"

"Yes, it is, Your Honor. And we have a request, sir, that I be allowed to read a comment after the verdict has been read. Will that be all right?"

"No, Mr. Foreman. I'm sorry it is not allowed, but you will be free to give it to the press if you wish after this court is adjourned."

"Yes, I see. Thank you, Your Honor." The foreman had short gray hair and stood very erect. He was dressed in a tie and jacket and he was dead serious.

"Please give the verdict to the clerk so that I may read it. Then he will return it to you so that you may read it aloud."

Judge Simms read the verdict and the clerk took it back to the foreman who had remained standing. The foreman, Mr. Blanchard, read the verdict.

"In the matter of the City of Mobile, Alabama versus Mr. Joseph Gore and Mr. Joshua Fuentes, we find the defendants not guilty."

There are no words for me to convey the flight of my long grief. I cried quietly, not wishing to draw attention. But I was not alone. Others cried as well.

Abe got pummeled by Joseph and Joshua, who were thrilled to be going to prison for several years.

Mike and I still had to leave separately. We, like Abe, were not finished.

Part 5

end game

CHAPTER

We met Abe fifty miles east of Mobile, near Pensacola, in a diner off the highway. As good as it felt to win one, it was only one and we all knew that.

I'd had plenty of time to think about our future during the trial, and I had a plan.

Abe shook off our congratulations. He said that anyone could have beaten Wes. That was not true, but it did bring us back to earth. Abe has a way of keeping himself totally in the game and objective. We understood him better by then and dropped the subject.

"I've been doing a lot of thinking Abe," I said. "Are you ready to talk about the next step?"

"Absolutely. The sooner the better, before those old boys catch their breath."

"Mike?" I asked. "How are you doing?"

"Fine, I guess. My wife's not too happy though."

"Tell her you were legally constrained not to tell her. I'll give you the words. She can call my wife. I never tell her anything. They can commiserate," Abe said.

"Abe, first of all, we've got to protect Mike. If they have any brains, they'll go after him right away. Mike stays on base where they have to go through channels to get at him. If and when they get through, Mike refers them to you, Abe, and you play serious hardball. He's a client and you will protect him from harassment. You will not make him available for anything unless they have a specific charge. If they try any chicken shit like charging him with breaking and entering, or anything like that, you cite that our evidence was admitted by their own prosecutor into a trial, therefore the point is moot. Then you tell them that Mike will be a prosecution witness in an upcoming trial where the police will be charged, and they cannot talk to him until it's their turn to take his deposition. If they persist, you ask them how they'd like a good dose of a U.S. Marine on TV talking about the local police tactics, including harassment after he fingered them." I looked to Abe. "That fly?"

He thought it over and then said, "Yes. I might add that I could call the D.A. and tell him to call off the dogs or I'll go after his office first."

"Would you do that? Go after the D.A.?"

"Absolutely. I am going after them. They're in on all this. Nobody skates on this one."

"But you'll do the cops first?"

"Yes. They could implicate the D.A.'s office. We'll have to see how that plays out. Go on."

"Well, I filed my story before I came out here and, while I told the facts, I did not hammer the cops. I went after Wes. It reads like the cops did it, but that any prosecutor worth a shit would have protected them better."

Abe interrupted, "That's actually true."

"I know, that's how I can get away with it, and it follows my pattern of pro cop, pro law and order. Our paper is conservative.

It'll fly fine. But that's not my point. The point is, I'll still be talking to them. Believe me, they'll appreciate my slant."

"Who's 'they'?" Mike asked.

"All of them. Frank and Ernie will be fine with it, I'd guess. At least it will be the kindest of all the articles and it will point to Wes as the fool. The other guys in the D.A.'s office will not be directly implicated so they'll probably cut Wes loose. The other cops, higher up, will see I was only doing my job and perhaps took it easy on them by comparison."

"Say that's all true. What can you do with it?" Abe asked.

"I can stay in. I can interview them. I can listen to them off the record. I can record them and perhaps even videotape them."

Abe rubbed his chin. "That could be dangerous."

"Prison is dangerous too, Abe," I replied.

"Not to mention escaping," Mike added.

We talked it out over supper and then went our separate ways. There was to be no communication unless Mike was being hassled or I had new information. Abe was staying in Mobile. He'd put his deputy in charge of the Atlanta office in the interim.

I asked him if he had anyone coming in to assist him.

"I would like to, but I can't tell anyone about you two bozos. We'll just keep it a three-man team. I know a couple of professors at the university here. I can get grunt work done by students. I'll be fine. Besides I can call in A.C.L.U. help on legal details over the phone."

"What about your wife?"

"We'll meet halfway on weekends. She's been down this road before. She has a business life of her own. She's smart."

CHAPTER

I called everybody I knew the next morning to request interviews or comments on the trial. No one took my call.

Ours is a morning paper, as is our competitor. We all write for the driveway and coffee trade.

I figured by noon all the news would be out and the police or D.A. would at least issue a press release. But there was nothing. The lid was on. I decided to force the issue and went over to police headquarters and presented myself again at the public information office to inquire about hearings which had been announced by the police commission.

I went through the receptionist and two other nice ladies until I finally got to the cop now in charge. He was an older man in uniform, probably putting in time before retirement, and he gave me the party line verbatim. He recited it distinctly and with an edge so that I would be suitably discouraged and leave them alone.

"We are not commenting publicly on this matter. It is an internal police matter and will be dealt with according to our procedures. These are confidential proceedings. The public will be notified of any actions taken."

My little risk taker was there in an instant and he was indignant.

"Sergeant," I said. "I am a journalist and an attorney. Do you have any idea what that means?"

He shrugged and then gave me his best cop stare. "Two assholes for the price of one?"

"Precisely," I said, not at all goaded by his surliness. "And these two assholes are going to a federal judge today and the odds are I'll be at the hearings. If I fail, I'll write a series of articles making this department look like the Gestapo. They know me here, Sergeant. Now go and tell Assistant Chief Burroughs that I'm here and I'm pissed, unless you'd like to be quoted on the two-asshole comment in tomorrow morning's paper. I can't imagine that would win you too many brownie points."

"Hey, who the fuck do you think you are? You can't come in here and threaten me!"

"Oh but I can. And I can put your face on page one for calling a member of the press an asshole when your job is public information."

"Well I ain't tellin' the chief a fuckin' thing. How do you like that?"

"Sounds good to me. Let me make sure I have that right."

I wrote his comment in my pad, then I took his name down from his name tag.

"See you in the funnies," I said cheerfully as I left.

He yelled after me, "Fuck you, asshole. You ain't doin' nothing if you know what's good for you."

I turned and looked to the ladies in the office. "You hear that ladies? Remember me?"

When the article was finished and ready, I held it waiting for a call from the police to come on over. It didn't come. The sergeant was calling my bluff. So be it.

The editor took some convincing, but he ran my article, complete with a file photo of Sergeant Norman Wade. It ran in the lower left of the front page under the headline of "Police Curse *Times* Reporter." It was the toughest piece I had ever written and I enjoyed it. In the article I said that this reporter was going to federal court to ask that the inquiry into police misconduct concerning the three-strikes trial be open to the public, just as the trial had been. The public had a right to know how this matter would be handled.

The chief of police called my editor at ten the next morning, trying to apply a little crony oil. The editor tried to call me off. I said he could stop using my stuff, but I was going to the federal court as a private citizen in any case, and if his paper was not interested, others would be.

"Harry," he said. "What's got you so het up over this? All I asked was could you let up on them a little. The chief said the cop would be reprimanded."

"It's not those two cops who are the problem. It's the whole old boy network over there, and in the D.A.'s office too. Listen, tell the chief he's got two choices, talk to us or not. His call. Nobody gets a pass with a phone call. This is far too serious. We're dealing with fundamental constitutional and public disclosure rights. Tell him I will listen to their side of it, but I am going to federal court today. I have an appointment with the clerk of the court at three. He already knows the subject and he's spoken to one of the judges."

"Jesus, Harry. You sound like a f—" he stopped short of finishing.

"A fucking lawyer?" I asked smiling.

"Well—yeah."

"I am a lawyer, Bob, and I'm an aggressive one. I've cut these guys some slack and they know it. Now I'm somebody they can just kiss off with the rest of them? Not me, Bob. They've never seen me pissed. I'm pissed, Bob."

He turned on his heel and said, "Hold tight, let me call him back."

My options were clear. I'd get back on the inside or I'd mount a one-man press barrage complete with legal ammunition.

The former seemed the more likely, but I started writing the next article immediately just in case.

CHAPTER

3

A ssistant Chief Joel Burroughs saw me in his office at two that afternoon. He was quite gruff and not at all the smooth get-it-done guy I was accustomed to.

"You see this yet?" he asked by way of greeting and handed me a paper. "Read it. We off the record here, Harry?"

"Sure," I said, "This too?" indicating the paper.

"No—that's already out there, or it will be real soon. Read it."

I did. It was a standard police public information form, saying that the Mobile Police Department had been named as the defendant in a suit filed in civil court alleging a conspiracy to violate the civil rights of the defendants in the recent "three-strike" trial. They were asking a hundred million dollars each for mental cruelty.

I handed it back. "They only need nine votes, you know, not twelve. It'll all depend on the jury," I said, regarding him closely.

He looked at me quizzically, not having expected that dry reply.

"I'm a lawyer, Chief," I said. "You have a big problem here, a big legal problem, and a big P.R. problem, too. You're not helping things much with your ham-handed public information office, either."

"You still pissed?"

"Very. That's the end of the off the record stuff, Chief. We're on the record now." I pulled out my tape recorder, pushed the on button and asked my first question.

"Chief Burroughs, when can we expect a full public explanation of all these three-strike entrapment allegations?"

"Can you turn that off for a moment? I'd like to give you some background, off the record, okay?"

I feigned reluctance, but I turned the machine off and sat back, waiting.

"Thank you. Harry, let me ask you a question."

"I thought you wanted to give me some background."

"I do, but I have a question first?"

"Shoot."

"Have you tried to check out this Mike Nevens guy? The Marine from the trial?"

There it was. The chief was always on the offensive. In one question he had changed the subject for the moment and essentially asked me if I was checking on the other side of the street as well. Was I being fair, was really his question. I hoped that was his motivation, in any case.

To collect my thoughts, I gave the standard response. "Chief, with all due respect, that's a matter between me and my editor."

"Come on Harry, you're starting to talk like a lawyer."

"That's what Bob said."

"Bob?"

"My editor."

"You giving him the treatment too, Harry?" It was delivered with a smile but the question remained, asked by the look in his eyes.

"You could say that," I said.

"You going to answer my question, Harry?"

"What? About the Marine?" I seemed to weigh the pros and cons of a reply and then continued. "Sure, in the spirit of cooperation, yeah, I'll answer it Chief. Of course I checked him out. He's a career Marine. He's the youngest at his rank in this command. He's a gunnery expert and his fitness reports are perfect. He has a wife and kids and lives on the base at Pensacola. He's as clean as fresh snow. He won't discuss the trial or anything else. His lawyer has him quarantined, so you guys can't even give him a speeding ticket. His lawyer said the only time you guys can talk to him will be at the depositions for the next trials."

"Plural?"

"Plural."

"You talked to him?"

"No. His lawyer," I answered.

"You check him out yourself? All that Mister Marine stuff?" Joel asked, now very interested.

"Twice."

"How?"

"That's a lot more than one question, Chief." I sat down, I'd said enough on this subject.

"I need the answer. Humor me."

"Fine. This is it though. There's no reason at all for me to be telling you any of this. One more only. This is way above the limit for me."

"I know, Harry, and I appreciate it."

"Fair enough. I know people on the base. They filled me in. This guy is the real deal and he has balls. I'm told he's very demanding of his students."

"Fuck! And I suppose his lawyer is still Abe Nordhoff and the A.C.L.U.?"

"It is."

"Fuck. You going to write about him?"

"Just a paragraph. I can't get anything from them."

"Them?"

"Him or his lawyer. That's it. If you wanted to know if I'm doing my job or if you just wanted to save some time, I don't care. I answered all your questions. Now you answer mine. What was the background you wanted to give me?"

"Harry, you got a real hard-on about this. What's going on here?"

The chief was stating a fact and asking me for my motives. He was good.

"What's going on, Chief, is that the Mobile Alabama Police Department is in serious jeopardy of federal investigation and its assistant chief is being purposefully evasive. It's your call, Chief. Talk to me or read about it tomorrow morning. I'm a lawyer, Chief. Police corruption pisses me off. Your guys are railroading fools."

"Allegedly."

"Allegedly, my ass. We'll take a poll for you. Trust me, you are railroading fools. And further to that you've got the A.C.L.U. on your trail and a lot of very happy journalists. Soon there will be more. Don't fence with me, Chief. I'm the least of your problems. But I am a problem. Don't make it worse. Make it better."

He stood slowly and walked out from behind his desk. "Can you give me a half hour, Harry? I have to talk to the politicians."

"Fair enough. Want me to wait outside?"

"No, no. Stay there. Use the other phone over there if you like. I appreciate your coming to me, Harry."

"I tried the easy way first."

"I know, I know. You're just doing your job."

"I'll wait here," I said.

He nodded and left, decidedly preoccupied.

When Burroughs returned he looked worse.

"You're going to have lots of company, Harry. The A.C.L.U. just called a press conference for tomorrow morning. There's TV crews coming from CNN and at least one of the networks."

"They give a topic?"

"Yep. They call it 'official law enforcement corruption in Mobile'."

"Oh, I see. Well, that will spread the heat out, won't it?"

"Huh?" He had been somewhat distracted but came back quickly. "What's that? Spread the heat? What's that supposed to mean?"

"What do you think 'official law enforcement corruption' means, Chief? Those are lawyer words. They didn't say police. It's a wider net. I'd guess the D.A.'s office, but it could be judges too. Cops can't pull this kind of stuff by themselves. But you already know that. They mention any federal guests?"

"What? What do you mean, guests? Oh, no, they didn't say anything like that."

"You better hope they don't."

"What?"

"Call in the feds. They love stuff like this."

"What, like what? Look, this is about a couple of over-zealous cops. These are good guys, Harry. This is getting blown way out of proportion."

"Are we on the record here?"

"No. I'll tell you when. Okay?"

"Sorry. I need a story. We're on the record as of now. All we've done so far is for me to answer your questions and give you what I've got. You haven't given me a damn thing. Fair's fair. Your free time is up."

I turned on the tape recorder. "Chief, either you don't get it or you think I'm stupid. Either way you lose. You're about twenty-four hours away from a subpoena and you're dicking around trying to con the friendliest reporter you have. I'm far from stupid, Chief. I made the dean's list at law school. There isn't one lawyer in your whole D.A.'s office who could carry my lunch. I happen to be a law-and-order guy so I don't sugarcoat criminals or vilify the cops gratuitously to sell newspapers, but believe me when I tell you that I'm pissed off. Imagine what else is in store for you. You think the politicians are going to go to bat for your guys? Not a shot. They'll all be card-carrying A.C.L.U. members by tomorrow morning. The D.A. has no doubt kept it compartmentalized, so he can probably skate. They'll take some low level hits, but that's all. That leaves the police and the judges. Believe me, it's easy to figure out, and believe me you will not like it. Now, are you going to answer some questions or not?"

The chief thought about that for a moment and then spoke. His face cleared and his eyes became fully effective. "Ask your questions, on the record."

"Thank you, Chief. Number one, are any of Frank Babcock's or Ernie Collins's superiors under investigation?"

"Not yet."

"Will they be?"

"Perhaps."

"Did you know what was going on?"

Chief Burroughs pursed his lips and thought that one over. When at last he replied, it was with tightly controlled anger. "Harry, this interview is over."

"Hey, hold on, Chief," I said. "I sat here for an hour answering your questions. Shit, I even gave you a half hour to—well—to ask the politicians what was up. I gave you information, Chief, good information. Now after one question, we're through?" I was actually angry, not needing my actor at all for this one. "We're not through. You owe me. I'm not standing still for this bullshit, not for one moment."

He stood and reached for my recording machine, but I was quicker and snatched it away.

The chief sat back resignedly and folded his arms. "This interview is finished, Harry. Call my secretary to reschedule. I'm out of time now. I have another appointment."

"Bullshit," I said. "You're afraid to answer the question. Were you involved in this, Chief? Yes or no. It's an easy one, yes or no?"

"Call my secretary, Harry. Now if you'll excuse me, I have a meeting to attend."

He stood as a signal for me to leave. So I stood, too, and I said "You have just fucked me over. I can't believe your nerve. Does this shit work for you? I guess it must. Well you have just fucked with the wrong guy. You go to your meeting. Be sure to read the paper tomorrow. You'll be in it."

He looked at me hard. "Don't get so huffy, Harry. This will all work out. I just can't talk to you now."

He had that practiced way of leaving you in doubt, but I'd seen it before and wasn't buying it. "I'm not one of your brown-noses, Burroughs. That's nonsense and we both know it."

"Hey, Harry, you're the big reporter. Report that I wouldn't talk to you. That's what happened here."

He turned to his credenza and starting sorting papers to signal my dismissal.

In times of extreme tension, everything slows so that our memory is seared by the emotions expended. I picked up my little recorder and bent to put it in my briefcase which was on the floor beside my chair. I saw the big L-shaped legs of the chief's desk, and with no hesitation put my recorder in the L, laying it against the dark wood. I opened my briefcase snapped it shut and rose to leave.

"One more shot, Chief," I said. "Fair's fair. I answered your questions."

He turned his head just enough to see me. "And I thank you for that."

"That's it? I'm supposed to just piss off like a good little reporter?"

"Something like that." He said in such a manner that it was a combined put down and dismissal.

I left without further comment.

The recorder had a new tape and it was good for a couple of hours. It was three-thirty, so I went to the newspaper and wrote my article and filed it with no fanfare or request for unusual placement. All I wanted was the article in the paper, not another contest with my editor.

At six o'clock, I went back to police headquarters to get my recorder. I'd simply say I'd lost it somewhere and ask them to look for it. If they caught on, so be it. I'd just stick to my story that I must have dropped it and see if they demanded the tape.

Burroughs was not there and his secretary had gone for the evening. There was a young Asian woman at a desk nearby and I told her my story and she very obligingly went into the chief's office and found my little machine for me. I thanked her sincerely and got out of there as quickly as I could without running.

When you are an escaped convict, you leave nothing to chance. If there is the smallest risk, you cover it. That was my training. I went to my room and immediately listened to the tape, while recording it onto another hand-held recorder I kept for my legal work. Then I re-ran the original tape up to the point where I was leaving the chief's office, and erased the rest. I mailed the original tape to Gwen's house in Jackson, with a note for her to put it in a safe place.

My pager buzzed right there at the mailbox. It was the newspaper. I called them from the car on my cell phone.

It was my editor. He had Chief Burroughs and a detective in his office and they were very upset. Could I come in at once?

I played dumb and he put Chief Burroughs on the line.

318 • Len Williams

"Harry, you're in a whole lot of trouble here. Now get in here right now and bring the goddamned tape with you."

"Hey. Hold on there, pal. What the hell are you talking about?"

"Stop the bullshit. I'm on to your cute little trick. That's not going to fly around here."

"Chief, what are you talking about?" I gave him all the indignation I could muster.

"All right, smart guy, play dumb. I'll spell it out. You planted your tape in my office. I want it."

"The tape? . . . Oh, the tape." I continued playing innocent. "I don't get it? What's your problem? I only had it on when we were on the record."

"Bullshit. You planted it."

"Oh, I get it. Sorry, I'm kind of slow. So you think I left my machine on in your office, is that it?"

"Yes, smart guy, that's it. Now if you know what's good for you, you'll get down here with that tape before this gets any worse."

"I'll be right there," I said aggressively and punched the off button on my phone. My alter ego had kicked in with the chief's threat. He wanted to do this in person? So did I.

When I got to the office, I turned on the second recorder and put it in my inside jacket breast pocket. It was a miniature and made little bulge.

They were in the editor's office waiting for me. Burroughs, a detective named Largent, my editor, Bob, and the publisher, Bill McNeill, were there looking very serious. After we had solemnly shaken hands, Bob told me how serious it all was and I was to cooperate fully with Chief Burroughs. He hoped I had not compromised the good name of his paper.

I listened politely to Bob and then asked Mr. McNeill why he was there.

"I received a call from the police commissioner about your little trick. Where's the tape? Let's get this over with." He was angry and dismissive.

I have to tell you that at that moment I was really enjoying myself, or rather my little actor friend was enjoying himself. I was watching, along with Billy Ray and TB18078.

"Okay," I said. "That's two constituencies heard from." I turned to Chief Burroughs. "What's your hit on this, Chief?"

"Where's the tape, Harry? I'm not interested in your smart-guy stuff. In case you haven't noticed, your employer wants their tape back."

"Oh," I said in mock surprise. "I see. That's it. No tape, no job. That it, Bob?"

Bob glared but said nothing. I was obviously pissing off the entire establishment.

"Fine, gentlemen." I said. "Here's the deal. Bob and Bill, you need to listen carefully to this. So far, no one has had the courtesy to hear my side of this. Fair enough. You are all nice and tight with the police. That's your prerogative. It's bad newspaper policy but perhaps that is not important to you. You should, however, listen carefully to the point of view of someone who writes for your paper before you abjectly surrender your constitutional rights to the Gestapo here."

It was out and they went nuts. No one tried to hit me, but it was all they could do to restrain themselves.

When their indignation subsided, I continued, overriding all their voices.

"Hey! Bill, Bob! These are the police! They are under investigation! This is a newspaper! They can't just pull a few strings and get my confidential working notes. Even you must know that."

"Well, that's where you're wrong, Harry," said Bill McNeill. "They are our notes, not yours and we do with them as we wish.

And I'll thank you to keep a civil damn tongue in your head. What you did was not the way we conduct business here. That is the issue."

"So the chief here comes over and tells you some cock and bull story and you just believe him? Just like that? No 'What have you got to say, Harry?' Nothing like that?" I asked.

With no answer forthcoming, I continued, moving into a higher gear of indignation. "Well, a real newspaper man might just ask why the chief here is so upset. Perhaps, if there was a tape, it would have something pretty juicy on it and that would be a good story. Did you think about that?"

I waited, staring at Bob and Bill and not at all at the cops.

No one spoke. They were all tight-jawed now, waiting to see if I'd give them the tape.

"Let me spell it out for you. One, I'm not anybody's employee. I am freelance. I sell one story at a time."

Bob started to talk, but I cut him off coldly. "Read the agreement Bob. I wrote it. Believe me, I am not your employee."

Now Bill McNeill started in with a threat to end my employment with his newspaper.

"Bill, do yourself a favor and pay attention. As I said, one, I am not anyone's employee. Just take my word for now, okay? Two, the tape machine in question is my private property which I dropped inadvertently in the chief's office. I went back to get it, and the chief and his secretary were not there so I asked another police department employee to see if she could find it. She did and I took it back. That's all there is on that subject."

Again angry voices rose but I yelled over them. "Three, the chief here conned me into giving him good information but refused to answer any of my questions on the record. Does that sound like a good story? I think so. You can read about it in the morning paper. This is a newspaper, and that is news."

"We are not running that piece, Harry. You're way out of line here," Bob said, but without hard conviction.

"All the bases covered, eh?" I said. "Very nice, Chief, very nice. Well, that is certainly not the response I had hoped for. So you gentlemen are not purchasing my latest offering and you are siding with the police in trying to force me to hand over my reporter's tape. Just to be perfectly clear, is that what's going on here?"

"That's it." Bill McNeill answered. "But that won't be the end of it if you do not comply and at once."

"Oh? What will you do, Bill? Not buy any more of my pieces?"

"Among other things," he said tightly.

"For instance?" I asked.

"I think you can figure that out."

"What? Indulge me, please."

He would not be drawn any further, but, it seemed, the chief would.

"Harry, we can make it very difficult for you down here. Now stop all this before you have burned all your bridges. Just give me the tape and we'll start over. I'll give the paper an interview tomorrow. On the record."

"What? Parking tickets? Harassment? Come on, Chief, this is America." I became really angry. It was all too absurd and too clear how this tawdry little establishment worked. "Don't ever threaten me, Chief. Ever. You understand me? Now listen carefully. This is my tape. I will not give it to you. I abhor the tactics used here tonight and you, Chief, will regret it. The rest of you don't matter a whit to me but I would never have guessed what self-satisfied little toadies you really are. At least I know that now. Chief, I am going to play the tape for you. I haven't even listened to it myself."

I took the recorder out of my briefcase and the chief grabbed it out of my hand.

"Thank you Harry, I'll take that."

"That is my property, Chief Burroughs, give it back at once. I only took it out to play for you."

"That won't be necessary. I can do that myself later."

"Afraid to play it here, Chief?"

"Fuck you, Harry, you're finished here."

"You mean with the newspaper or the town, Chief?"

"Both."

"You all saw him take my tape recorder. Chief, that's theft. Give it back at once."

"They'll buy you a new one."

"Will they? Well that won't do, Chief. You have just stolen my property and trampled all over the Constitution."

"Go preach that shit someplace else." Burroughs said.

I turned to Bob. "Hey, Bob, mail the stuff in the desk I use here to my law office in Jackson. I'm out of here. Chief, I'll see you later." I turned and left them where they were standing, the four dark figures together in the office.

I got in my car and drove to Jackson to put the new tape in my office safe.

Two days later it was joined by the first one.

CHAPTER

When I told Abe Nordhoff what had happened and what I intended to do, he was pleased.

We decided to leave the A.C.L.U. out of it entirely and just open up another front for the authorities to deal with.

There had been good initial coverage of the suit which the A.C.L.U. had brought, asking damages from the Mobile Police for Joshua and Joseph. The proceedings had been scheduled for three months hence, awaiting court time. After a few weeks the furor had died down, which suited our purposes just fine. Abe could stay in Mobile, working on the real case and I could stay in Jackson, as a seemingly penitent transgressor.

Slowing my reporting for the Jackson paper to a trickle, I concentrated on my law practice. Anyone could see I'd returned to my legal work.

The day after I'd left Mobile, I had filed a complaint with the police about the assistant police chief taking my tape recorder, but

I'd never been called, nor had I followed up. The really good news was that my tape machine had not been returned to me. That had surprised me, but I suppose it shouldn't have. They were in charge down there in Mobile. That had been abundantly evident.

Six weeks after Chief Burroughs had taken my tape recorder, I went to Montgomery to sit for the semiannual Alabama bar examination.
Two weeks later I could practice law in Alabama.

CHAPTER

Back I went to Mobile and made the rounds to the police department, the D.A.'s offices, and the newspaper. None of them would give me the time of day regarding my stolen tape recorder.

The police had nothing on file, the D.A.'s office told me to stop annoying them, and the publisher of the newspaper would not take my call. They all turned down Harry Brown, the former reporter.

On a Monday morning, I filed suit in civil court, naming the Mobile Police Department and the *Mobile Times* as defendants. One claim was for a million dollars for having denied me any due process before illegally seizing my tape recorder and tape, thereby trampling my constitutional rights. Further, I said, they had deprived me of some livelihood and reputation, and for that I asked another million. The charge was general, and on the surface was meant to look like a nuisance suit that any able lawyer could have thrown out of court.

But there are two courts in America, and it was to the other that

I really appealed. On Wednesday, having given ample time for the serving and reading of the legal papers, I gave an interview to one of my former competitors on the other Mobile daily newspaper. They were conservative as well, but sufficiently competitive to run it. In it, I told the reporter that I had proof of collusion between the *Mobile Times* and the local police force. I told him about two tapes: the one the chief had stolen and the one I had of the confrontation at the newspaper. The article ran in the metro section on the cover page as a secondary article. By then, I had returned to Jackson.

The *Mobile Times* still had my office phone number and I guess that's how Chief Burroughs got it. He called me before noon on Wednesday, all huffy and official.

All I had to say was "Oh, hello, Chief, nice to hear from you," and he took off on a tirade about the newspaper article. I listened carefully and then told him I couldn't speak with him just then because I had a previously scheduled engagement. He could call my secretary for an alternate date and time when I would be available, and I hung up the phone.

Since I had named myself both as plaintiff and plaintiff's attorney, they had no recourse but to eventually talk to me.

Chief Burroughs apparently felt slighted and had a succession of public and private lawyers call me. They all got the same response. I was serious, I had tapes, and they could hear them when I stipulated them as evidence in the pretrial discovery phase. They would get nothing before. I was unfailingly polite, cheerful in the anticipation of receiving a couple of million dollars for their clients' abject stupidity.

I knew the *Times* lawyer because occasionally he'd had to check out some of my articles. He was a pleasant low-key guy, making a very soft living at the paper. I was happy to take his call.

"Hey c'mon Harry," he said. "This isn't going to do anybody any good. You know those tapes are not admissible, even if you do have them, which I doubt."

His name was Russell Ferguson. Everyone called him Fergie. "That's right, Fergie," I said. "Just like the videotapes from that three-strike trial? Don't worry, I have them and they'll be admitted. No problem there."

"Don't be too sure. That was a fluke. A good lawyer would never have let that stuff in. If we go to trial on this, and I don't think we will, you won't be facing any Wes Wentworth."

"What, you going to take this one yourself, Fergie?"

"Very funny. No, Harry, but I can tell you confidentially that we will call in the best for this one. The paper's reputation is at stake. You'll have so many good lawyers to deal with, it will be hard just to sort out the documents. You understand what I'm saying here, Harry?"

I had intended to confront Chief Burroughs directly, but it seemed he might never call me. I decided on the spot to lay it on Fergie instead.

"Tell you what, Fergie. You're a good guy. No reason why you shouldn't get a few points out of this. Here's the deal. This is a one-time offer."

"What, we give you the million and you go away?" Fergie laughed.

I liked him and so I laughed too. "Look, Fergie, please write this down for them. I'm serious."

"Okay, sorry. Shoot. This I have to hear."

"Thanks. Fine. I have three tapes. A copy of the one Chief Burroughs stole from me, a second one I had on in his office, and the one on which I recorded Bill, Bob, and Burroughs in Bob's office. I am willing to play the third tape for you and one of your outside lawyers, no one else, but you cannot have a copy. When you hear it, you will probably agree to having the paper removed from the suit and settling with me for a million dollars. If not, we go to trial. I should tell you, however, Fergie, that the justice department has a copy of the tapes. They have been informed and have agreed to await the outcome of the civil suit before taking any action. My sense of it is that they would act if pushed hard enough. I can provide that push but I won't tell you how. That's it, Fergie, your call."

"Hey, how come you're the attorney on this? I thought you were only licensed in Mississippi?"

"I took the local bar exam just for this, Fergie. It's not often that a person can get rich and even at the same time. You want to call me back on this or can one of the guys on the speaker phone there make a decision right now?"

"How the—?" Fergie bit his tongue.

"So," I said. "Who else am I talking to?" I could hear the phone click and then all was quiet for thirty seconds.

"Mr. Brown?" A new voice.

"Yes, who's this?"

I met the next day in my office in Jackson with Fergie and Nathan McAndrews, a heavy-hitter corporate attorney from New Orleans.

It did not take long. The chief would be on his own. We settled on six hundred thousand and they were out of it completely except as witnesses. I had the papers ready for them to sign. They were not at all complicated. In a pinch they could look like victims as well, if it came to that.

I never said it, but they seemed to understand that I was after Chief Burroughs, not their newspaper.

CHAPTER

It had seemed strange to me that Fergie never mentioned the other tapes. All he wanted to know about was the one recorded at the newspaper office. I had put it out to him that there were three tapes because I wanted Chief Burroughs to feel fear himself for a change.

After my settlement with the newspaper, I could only wait for the pretrial process of my lawsuit to kick in.

For two weeks nothing at all happened. I had several small cases brewing, which kept me occupied, and at night I would go home to Gwen. It was a pleasant interlude.

"My name is Joseph Costello, Mr. Brown. My firm is representing the City of Mobile in the lawsuit you are attempting to bring against them."

The message had said urgent but I didn't know who J. Costello was. He immediately took the offensive with a deep, strong voice. I love dealing with guys like him.

"We want to meet with you right away, Mr. Brown, to resolve this thing before you take it to a point where we cannot be reasonable."

Again he waited for my reply. I punched the speaker-phone button and put my feet up.

"Are you there Mr. Brown?" came the big voice.

"Yes I am."

"Well sir, what do you have to say?"

"About what?"

"Well, since you ask, about withdrawing your lawsuit. That's why I'm calling. We should meet and end this thing before it gets away from you."

"Who exactly is 'we'?"

"Our side will have four attorneys present. Myself, one of my senior partners, the district attorney, and the insurance company attorney."

"And what would you wish to discuss, Mr. Costello?"

"I'd rather wait until we meet, if you don't mind."

"Where would you like to meet, Mr. Costello?"

"At our office here in Mobile. That's the easiest spot for most of us to get to."

"So you have in mind that I would come to Mobile to listen to your proposal in your offices. Is that correct?"

"That is correct. If you have your calendar handy, perhaps we could set a date."

"Mr. Costello, did someone tell you that I was stupid? Perhaps one of the people in the office there with you?"

"Really, Mr. Brown. There's no need to be hostile here. We're trying to make this as easy as we can."

"Mr. Costello, if you are not recording this, please write this down. Your client has a senior employee, the assistant chief of police, who stole my tape recorder. There are witnesses and a

tape of his theft and threats. He has also trampled all over a reporter and taken his confidential notes, which are specifically
protected by the U.S. Constitution. The newspaper has settled
with me. I am dead serious about this lawsuit, Mr. Costello. I will
take it to trial before a jury and I will prevail. I don't need to tell
you how some juries react when the little guy is injured by the
big guy. Read the lawsuit. I asked for one million for specific
damages. I did not ask for a specific amount on the penalty
phase. I will leave that for the jury. Now, Mr. Costello, I'd be
happy to meet with you one on one in my office here in Jackson.
I would even meet you halfway, in Meridian. But one on one.
Otherwise we will not meet. Is this all clear to you?"

I had purposely kept my voice matter-of-fact and business-like.

The line went silent as I guess he pushed the hold button. I
hung up.

He called back in a few minutes, all indignation. "Mr. Brown
did you hang up on me?"

"Mr. Costello? What's your answer?"

"See here, Mr. Brown. We are representing the City of Mobile
here. We can't be—well, we have to do things correctly. We think
you should come to meet with us here in Mobile."

"Mr. Costello, the next time I come to Mobile, it will be for the
trial. I will be escorted by two off-duty state troopers in an un-
marked car so the local police can't set me up for a hit and run. Mr.
Costello, your client has a big problem. If you don't know that, you
are missing the point here. It's me against the Mobile Police Department and Chief Burroughs. By the way, the U.S. Attorney will
be watching every step of this. Now stop all this nonsense. My patience is at an end. If you have an offer, send it to me. If you want
to meet, one on one, I'll arrange it. Otherwise, Mr. Costello and
gentlemen, I'll see you at the pretrial deposition."

"You are forgetting one thing, Mr. Brown."

"And what is that?"

"We have huge resources here. There's the city, the insurance company, and our firm. I'm sure you know what I mean."

"Absolutely. You have lots of lawyers to put out reams of paper to bury one lone practitioner like me. That it?"

"You really need to be more accommodating, Mr. Brown."

"You know what I'm going to do with the tape of this conversation, Mr. Costello? I'm going to take it to the U.S. Attorney in Mobile and to the National Association of Newspaper Editors. Perhaps their lawyers can handle yours. I'd bet on them, actually. If I cannot get enough help, I'll spend the big settlement I just got from the *Times*. You have threatened me, Mr. Costello. On tape."

"Hey, there, you can't tape this without telling us."

"Ask the D.A. there. What are you, Mr. Costello, a real estate lawyer? This is hard ball. You have just succeeded in upping the ante here. Thank you. I work much better when I'm upset. Look, do me a favor and put the D.A. on. You're out of your depth here."

This time I waited on hold.

"Harry?" It was the D.A., Dave Harris.

"Hi Dave. How's it going?"

"Very funny."

"We on the speaker phone?"

"Yes."

"Take it off. Okay?"

His voice became clearer. "Okay, we're off."

"Who hired Huckleberry Hound there? He sounds like a bad movie."

"Not me."

"That's what I thought. You want to meet, Dave?"

"Sure. Where?"

"Meridian, okay?"

"Yes. When?"

"Anytime I suppose. You can bring Chief Burroughs if you like."

"Really? How come?"

"I think that's the only way you'll see what you are up against."

"Meaning?"

"Meaning I'm not very interested in any second-hand negotiations and you may not know his whole story."

"And you can get it out of him I suppose?"

"I can try."

"I'll let you know. Okay?"

"Sure. I'll wait for your call."

When you know what you want, your energies go in that direction. I had wanted to confront Chief Burroughs. Now perhaps it would happen. Court would be acceptable of course, but under oath with lawyers preparing them people were not themselves. I wanted this guy natural.

What I wanted was a face-to-face with one of my tormentors. Frank Babcock and Ernie Collins could not have operated without Chief Burroughs or the D.A.'s office, could they? I certainly didn't think so.

CHAPTER

C hief Burroughs was highly polished in a neat civilian suit and white shirt. He was freshly shaven and seemed in good spirits.

I had borrowed a small boardroom in a law firm's office in Meridian. It was ten in the morning and there was coffee and rolls and a pretty view of a small downtown park.

We had shaken hands coolly but not unpleasantly. Everyone took coffee and we actually talked about the weather for a moment. It was a gorgeous day.

Finally, I said, "Let's get started. First, I am making no tapes of this meeting. I state clearly for the record that in no manner am I recording this meeting except by the notes I take. You can tape it if you wish."

They looked at each other and Chief Burroughs smiled. "No, we won't tape it, either." He turned to Dave. "Should we get him to sign something?"

Dave let out a snort of nervous laughter. "No, I have it on tape."

He opened his briefcase and took out a small black tape recorder, and with some ceremony, turned it off.

We had a little chuckle over that.

"Good," I said. "Dave, do you have a proposal to offer me?"

"Not so fast, Harry." The chief interrupted. "I want to hear more about the tapes, the ones you told Ferguson about."

There it was. I'd put it out and he'd taken it. I couldn't ask, nor could he. Not until now.

In negotiation, the best tactic is to listen. Your opponent will tell you what's important. The chief had just told me.

My intention had been to hold the tapes out of his reach as a threat but not to use them in the civil case at all. They were for tho larger trials to follow.

It occurred to me, on the spot, that perhaps I could use them in another way.

"Dave," I said. "Who do you represent here?"

"The city."

"Not Chief Burroughs?"

Dave became wary. "Yes, him as well, but only insofar as he works for the city. I'm not his lawyer, if that's what you're asking."

"Then we have a problem. I'd like to tell the chief some things and he might want to tell me something as well. You shouldn't hear it unless it's privileged. But I want you here, so what can we do?"

"You want me here? Why?"

"Take my word for it, Dave. Can the chief's comments be privileged?"

"I can stipulate that for this meeting I have agreed on behalf of the city to represent him personally."

"Good. Write it down and sign it please."

Dave was puzzled but curious, so he scribbled a note. He and the chief signed it.

I should have called Abe Nordhoff, but the spirit moved me right there and then to get it over with. For some strange reason, while Dave was writing the agreement, I flashed back to the morning I had decided to stay in the swamp for three weeks instead of three hours or three days. It had just happened. Now this was happening and I was almost powerless against its inevitability.

I just started in. "Chief, I have you on tape talking to Frank Babcock after I left."

He started to swear, but I politely asked him to hear me out. He stopped.

"I rerecorded the tape and let you steal the original after I had erased all the stuff recorded after I left."

The chief just sat there, his cool eyes fixed on me.

"You guys are the masters at taping. Now you're on the other end. But let me be clear. I am not after you personally, and I'm not after money. This is part of a much bigger thing. You are both neck-deep in those three-strike scams. What I want is your cooperation to set that right."

There ensued all manner of protests and posturing which I endured as best I could. We debated for most of the morning. Finally, I said. "Look, there are two ways this can go. One is that I proceed with this suit and prevail. That is very likely. Then we'll have an assistant police chief guilty of theft and politicians leaving you like rats. After that, you have the A.C.L.U going after a couple of hundred million, reminding everyone about the police scam. They'll win a few million, perhaps more. There's no way they lose, especially with my tapes. The D.A.'s office will be included in the conspiracy. They had to be in on it. How else could it happen? I'm sure Wes Wentworth would welcome a shot at you guys. After that the A.C.L.U. and probably the Department of Justice will force retrials or reviews of the seven other three-strike scams. By then there will be a new police chief, assistant police chief and D.A. The new guys will want to set things right, so they'll bury anyone involved." I paused to let that scenario sink in. Dave did not look up, but the chief did.

"What's number two?" he asked.

"You guys see the error of your overzealous activities and ask for the reviews or retrials yourselves. I'll make sure the A.C.L.U. and the Department of Justice applaud your efforts and we get the last convictions vacated and those poor bastards out of prison. Believe me, it's the right thing to do. You'll come off as tough law-and-order guys who went too far. Maybe you even keep your jobs. Oh, I forgot, in scenario number one, the A.C.L.U. goes after you on criminal conspiracy charges. You would be convicted and get a minimum sentence of three years, probably more.

"What's all this A.C.L.U. stuff?" asked Dave. "How can you—?"

I held up my hand. "Dave, I'm their client."

"You're their what?" yelled the chief.

"I hired them. They work for me."

"When?"

"After I helped Mike Nevens tape your boys getting those lousy double convictions."

They stared at me, struck seemingly dumb for several seconds.

"Who the fuck are you, Harry?" It was Dave who finally asked.

"I'm a lawyer, Dave, and I'm a goddamned unhappy one. Your call. I'll get the A.C.L.U. on the phone if it helps."

We sent out for lunch, I talked to Abe, first in private, and then we talked to him on the speaker phone together.

You had to hand it to Abe. He just wanted what I did, to get those men out of prison.

He had asked a few questions and then just said, "It's your show, Harry. You pull this off and you're my hero. Go get 'em." I could have wept.

With that support we worked our way through the whole thing by dusk.

We really still held all the cards. The lawsuits and any future charges stayed valid until the prisoners were out.

CHAPTER

Some things just cannot be planned. All the time I studied law and all the time I practiced it and worked as a reporter, I had one vision. It was such a true, clear vision that it could have been a memory. I stand at the rail while the jury watches and listens, completely absorbed. The summation is short but true. I have them.

Now on a whim, I'd played my hand to avoid that which I craved. Strangely, I feel no loss. Perhaps Abe did it for me defending Joshua and Joseph. My desire, I find, is not ultimately for theatrical flourish. But perhaps I am too impetuous.

My greatest fear—while I waited for Harris to act during the days after our agreement—was that I would be found out. I suppose I had wagered on that. The D.A. had asked me, "Who the hell are you, Harry?" When he said that, I thought they would throw all their resources into checking me out. What about my prints, my background before Jackson?"

All I could do was work at my office and wait. We had no

written deal. Either they would take over the situation or my suit would proceed.

For a week I waited, becoming more fearful of discovery and more jumpy as the days wore on. A week is a long time for a thorough search. But, I reasoned, the fingerprint check would bring up Harry Brown, the car driver in Jackson. What about my draft status? There was none. Would they check the high school in Canada?

I hated not being myself and proud of it. Billy Ray had nothing much to be proud of, TB18078 could be proud of graduating high school, and Harry Brown was a little dead boy in his grave. I couldn't even tell Gwen who I was. Abe Nordhoff must have had some idea of how important he was to me. He was the only person alive, other than Mike and my brother, who knew who I was.

The district attorney for Mobile, Alabama called a press conference eight days after our meeting. He phoned me so that I could attend, but I was still too nervous to take the chance of delivering myself up to them. If they had found me out, it could be a trap.

I said I'd go, but in the end I asked Abe to tape it for me. If the conference was a scam, I'd know in enough time to escape. He had my cell phone number and I waited in my car a long way from my office. Once caught, twice shy. Abe took me seriously, or at least he pretended to.

The cell phone rang a half hour after the press conference had been scheduled to start.

"Harry?"

"Hey Abe. How'd it go?"

"I sat right up front so they could see me. You want me to tell you or do you want to hear his statement? It's short."

"Can you play it for me now?"

District Attorney David Harris spoke as the recently converted. His voice was full of righteousness. They had been taken aback by the recent trial so ably won by the A.C.L.U. It was a great thing to be an American. The glib bastard wrapped the whole thing in the flag. The police had been overzealous in their application of the three-strike rule. Bear in mind that all these men were convicted three-time felons. All they were trying to do was protect the good citizens of Mobile. And, yes, his office had helped too, perhaps unwittingly, but nonetheless, to some extent they had been guilty of a little excess in their crusade.

Well, this was America and America is built on laws. Just as his department and the police had been zealous to convict known criminals, now they would prove just as zealous in protecting their rights. These remaining seventeen felons were in prison, without recourse or resources. He obviously had not checked his count—I was gone—there were only sixteen. I took great heart from that.

He would personally, along with his compatriot assistant chief of police, Joel Burroughs, try to set things straight. First, they would renounce any further attempts to split felonies, and secondly, he would, himself, on behalf of the good citizens of Mobile, file an appeal covering all seventeen previously convicted felons to attempt to have the fourth convictions set aside. The case law was now clear to him and he could do no less. The appeal would be filed that very day. His office had been working on it for some time and he had faith in its merit. The letter of the law would be served.

I listened to it all and then told Abe that this guy should run for mayor, he was so full of shit.

Abe said it was a masterful and artful performance. The D.A. and Chief Burroughs stood there like crusaders and the press had eaten it up.

I had asked Abe previously to go to the state prison to see Maynard and Eddie. He had told them that they could be released if everything worked out, and he had signed them up as clients, not mentioning Billy Ray or Harry Brown.

Abe said they were very excited but felt terrible about their pal Billy Ray who had to die because of this. Eddie said that if he got out, those two cops were going down. Abe gave him the five-cent talk concerning the stupidity of that and Eddie said he'd do it anyway, for Billy Ray. It was only fair.

We got their signatures, which was all we needed to represent them at the appeal.

It was a surprise to Dave Harris, who had expected a solo performance. He got all pissed off and agitated when we met with him after we declared that we would represent some of the felons. We met in Montgomery where the court was sitting, the day before the hearing.

He accused me of reneging on our deal. I told him I wouldn't trust him as far as I could throw him and that we would be there for all of the defendants to make sure that they weren't shafted.

Abe finished him off. "Mr. Harris, let me be very clear. Our deal was not that we have this appeal, it was that these men receive justice. By that I mean freedom and compensation immediately. Anything less than that, and I go after you. You are guilty by your own admission. I'll get you three to five without working up a sweat. Your pal Chief Burroughs goes down too, but probably for more. Now, we don't know if you planned to act in good faith or not, nor do we give a rat's ass. You are obviously not to be trusted. We will represent our clients. You follow our lead or so help me God, I will put you down."

Abe spoke firmly but not with any excess. His eyes never left Dave Harris.

"Are we clear on this, Mr. Harris?"

Dave sighed. "I'm not planning to fuck anybody over on this." All his air was gone. Whatever he had planned, we were now in charge. We had to be. There was some tricky wording needed in the decision, and we knew by Dave's performance at the press conference that he was perfectly capable of sugarcoating his activities and those of the police.

CHAPTER

In his opening statement, Abe told the Alabama Court of Criminal Appeals the whole tawdry story. He said he could call all of the police officers and felons and their previous lawyers and all the city prosecutors; or the assistant police chief and the Mobile district attorney would stipulate the accuracy of the charges.

Dave Harris went at once from hero to villain. At the recess he was livid at this tactic and Abe told him his choice was to stipulate or to climb up on the witness stand after a parade of dumb-looking cops and prosecutors.

Although I did not represent Maynard and Eddie, I sat in on all the sessions with Dave. He looked at me and yelled that I had set him up.

With Dave and Chief Burroughs, I had always played the game of calm attorney, in control of the situation and unflappable. This moment seemed right for Billy Ray to finally have a say.

"Dave, you're a glib government employee who has fucked over the law and the lives of a lot of men. I could give a shit what you think, and don't think for a moment when those men are free that you are finished with us. We're going to watch you like fucking hungry eagles. Don't ever accuse me of setting you up. You're lucky you're not dead."

He turned chalk white. Then, I guess his lawyer mind clicked in and he asked me who "we" were.

"We is anybody I say it is, Dave. It's me, it's the A.C.L.U., and it's the U.S. Department of Justice. If that isn't enough, I have other resources."

He sat back and finally a wan smile came. "Well you really are one hard-assed son of a bitch, Harry."

"You have no fucking idea." I answered.

Abe took over before I got any angrier, taking the opportunity to brief Dave on our strategy.

After that, Dave was docile and even, at times, fervent in his plea for clemency. We could never know if he was sincere or not. All we cared about was the effect it had on the judges.

Abe wrapped me up in his final motion. Any and all seventeen felons still incarcerated as of the date of the appeals court's decision should be freed and given a lump sum compensation of $100,000.

Court was adjourned. The decision would be forthcoming in two to three weeks.

Chapter

I could take no chance that a decision would come down early. It had happened before, and this case had achieved some notoriety.

The court had adjourned on Wednesday. On the following Monday morning, I drove to the state prison just outside Birmingham, Alabama. I had read the law regarding escapees and knew that by giving myself up, they would take me in immediately and that they would automatically add years to my sentence. For a lifer with no parole, that was precisely nothing. I would be back in prison and still a lifer.

I did try to look as different from Harry Brown as possible. In anticipation of this, my hair had not been cut for over a month. I washed it and just let it dry wild. I had not shaved since Wednesday. My regular glasses were replaced by an old pair of those ugly yellow tinted jobs with old wire frames. I wore jeans and an old plaid shirt and sneakers and a baseball hat.

Leaving my car in town in a parking garage, I took a taxi to the prison.

The south Alabama twang I'd long ago discarded came back gratefully. I had practiced it all the way from Jackson in the car. It brought me back to Billy Ray.

I walked the last five hundred yards up to the prison. It was a bright cool day and I could not believe that I, Billy Ray Billings, had walked so far to have come right around the world and end up at the beginning.

The administration building is inside the double-wire fence and guard towers. I walked to the main gate where visitors and delivery trucks came. There was one big white truck there.

Three guards, one standing aside with his hand on his pistol, one looking inside the truck, and the third in a glass booth, checked out the truck.

I waited until the truck was allowed to leave, the gate had been closed, and I could have the full attention of the three officers.

"Hey, buddy, how ya doin'? What can we do ya fer? Visitin' was yesterday."

"I'm givin' myself up." I said, not looking at him.

"Yer what?"

"Givin' myself up. I used to be in here. I escaped."

They thought I was a nutcase, until I told them who I was— Billy Ray Billings, TB18078, escapee, believed dead. I told them that I missed my friends inside.

The warden was a recent arrival, but the captain of the guards was not. He remembered me and told me that I was certainly one crazy son of a bitch. I agreed with him.

Over the whole of that Monday, I was fingerprinted, had mug shots taken, and was finally, officially, back in prison.

The warden asked me what I'd been doing all these years. I told him in my best twang that I'd gone to law school and then I'd been a reporter for a great metropolitan newspaper.

He smiled. "Kind of like Clark Kent, eh?"

I didn't want to appear too nuts, for fear of a psychiatrist, so I smiled back. "Just kiddin', Warden, it weren't no great metropolitan newspaper, more like a midsized job."

"Oh, I see."

He didn't seem to know what to do with me at first, but the system took over when he gave me to the captain of the guards. I was admitted just like any other convict and assigned a cell. I'd expected solitary for the escape and perhaps some guard brutality. Actually, they were rather respectful, probably because I had to be one really crazy son of a bitch to have come back.

For four days, nothing happened to me. I was not integrated into prison life as I had anticipated. I just sat by myself in a double cell, only getting out for meals by myself, or to shower. There was always a guard on a chair outside my cell.

Later, I learned that I was the first one ever to come back to that institution from the dead and there was nothing covering that in the manual.

On Friday, in the afternoon, the warden himself came to my cell. He was very formal. There were two guards with him.

"Come with me, please," was all he said and he marched off down the steel walk past the other cells. All were empty. It was chow time.

He took me to the admitting office and had me change into the clothes I'd arrived in. All the while he sat and looked at his shoes.

Then he asked the other guards to leave us alone.

"Billy Ray. You are a free man, but I suppose you expected that. Am I correct?"

"You are," I said, back to my lawyer accent. That jerked his head up.

"Would you mind telling me what's going on?" he asked.

"Not at all. Can I see my release documents first, please?"

He went out of the room, came back and handed me the papers. I read them quickly.

"You came back for the hundred thousand dollars, right?"

"No, but I'll take it. I came back for my friends, warden. Are there any reporters here?"

"Two TV stations is all, plus a dozen radio and paper people."

"Warden, you folks have treated me very civilly and I won't forget it. You seem to have a good hold on things here. Thank you. I expected much worse. Now if you'll come with me, I'll tell the TV guys some real news."

We walked into the next room. Abe was there with Maynard and Eddie.

"Hey Billy Ray," Abe said, "I thought you might want to see these guys first."

I did, but I kept it to some hugs and let them keep wondering. They would hear all of it in a minute, I said.

The main meeting room was filled with people. Gwen was there. That took my breath away. She hugged me and whispered that Abe had told her everything on the way down and how much she loved me. I cried with her.

When I looked up, everyone was quiet and looking at me.

Abe came to us and told me it was time to tell my story. I looked around. There were about a dozen men staring at me. They had to be the other cons. Maynard and Eddie still looked shocked because I'd not told them about Harry Brown yet.

I took my real glasses from Abe and went over to the TV guys.

"You guys ready?"

They nodded, not knowing even what to ask.

"My name is Billy Ray Billings. I escaped from this prison over ten years ago."

I looked up at the silence, having expected uproar.

"Time is finite," I said. "It must be spent. There was a rare man in this prison. He taught me how to spend mine wisely. His name is Leonard Mossgrove and is the savior of all my brothers here."

epilogue

Billy Ray Billings does some work for the A.C.L.U. and writes crime novels in Jackson, Tennessee. He is married to Gwen and they have an infant son, named Leonard.

Mike Nevens is the ranking warrant officer at the Marine Corps Camp in Oceanside, California. His cover is intact.

Leonard Mossgrove teaches English at a high school in Huntsville, Alabama. He is married to a large woman who cooks well.

Maynard and Eddie are the proprietors of Orville's pool room, which they bought with their prison release money. Neither has married and they still live at Maynard's house.

Joshua Gore and Joseph Fuentes are still in prison at this writing. Joseph is finishing high school.

Frank Babcock and Ernie Collins are still with the Mobile Police Department.

Joel Burroughs is now the chief of police.

About the Author

LEN WILLIAMS has been CEO and/or president of retail companies in Canada, New Zealand, Belgium, and the United States, including Caldor; Gold Circle; Lion-Nathan and Coca-Cola, New Zealand; and the Pic'n'Save Corporation. *Justice Deferred*, which was optioned by Warner Brothers for Maguire Entertainment to produce, is his first novel. Originally from Prince Edward Island, Canada, he divides his time between Rome, Italy, and Los Angeles, California, with his film and theatre producer wife, Christine La Monte, and is currently at work on his second novel, *The Good Sisters*.